STORY OF THE SAND

STORY OF THE SAND

A Novel

Mark B. Pickering

iUniverse, Inc.

New York Lincoln Shanghai

Story of the Sand

iUniverse books may be ordered through booksellers or by contacting:

iUniverse
2021 Pine Lake Road, Suite 100
Lincoln, NE 68512
www.iuniverse.com
1-800-Authors (1-800-288-4677)

Because of the dynamic nature of the Internet, any Web addresses or links contained in this book may have changed since publication and may no longer be valid.

This is a work of fiction. All of the characters, names, incidents, organizations, and dialogue in this novel are either the products of the author's imagination or are used fictitiously.

ISBN: 978-0-595-47205-5 (pbk)
ISBN: 978-0-595-70892-5 (cloth)
ISBN: 978-0-595-91485-2 (ebk)

Printed in the United States of America

My many thanks to the staff at iUniverse, my family, my friends, my dog, and the soldiers—past, present, and future—who endure terror and its aftermath for strangers everywhere.

Contact me at litpick@gmail.com.

This novel is dedicated to Rita, for everything.

God is an American.

—David Bowie

Chapter 1

Sampson was a drinker, and the night before he had a fill that would disable most men for days. But his pants weren't wet. He felt under his lower body, which rested on his tent bottom, and could feel no dampness, so he figured a wayward hiker or maybe he himself had taken a piss outside that was now spreading its aroma with the help of morning sun's heat.

The smell was awful, but paranoia had awakened him. Sampson's head ached. The empty pint bottle of Evan Williams and empty liter bottle of Rumplemintz lay by his feet. They clinked together as he moved his legs, cradled his head, groaned, and fished for the cigarette pack that was indented into his upper back.

Sampson took out a flattened cigarette and lit it. He sucked it in, blew out the smoke through his nose, and sighed. The tobacco provided his brain some relief by numbing his paranoia, if only for a little while.

The stench of urine still hung in the air even after Sampson seared his nostrils with tobacco. Someone else might not have detected the odor. But the smell that entered his brain was as real to him as the ground he slept on. It was not from an animal. He knew that. Animals pissed and shit all around him. But they never made this smell. And Sampson didn't smell it when he went to sleep the night before.

Did someone know he lived out here? Was someone watching him? Was someone taunting him?

He had trekked far in the woods surrounding Kennesaw Mountain, so far he'd lost all bearing of direction, but that's what Sampson wanted. When he was hungry, he left his tent. When he was thirsty, he did the same. He figured out eventually how to get through the dense woods to a street and then a store. He didn't care that perplexed faces stared at his unwashed, unshaved face everywhere.

Sampson smelled. He knew that. His hair was matted. His beard was an unattractive, spotty reddish brown. But he had money, so he could buy what he needed—usually with a smirk. He didn't sit down in a nice restaurant. That's the last thing he wanted to do. Sampson wished food and clean water would rain down from the sky so he never had to see another living soul.

Archie was dead. Alan was dead. Alvin was dead. The three A's, he always called them. He became friends with them in boot camp, and all ended up in the same unit together. The three A's didn't have a morose bone in their body, and Sampson didn't think he did either before the war, so he stuck by them for the likeminded camaraderie. He was thrown clear from the Humvee with just a concussion, while they died beside the road.

Grouchy was alive and back home in Kennesaw. His left leg was gone, but that was all. Sampson had known Grouchy (his real name was David) since they were kids. Sampson had given him the name "Grouchy" before they could even grow stubble. No one else called David that. Sampson figured Grouchy must be even grouchier now without his leg.

Grouchy hated the army, but Sampson loved it—until the three A's died. After that, Sampson loved nothing and nobody, not even his wife. So she moved back to Ohio to try to find another love.

The rain from last night stayed out of Sampson's tent. But once he left it, the cold, wet ground stung his bare feet. So he returned to the tent and put his boots on. His boots were nearly useless by now. He had taken them from the closet he once shared with his wife, along with the tent and another pair of warm clothes. He left everything else, except a wad of cash he had hidden inside his sock drawer.

A moving branch caught Sampson's attention as he returned outside. He thought he saw a hand and gripped the hunter's knife that he carried in his back pocket for emergencies.

"Who's there?" Sampson called. He heard nothing. "This is my spot! Find your own damn spot! You do anything to my tent and they gonna find pieces of you from here to Atlanta!" He loosened the grip on his knife and put it back in his back pocket.

The holes on the bottom of Sampson's boots and the crusty-thin socks he'd put on sucked in a good deal of rainwater. He made a mental note to buy some duct tape. The sky was still hazy and threatened more rain. A downpour was an opportunity to clean some of the crust of dried sweat that grew until he scratched it away.

He was watching his steps a bit more carefully lately. Sampson had surprised one too many a snake and was afraid the next one he encountered would be poisonous and bite. He remembered watching a small boa constrictor when he was young; it was fascinating to see it kill mice and swallowed them whole. But these days the sight of blood made him sick. He didn't eat meat anymore. He wished he could close his eyes and taste it without imagining the slaughter.

Kennesaw Mountain loomed ever closer as he stepped on to an established footpath. A female jogger in the skimpiest of clothes ran by him. His lust was coming back.

After he returned from the war in the sand and before his wife left him, Sampson couldn't even sleep in the same bed with her, let alone hold or kiss her or make love to her. But the inviting site of a well-rounded bottom or ample breasts had him staring lately and scaring many a young woman. He fantasized of going to Atlanta and finding a cheap prostitute. The grip of sexuality around his penis was lately only his hand; even if it could just be someone else's hand, he would take it. His hand was cold most days.

More rain did come in a mist, and all Sampson could think about was the female jogger. She had on a white top, and Sampson wondered if the rain displayed a clear picture of her breasts. He knew he'd think about her when he next masturbated; he would picture her seeking him out inside his hidden tent and not minding his smell. Perhaps his smell would even turn her on. It was the only fantasy that seemed to ever work.

A cop was on the road. Sampson ducked his head down, hoping the cop hadn't seen him before. He had to take different routes to town every day so he wasn't spotted too often and reported. He'd been warned before. The cop had no evidence he was living there, but still told Sampson the park wasn't meant to be anyone's home, except for the animals that already lived there.

If he were living on the streets of Atlanta, no one would care. The cops might hassle him a little, but otherwise see him as just another section of concrete or a tree. But Kennesaw was smaller, far more conservative and vocal. None of the mountain's regular hikers would stay quiet if they learned someone slept, defecated, and masturbated within a camouflage of pristine woods that was supposed to shield them from the troubles of the modern world.

The day will come when he will become a priority to local officials. Sampson is sure of it. They will seek him out and throw him in jail. He can only hope he'll go peacefully, but he can feel the knife itching in his back pocket just thinking about it. It would beg to be used. Maybe he'll just kill himself when that day comes.

His destination this morning is a store, the closest one to him. This had been his destination every day, or every other day, since he started living in the woods. The owner sneered every time Sampson walked inside. He was an older, deeply southern man who kept a signed picture of George W. Bush above his cash register. That would have pleased the old Sampson. Now, he had to grin and bear it. The owner's son worked with him during the day, and they always spoke about Sampson behind his back, purposefully loud enough for him to hear.

"Maybe this rain'll clean some of the filth away," the owner said to his son.

"Some filth need a hurricane to get rid of it," his son replied.

"Be that time of year soon. Maybe that filth should think about botherin' another store in a state with no hurricanes."

Sampson approached the register without seeming to notice their words. He never gave them the satisfaction. He always wanted to tell them that the mother-fucker pictured above the counter made him like this, but he knew that could lead to violence and knew that violence would lead him to a jail cell.

Sampson placed a role of duct tape and a large bottle of water on the counter. He grabbed a half a dozen packets of peanut butter crackers from a labeled case on the counter. Taking a soiled but usable $20 bill from his front pocket, he set it down within reach of the storeowner's left hand. Sampson then monitored his cracking boots while he waited for a ding and the rattle of coins. But he stood longer than he'd expected, so he raised his head. When his eyes met the owner's, the owner chuckled.

"Doan know what you waitin' for."

"My change," Sampson said with obvious annoyance. He wanted back in the woods as soon as possible. *What* was the holdup?

"There ain't none."

"How much all that cost?" Sampson said passing his hand over the goods he just bought.

"Doan know. Doan care. Consider this a fee for lettin' you shop here."

"What?"

"What I just said. Maybe you'll pick another place now."

"I want my change," Sampson said calmly, though the edge of his eyes tightened.

"Told you there ain't none."

"Give me my change."

"Or what? You gonna call the police? Complain to the Better Business Bureau?" The owner looked back while he and his son enjoyed a quick laugh. "Look at you, son. You think you credible against me?"

The hunting knife's pleas were too insistent, so Sampson grabbed it from his back pocket. He thrust the blade into the dense wood of the counter; it stood quivering while Sampson monitored the owner's changing expression.

"Go ahead," Sampson said. "Reach for it. Give me an excuse. You ain't gonna live if you do."

The owner and his son both stared at the handle. His son, six feet behind, started to shift his shoes in the direction of the store's phone, which was hanging on a wall just out of reach.

"Now, I want my change," Sampson said calmly.

The owner peered up into Sampson's face. After seeing an unwavering insistence and knowing he didn't have the strength to compete, the owner opened the register.

"Might as well give me all of it," Sampson said. "I know you gonna say I robbed you anyway."

The owner's son dived for the phone and Sampson hoisted his blade out of the wood, grabbed the top of the old man's limited hair, yanked it towards him, and put the tip of the blade close to the old man's throat.

"You think I won't?" yelled Sampson as the owner's son maintained a grip on the phone but didn't take it from its base.

"Take it easy. Take it easy," said the owner.

"I'm a veteran!" Sampson continued to shout. "*That* man!" he said, pointing up at the picture of the president. "You like that man. That man sent me. You tell everyone you support me, I bet, but I get *hell* when I walk into this place!"

"How am I to know you a veteran?" the owner asked timidly.

"It shouldn't matter! I never stole nothing! I can't be the only slime bag that walk into this place. I'm looking at *two* of them now!"

"We was just having some fun," the owner squeaked.

"Fun? You call that fun, huh?"

"Well …" The owner was embarrassed.

"All of it. All the money. On the counter. Now!"

"Could you … let go of my hair? You holdin' me tight, son."

Sampson did, but darted his eyes between the old man and his son, ready for any questionable move to retake the elder hostage.

"Get away from that phone, Glenn," the owner said, motioning behind him with his free hand.

Glenn did, but glared into Sampson's eyes. He licked his lips and said slowly, "Don't you think you gonna get away with this."

"What you saying?" said Sampson. "You saying I should eliminate all witnesses?"

"Why don't you-" Glenn began, but his father silenced him. "Shut the hell up, Glenn!"

"There it is, son. There it is," the owner said, motioning to the pile of paper bills and change sprawled on the counter. "Do you want me to show you the register? There's no more, I'm tellin' you."

Sampson swiped the change onto the floor behind the counter, and Glenn's nerves made him do a little jerky dance. His legs soon stopped quivering, and Glenn resumed his defiant stare at Sampson's eyes. Sampson scooped up the bills and stuffed them in his front pant's pocket, too busy to notice Glenn's stare.

"Who owns that Hummer?" Sampson said, motioning with his chin at a hulking yellow vehicle that took up two spaces.

"That's … uh … that's Glenn's. Why?" the owner replied.

"You wanna be a solider, buddy. Then sign up," Sampson barked at Glenn. "You look to be the right age. Make your daddy proud. Make the man that sent me proud of you, jackass!" he said as he walked out the door, noticing Glenn diving for the phone.

Sampson knew he had some time, so he plunged his knife into each tire of the Hummer and watched as the great mass sagged ever closer to the ground.

He raced across the road with his supplies and the money while muttering to himself, "Why'd you do a thing like that, Sampson Roy? You gonna be another target now for sure."

CHAPTER 2

It wouldn't stop raining the day Sampson held up the convenience store, and it wouldn't stop raining that night. Sampson hadn't dreamed these dreams in so long; the alcohol had burned them away. He was afraid to close his eyes. But they closed.

The dreams held on to him tightly. Sometimes, they were exaggerated. They were as bloody and hopeless as he felt. Sampson would have to scream to be released from sleep. His screaming bounced echoes off trees that had stood since before the Civil War.

The money in his pocket felt like a poison in his body. He was chained to his tent by fear.

"Why did you let those two rednecks rile you up? Why?"

He imagined helicopters and tracking dogs. They wouldn't miss his scent.

Maybe I should use this knife. Maybe take care of it myself, Sampson thought putting the teeth of the knife on a wrist.

This time, unlike when he returned from the war, the news could save him.

Sampson was on the news when he came back from the war in the sand. He stood among the wounded. He stood with all his limbs. The other just-returned veterans wobbled around. Their wheelchairs were too old. He tried to smile. They tried to smile. What were they smiling about?

Some woman asked him how it felt, and he told her, "Great." She wrote it down. He wondered if that was his quote, if that was enough of a quote. What would the quote be now?

"Why did you stick up that store?"

"They made me mad."

"Why didn't you just leave and never come back?"

"They needed to know."

Was that an excuse? Would, "I'm a veteran" make his crime not a crime anymore after this imaginary interview?

They must have had some money in a safe, Sampson thought. *They weren't stupid enough to put it all in the register.*

Sampson reached in his pocket and counted how much. $104 in all.

You can't keep a store open on that. They let it go. They know who I am now. They believe me. They let it go. Let me go. Just let me go!

This wind, it reminds me—but the sound of footsteps interrupted Sampson's memory. He gripped his knife.

"Soldier," someone called outside. "Soldier, I come in peace."

"Who is that?" Sampson asked.

"Just a friend."

"If you a friend you can say your name."

Sampson looked out his flap. A part of desert-designed camouflage jacket blocked the sun.

"It's David Tree."

"The only David Tree I know I call Grouchy."

"That's me, Sam."

"He'd never identify himself as David to me."

"No, *you* never identified me as David. I always did."

"That ain't true."

"You have a selective memory, Sam."

"Not anymore."

"I prefer to be called David, always have," said the voice outside. The man started to put a hand into a flap.

"I wish you wouldn't," Sampson said and backed up using his forearms. He held his knife firmly as the previously unknown body revealed itself in full.

"Small tent," Grouchy said, looking around. He steadied on his haunches. Two legs were attached to his body. Sampson had seen him just after that left leg was blown off.

"Must be my imagination," Sampson said.

"Why do you say that?"

"You got two legs, Grouchy. Two legs. I know you left without one."

"Maybe *that* was your imagination, Sam."

Grouchy looked clean. His hair was cut short, no stubble was on his face. Sampson couldn't smell any odor. He told himself he was trapped inside a dream—though he could never control his actions in his dreams and he could now.

When Grouchy moved, the tent seemed to move with him. As Grouchy breathed, Sampson thought he could smell his breath. There was no blur, no numb feeling of powerlessness. Sampson could break outside of the tent and run away. This wasn't a dream.

"No, Grouchy. I know that was real."

"I prefer to be called David, Sam. Just me call me David from now on, OK?"

"Why? You ain't grouchy no more?"

"Now? No. I guess I'm … sad. Yeah, I'm … sad most of the time. Actually, all of the time."

"Which one of them dwarfs was always sad?"

"I don't know … Sneezy?"

"Sneezy don't fit you. You always been Grouchy to me. You can't be nothing else now."

"I never liked it, Sam."

"You never told me that."

"Yes I did, Sam. But you never listened, so I just stopped wasting my breath."

"'Cause you knew it was a good nickname."

"No, Sam," Grouchy sighed. "Tell me when the hell I was ever grouchy?"

"Always playing war, man. You one grouchy mother when you playing war."

"I didn't like playing with you, Sam. You roughed us up like it was real. No one was too happy with your way when we were playing war."

"Rough? Shit, we was kids, we was boys."

"You took that game too seriously, Sam."

Grouchy's eyes seemed clear. There were pupils. There was something to look into. But, a type of translucence appeared from the side anytime he looked away.

"Are you a real man or a ghost, Grouchy?"

"I'm a ghost, I suppose you'd say. Well, I'm dead at least. I'm dead but I am really in front of you, Sam."

"But … I heard you was fine. I heard you got home OK."

"I did get home fine. I got on fine for a time. But there was an infection. It killed me, Sam. Real quick. No one expected it. Just happened."

"But your baby …"

"What about my baby, Sam? People with babies die too. Many guys we knew had babies, and you saw a lot of them die."

It was true. Sampson saw *a lot* of them die. It seemed to replay in his head all the time, even when he was drunk. But when he was drunk he was void of all emotion. He saw men die in explosions, and their corpses resembled pieces of blackened meat rather than anything human. Sometimes he thought those men were never men, just phantoms of some kind that turned gruesome. Sometimes Sampson thought he had died and went to hell and would spend eternity entering sandstorm after sandstorm, where brains and blood splashed on his face continuously.

The thing was it didn't bother him. Not until his head was rocked. He could handle hell. He'd adapt to the conditions. If it meant the same monotony of waiting and death, then he'd relish the death when death came.

"What are you doing out here, Sam?" Grouchy asked.

"Don't know really. Guess I'm here now because I held up a store."

"No. Why did you start out here in the first place?"

"Nothing seemed like it used to be."

"And here it feels like it used to be?"

"No, Grouchy, but here no one has to worry about me."

"What did I tell you about the Grouchy business? Call me David, Sam. Only David. I never liked anyone giving me nicknames."

"Sorry. I'll try and remember. Not promising anything, though."

"You let a good girl get away, Sam."

"She's better off."

"She's pregnant too."

"She's what?"

"She's pregnant, I said."

"Who's the father?"

"You, Sam."

"No, that ain't right, Grouchy. Not me. I never could get it up when I came back. I tried, but I couldn't. I know she took it personal. You got your information wrong. Some other man's the father of her baby, not me."

"You got it up once, Sam. You were drunk, but you did it."

*   *   *   *

Two empty bottles lay by Sampson's side: a bottle of Beefeater gin and his trustworthy fifth of Evan Williams bourbon. He was opening a third, some swill that was only four dollars, as Mary opened the door, quietly calling her husband's name.

Mary looked in the mirror and told herself she would try one last time. She undressed in front of that mirror and wanted to find the reason Sampson wouldn't touch her. There seemed no reason. She wasn't fat. She had no scars. Mary was young and wanting; she wanted him to hold her like he used to.

Her unveiled body was just a blur until Mary let her breasts fall to Sampson's face. Mary fumbled with his zipper and maneuvered Sampson's penis so she could let it glide inside her. Sampson looked into her eyes, but didn't know whom he was seeing. Mary closed her eyes and made love to a body that couldn't react. An oldies station started playing "Cecilia," by Simon and Garfunkel, in the background as her motions grew in momentum.

Mary thought she'd reached him again until he called her Susan. Sampson cooed "Susan" over and over. "I love you, Susan," he said, sounding like a scratchy record. Sampson never loved a Susan. He didn't know many either. The bliss Mary had manufactured was shattered and she started to cry. But she continued making love to Sampson until he climaxed and his head fell backward and into sleep. She left the next day.

✳   ✳   ✳   ✳

"I'm saying for sure you a fantasy. You ain't a ghost. You the shit in my mind getting worse."

"Your mind is getting worse, Sam. But I speak the truth. She'll raise it alone, or find some good man to be its daddy. I don't think you'll get that chance no matter what you do to clean yourself up."

"Goddamnit, Grouchy! I just got back from a war!"

"You lost something in that war, Sam. You can't get it back. She knows it too. She's smart, that one."

"So it's my fault!"

"No, not necessarily. Probably barely. You had to become something else. But when you become something else, you leave what you were behind. She wanted what you left behind. It's like shedding a skin, Sam. You can't wear it again. It's loose. It'll crack, boy. You ain't that man anymore."

"Will I ever leave what I am now behind?"

"Hard to say."

"The next step is jail, I guess."

"Well … you are mentally disturbed, Sam. Authorities might give you a break, especially since you were in a war."

"So that means I get drugged until I'm drooling all day? It don't mean they'll leave me alone, does it?"

"No, it doesn't, Sam."

"Then … no, thank you, Grouchy. Forget it. Nothing they can do for me. You know that. Can't do a thing for us can they? Unless they take it all away."

"So, no more looking for food, Sam? No more looking for water? Are you gonna try to hunt these animals out here? You only have a knife. You ain't that fast."

"I wouldn't even if I could."

"So you're just gonna waste away? Stick it to them that way, huh? Some fella will find your body out here, all skinny and gross."

"I either waste away on my own or with the help of the government, Grouchy. And the government already gave me all the help I need in that department."

CHAPTER 3

Mary knew Sampson would leave her for the war, soon, and maybe be killed and buried before her eyes before she gave him the most of her physical self. She never let a man touch her this way, love her this way. But he was different, different in every way. Sampson said he'd marry her, and a judge did the next day.

Sampson wrote Mary emails when he could. He called her from a phone on base when he wasn't too calloused to think. Sometimes things happened that made him want to stay quiet, and sometimes that lasted weeks.

Mary was smarter than he was. She wanted a degree. Ohio was her home, but Kennesaw State was her school. Sampson thought she'd find someone better and tell him as much in an email. But every message back just said she missed him. He wished it said she'd left him behind.

It would be easier to die if she did. Sampson knew he was only lucky so far. He got too close to danger many times. Grouchy had already gone home. Sampson saw that bandaged stump.

The medics wouldn't look at him. They only looked at who they had to. Sampson feared acknowledging their eyes, thinking if they looked at him square that meant his end. Every day he heard news of someone else's death. It didn't matter if Sampson knew the soldier or not. It was one more death closer to him and then his Humvee exploded. As he flew through the air, he thought that bright light or big nothing awaited him.

He woke up somewhere else, in some other country, he knew. He couldn't hear any rifle fire or explosions. He couldn't hear all the swearing and tension. Sweat, blood, and death were no longer surrounding his life, but they were burrowed deep inside his soul. Sampson was asked questions and answered them without the clarity the doctors were seeking.

"When am I going back?" he would ask, and the heads would shake.

"You're going home," they always said.

"But why?"

"You're too damaged, Sergeant Roy. You're a liability."

"Every part works!"

"Your mental trauma makes us think they won't."

*   *   *   *

Mary was crying when he got off the plane, and so was he. But Sampson wasn't crying for her. He was crying for all of those he left behind. They didn't have a wife to hold. They didn't have anything to hold but a rifle and the hope of leaving soon.

Returning from battle wasn't at all like Sampson imagined when he was young. He didn't feel the pride. He didn't know when he would. He wasn't a hero, not to himself anyway, but his father told him he was. The pats on his back all felt like a sucker punch.

Mary undressed in front of him. Sampson's uniform was still on. It was pressed and clean. He wore his Purple Heart. She cooed and whispered in his ear, and he felt full of bile. Sampson didn't want her to think his attitude was her fault. It wasn't. He didn't want her to think he'd never be the same. He wouldn't. So Sampson sat like an overstuffed scarecrow and heard Mary's tears when his lips couldn't kiss back.

"Maybe spend some time in the hospital?" said his buddies, who didn't go. "Maybe a shrink? Maybe some drugs?"

Memories—and his attempt to remove them—became his only chosen companionship. He could empty a bottle within minutes—and another bottle just minutes later. Mary gave him some time, gave him his space; but when she looked in his eyes she saw no feeling or even much life inside. She was starting to believe every trigger over there had made him as dead to her as some of Sampson's friends were to the world itself.

Her friends told her to be patient, but Sampson was like an old dog without the use of his back legs. She could watch his front legs drag his belly on the ground, or she could be the muscles of his back legs. Mary tried, but he called her Susan. He called her *Susan. Who* was Susan? It didn't matter if he was drunk. She was his *wife*. *Who* was Susan? Sampson didn't know her anymore. Mary didn't know him. That was that. She couldn't do this anymore.

Sampson didn't even hear her leave. It might have been days before he noticed she was gone. There may have been a note, but he didn't look. He left for the woods instead.

CHAPTER 4

Sampson had to wait until it was dark and the roads were quiet. When a car approached him from the front or from behind him, he crouched behind a mailbox or a fence. Sometimes he stood still against a tree. Sampson wasn't seen or looked for. He walked among such graceful surroundings that drivers wouldn't imagine anything might blight the landscape—not at this time of night, at least. He was lucky. If he were seen, his appearance would be so shocking that a driver would undoubtedly call the police.

He tried scouring trash cans, but the smell of rotting meat repulsed him. Even if the most succulent meat were thrown at his feet, Sampson wouldn't eat it. Instead, he survived on backyard gardens, where he found tomatoes, carrots, and vegetables he hadn't eaten in years. Sometimes he found a peach tree and ate of its fruit.

Sampson was caught only once. He was sighted, but not apprehended. Some old woman in curlers and a too-short white nightgown came out screaming at him to get out of her yard. With floodlights shining on top of him and the woman swinging her sagging breasts as she ran behind him, Sampson escaped. His shirt was full of ripening tomatoes and cucumbers, and he didn't drop a one.

"A raider?" asked Grouchy, who had yet to follow Sampson outside of the tent.

"You saying I'm a thief?" Sampson answered defensively. "I ain't no thief, Grouchy. I earned a little something for my service. I'm just taking what I'm owed."

"Yeah, and you also took $104 to allow you to buy what you're owed, Sam."

"Right and if I go and buy it, I'm locked up, Grouchy. They gonna feed me rabbit food and dope. Then I'll be a hundred eating rabbit food and dope."

"I've been asking you politely to not call me Grouchy-"

"Just can it, man! I'm *still* gonna call you Grouchy. Just *deal* with it. I started when we was ten and it ain't gonna change now."

"Suppose I have no choice."

"You can go anytime, Grouchy. Anytime this don't suit you."

"Sam, I'm dead. Nothing does or doesn't suit me."

"And that's all?"

"Sure. Call me whatever. Strange for me to be so picky, considering I'm out of population."

"No. I mean it's that simple? You just floating or something? This just no big deal? I mean, tell me what it's like is what I'm saying."

"Sam, it's the word itself. Dead is dead. Useless. You don't feel anything out here. Everything you see me do, I'm not doing. You're just seeing it."

"So how do you move?"

"Just think. I can think. I can feel things, you know, inside," Grouchy said, tapping on where his chest would be. Sampson had to remind himself he wasn't really seeing it. "Maybe that means we have a soul. I don't know. I can only talk to the dead that stick around like me or the near-dead like you that are real close to saying their good-byes. I wish I could say it wasn't true, Sam. But you are if you keep on like this."

"So, I'm one of the near-dead, then?"

"I *said* I can only talk to dead people or near-dead, Sam. And you know all too well you're not dead."

"No. I don't know that, Grouchy. This could be one mind-fuck. You could be some imposter. What do I know? Told God a long time ago I didn't believe in him. If he's true, maybe he's making me pay the price."

"Sam … trust this or not, but you're not dead."

"So then you must be getting me ready to be dead?"

"No. I'm just here, Sam. I'm lonely. I don't like what you're doing to yourself. But mostly, I'm just lonely."

"Do you ever watch your baby?"

"No. Why should I? Can't do anything. She doesn't see me. She doesn't feel me."

"Maybe just to know what's happening."

"I know what's happening: a lot of sadness."

"And that's what's in this tent, Grouchy!"

"Yeah, but figured you were lonely too."

"I don't know how my loneliness goes away by talking to someone who's dead!"

"Yes you do, Sam. Because you're talking to someone besides yourself."

*   *   *   *

The tail end of Grouchy's service was shadowed by the knowledge that his daughter might never know him. In a way he was relieved when the explosion ripped into his thigh and cost him his leg—not when he saw the limb blow, but after he woke up in the German hospital. Grouchy couldn't serve without a working leg. He'd see his daughter. He'd get to watch her grow up. Being out of the line of fire meant he would, or that's what he thought.

Grouchy's brother, Teddy, was always around when Grouchy came back from the war. Teddy carried a heavy guilt by being the smarter one, or at least smart enough to get a scholarship and avoid having to decide if the military was an option. Grouchy enrolled in the army just to go to school. He wanted to do something with design. Maybe be an architect, though he figured he'd settle for just working with one if the money from the army didn't cover the rigorous schooling.

Teddy was two years older than Grouchy. He was a lawyer and had a nice house in Atlanta. He was unmarried, but being rich and successful gave him the opportunity to date many women. When he saw Grouchy without a leg, he felt too gilded to live. Teddy tried to assuage this guilt by visiting Grouchy almost every day, on his lunch hour, thirty minutes north of his office. Grouchy wanted to tell him he didn't have to. He wanted to tell Teddy that just the touch of his daughter and the smell of his wife was enough. Grouchy could bask in the love of these women, this gentle change of pace from so much misery and barbarity, until he was ready for the grave.

"Sometimes I wish I were in a car accident," Teddy said to him one day.

"That's a dumb wish."

"One bad enough that I'd have to have a leg taken too."

"Teddy," Grouchy sighed, "appreciate what you have. Your life is yours and mine is mine, for better or worse."

"But ... you didn't want to go, David."

"A lot didn't, Teddy. War ain't a place you really want to go to."

"Some want to go, David. You know that's true."

"*Morons*, Teddy. Morons also want to light themselves on fire sometimes."

"I'm the older one, David. *I* should have gone. You should have gone to school. I was done with school. I had money in the bank. I'm not too old to do what you did."

"Hey, Teddy, no one's stopping you. You're far away from forty-two, man. They'd be glad to have you."

"Leave my practice for a year, David? I'd have to find all new clients, another office. The deal I got was *amazing*, I won't get-"

"Right, Teddy, you have things to do here. You have a choice and you were never much interested in not having one. And that's good. You earned what you have, so just enjoy it. Don't keep moaning about me. That's one thing you can't do anymore. If you feel bad just deal with it, 'cause I can't do nothing about this leg and it doesn't make me happy thinking of you fighting just 'cause you want to look just like me."

Grouchy didn't understand discontent anymore. Especially from the healthy with four working limbs. He'd lost one, but what he kept was worth it. The memories, too, even the bad ones. He'd be a better man for it. A lot of soldiers had daughters. A lot of soldiers had them and died before they ever saw what was theirs. Grouchy woke up to his daughter every day. He put her to bed every night. All day long he held her, cuddled her, and told her how much he loved her. Grouchy didn't mind if he never had to work again.

The infection seemed nothing at first. Just a little itch. A little redness from time to time. But Grouchy began to wake from the pain. The doctors at the VA hospital gave him medicine, but otherwise shooed him away because of the volume of veterans that came through those doors every day.

The infection traveled to his bloodstream, then to his heart. It killed him quickly. Grouchy stood over his body with the missing leg. He watched as his wife cried into his chest. His daughter cried, too, because mommy was crying. If it meant having no legs, no arms either, he would have traded death to have again what seemed such paradise after war.

The military claimed Grouchy's death wasn't their fault. Sheila, Grouchy's wife, received a ten thousand dollar check, and that was all. It was for his missing leg. His missing self wasn't their responsibility. If she wanted more, she'd have to sue, and she wasn't going to sue. Teddy compiled a list of lawyers who specialized in getting her more, but Sheila just stared at the list. She never picked up the phone to call a one. None of them could bring Grouchy back.

Sgt. Sampson Roy was in the woods. Grouchy had heard about him deserting his home. He'd heard about his wife leaving. He'd heard about that night she and Sampson conceived a child.

Grouchy remembered Mary. He'd met her once. She wasn't like Sampson. The girl with tight jeans and too much makeup whom Grouchy remembered Sampson dating in high school didn't resemble her. Mary was open-minded. She hated guns. George W. Bush would never be on her bumper. She loved Sampson, though. She loved him with a devotion that could strike others with envy. She looked at Sampson in a way that no woman had ever looked at Grouchy. Sampson seemed a worthwhile mission, a worthwhile discursion for Grouchy to avoid the true death.

True death was beyond the world of any sight. True death shed any image of clothes or body. True death was a mystery. It promised its victims nothing except the end to what they thought they knew.

Grouchy would go—he had to go but not yet. He didn't know if he would perhaps comfort Sampson until Sampson's end or travel back to the sand to comfort someone dying alone from a bullet wound that was fatal but slow.

"Time stands still to me," Sampson said. He was eating a tomato that wasn't quite ripe.

"Time is very real, Sam," Grouchy said to him. "It will ravage you with advanced age if you remain defiant to what the sanity in your head is telling you."

"And what's that?"

"Surrender. Surrender and find help."

"Then would I still be near-dead, Grouchy?"

"I don't know. You'll know you're out of danger when you can't see me anymore."

CHAPTER 5

Ed Roy was a cop. From age six Ed fired guns at a target his father personified as "Get the gook" or "Kill the nigger" or "Get that Nazi." When the war broke out in Vietnam, he couldn't wait unit he turned eighteen; and when he did, he didn't wait to get drafted.

Ed arrived at the recruitment office and stood in no line. The recruiters looked blessed from above. They blessed Ed with their smiles that looked lined with God's pixie dust. As Ed filled out the paperwork, he dreamed of his first kill. He dreamed of seeing the squirt of blood and a dead gook that looked in his mind just like a dead buck he caught between the eyes. Pins and medals were in those fantasies. He'd come back to a waiting crowd so happy for his service. Ed dreamed of all the women he could lay.

But Ed Roy's back had been giving him problems since he was young. His mind was suspect from the age of sixteen, when he started drinking hard liquor like it was water. So the form was stamped "**DENIED.**" The recruiters said they were sorry. All his friends went, and the ones who came back with limps or catatonic minds Ed envied just the same.

In the woods, Ed brought five-year-old Sampson to a body, a black man full of holes. He smiled at his son, though Sampson was afraid. The man had escaped, Ed said. He told Sampson the man had raped a white woman, though the truth was he held up a liquor store.

On horseback, Ed tracked the scared young man through the woods. The young man was cornered and begged Ed to treat him mercifully. Ed played sympathetic and told the boy he wasn't going to do anything, told the boy to keep running, and then shot him in the back. His twisting, dying body gave Ed more pleasure than he could ever imagine.

Then there was that time when Sampson was eleven years old. His mother had locked him and his sister in the house. They heard a commotion outside, mostly banging on the back door interrupted by brutal swear words. A shot was fired and Ed came in through the hole the shotgun blast had made into the kitchen's back door. His wobbling gut was bare and his eyes were red. He held the shotgun to his wife's head. Ed would have killed her if Sampson didn't yell, "Stop!"

Ed Roy quit drinking after that. He became a churchgoing man. But none of the churches he attended ever said a word against war—no war America was ever in, at least. Ed wanted Sampson in a fight. He had said this since Sampson could talk, so Sampson figured he was right. Sampson liked to fight. He fought boys around the neighborhood. His used his strength in any way to impress others: helping people move or cutting tree branches down. When he cut those branches down, all the girls around found reason to linger over his naked upper half. Sampson felt good being tough. Everyone wanted to be his friend.

Sampson didn't keep girlfriends too long. They weren't his prize. Glory was. Girlfriends were fun as long as they kept it fun. When they started talking about marriage or kids, he found a way to cut them loose. Marriage and kids were for after he earned all the respect, the medals, and the news that could catapult his fame.

Meeting Mary didn't change his mind at first. They met in a bar. Sampson had wowed many women in the bar; he slept with nearly half a dozen, just there, not to mention the other bars he hunted. Mary's eyes were almost purple behind the glasses she wore. Her hair was obviously colored, but it didn't contrast to any degree Sampson's want of those eyes staring back at him above her sweaty, naked body.

She didn't like him at first. Sampson just wanted Mary naked. He delivered all his lines, sprinkling "the enemy" throughout. He relished getting a chance to kill "the enemy." The others girls liked his toughness, but not Mary. She told him she didn't agree with the war, and Sampson's smooth delivery faltered. The argument became a shouting match, until Mary stormed out.

Mary promised herself she'd find another bar. But she was back two weeks later. She was looking for him. She watched all the Sunday political programs, and took notes as those protesting the war made points she couldn't imagine anyone refuting. She had a better argument than Sampson in spades. She would force him to hear it. But the discussion didn't happen the way she was sure it had to.

The bar was mostly empty, and Sampson looked depressed. Mary started towards him quickly, but when she came close enough, he looked decidedly different than the last time: softer, almost sad. He was alone and seemed to be pleading silently for someone to help. All thoughts of venom vanished from Mary's insides. Was that tenderness she saw? Her passions shifted, and Sampson became something she had to explore.

Sampson didn't try anymore. Mary was different. Getting her naked with the same tired lines seemed almost pathetic. She was the opposite of easy. Mary was smart, and Sampson didn't think he could keep up. But he wanted to listen to her. She needed someone to listen. Being near her was better than sex. He didn't know why. He thought maybe before he died he could be the man his father never was.

When Sampson promised he'd marry her, she allowed him the closest touch.

Over there Sampson missed Mary until the shooting began, and then he was tough again. He was who he was bred to be again. Death just seemed part of the day. A drug-like rush coursed through his body when he saw his bullet hit. He was still just a sportsman and his game was the enemy. The brown enemy. The cloaked enemy. The enemy from within. The soldiers who complained. Anyone who contradicted what he had to believe. If Sampson could have killed the men who had different opinions from him, the men in his unit who wore the American uniform, he would have.

He hated himself.

The hate spread from his core into every facet of his life. Sampson was ruined. He'd hardly become a soldier, let alone a man. Killing was his only real action. It didn't discriminate. It didn't want truth. *Fairness* was just a word … usually.

Sampson was sure he'd killed the innocent. He knew he had. Standing over a crippled boy who had waved his cane in the middle of a dusty room almost brought tears to his eyes. Sampson felt a pang of disgust, and when the boy's mother entered the room screaming in a tongue he hadn't learned one word of, he screamed back.

"This is a war!" he said. "What he doing with that fucking stick? That stick look like a gun to me!"

The mother didn't understand. She held her son's limp body. Sampson left the room. A report was filed, and his commander told him accidents happen.

*   *   *   *

"Are we the bad guys now, Grouchy?" he asked Grouchy inside that tent, which was feeling smaller each passing day.

"No. But when you tell the world how good you are and then act bad for a time, it's worse than if you're always bad. They wonder which country is gonna show up: the one handing out food and candy, or the one dropping bombs on little children from the sky."

Sampson had seen those bombs. The ones that hit the wrong target. Sometimes they hit nursery schools or hospitals. Anger filled the streets. Foreign voices shouted in his face. He hid his face behind his black sunglasses. If Sampson had no gun, he would have been trampled to death.

"We're fighting for *them*!" he would tell fellow soldiers who were starting to lose the faith. "You gotta break some eggs to eat breakfast!"

When Sampson roared, almost no one roared back. He was their sergeant. He dictated to them what they were to believe. War wasn't a debate, not while you were in it. He told them people could debate all they wanted back home, but *they* would follow his orders and be glad doing it.

When he came back home, every day they came to him. They were now just images. Which ones were just a statistic now? Who did his job now? Who told them what to believe and when to believe it? Who *still* believed?

Sampson watched his president, the one who he voted for twice. The one who he defended and the one who he believed in so much that if he even *heard* someone had voted against him, that person was liable to receive a black eye—two black eyes sometimes. Sampson didn't care if that meant fewer fighters. Half a dozen patriots were better than a half a dozen more traitors to him.

Sampson watched this man, his president. Sampson saw no idea in his eyes. Sampson saw a fool. Sampson felt a fool himself. His father wasn't a relative anymore. In all phone calls, in all visits, Sampson told Ed Roy to go to hell. Another fool was like another injury, and he considered armchair warriors as vile as the enemy, if not more so.

The stings of war were increasing. Sampson felt as if he were in a burning building, and all his adrenalin had finally dried up. In its place was revulsion—not for the war, not for what he had to do, but for how he had convinced himself to do it.

Anyone who loved him must be as vile as he felt inside. Sampson erased that bile with liquor, but the liquor became the bitch goddess of regret when his aching head saw who he was hurting those few moments he was sober.

Mary's head popped in sometimes. If Sampson weren't too far gone, he'd turn his head away. If he was too far gone, he had no idea what he said, if anything. Sampson wondered if he cursed her. But he never did.

*   *   *   *

"You serious that she's pregnant, Grouchy?"

"Why would I make that up?"

"How's she holding up?"

"Don't know. Just heard through the grapevine that she's pregnant. She'll hold up fine, though."

"But I'm not dead yet, Grouchy! It ain't right. I should try and find her. I should try and get it together."

"First you have to surrender."

"Then that means years inside some institution. She'll find someone else for sure, Grouchy!"

"You tell me which way she'd rather have it—you on the lam, or your crime paid for?"

"Which crime is that?"

"You held up a store, Sam. I know you didn't forget it."

"I killed men, too, Grouchy. Which crime I need to pay for first?"

"That wasn't your crime, Sam. That was your duty. Someone else needs to pay for it if that was wrong."

CHAPTER 6

The two-story building seemed too bombed to hold any man. But it still stood. And men sometimes stood inside. The pipes that once carried water stuck out from where cement used to shield them from the sun. Coiling electric wires sprung out from each impact and dangled all day like a dying man. Black clad individuals ruptured emotion by standing and firing at an American target through windows that had long ago lost their glass. A boy hidden on the street signaled these snipers by radio.

Electricity to this building had been cut off. Sewage too. No one flopped there at night. U.S. and native troops held big floodlights at the top of their scopes to make sure. When all troops had left, the squatters came back with their guns and any other weapons they used to cripple or kill.

With faces shielded by black cloth, they had cut down two Americans and wounded three before Sampson and his crew were ordered to stop all that. Sampson was driving the Humvee. He'd done this before. But this building was a successful camouflage and hadn't been defeated since the war began. Sampson didn't know that. Alan, Archie, and Alvin didn't know that either. They were all sure this assignment would be simple, like all the rest, and they'd be sharing high fives within the hour.

It was dusty. The sandstorm had kicked up fierce. The people on the street covered their mouths and eyes with shawls. They walked about without any suspicious movement. This wasn't anything Sampson and the boys weren't used to. They snugly tied their own American flag scarves around their mouths and looked up at one of the windows, ready to destroy who crouched beneath it.

A rat-a-tat round came from that window as soon as Sampson and the three A's raised their weapons. The Humvee bounced with all their firepower until more people came into the street to blur their target. They held their fire, but the insurgents' fire didn't stop. It killed two children begging for candy. Sampson and three A's shouted for everyone to make way. The women looked scared. Behind them masked men in doorways made sure they remained an obstacle, even if it meant being struck by an insurgent bullet.

Sampson wasn't sure how the explosion happened. It wasn't an IED. It was from some rocket-propelled grenade, he was almost sure of it. The Humvee was blown apart and the force sent all inside flying. The three A's they were dying or dead. Archie was a headless, blackened torso. Sampson lie on the dusty ground and felt the culmination of his duty in a land where nothing made sense except to shoot to kill.

Sandals ran before him before he completely blacked out. Sampson wanted to grab an ankle. He wanted it to feel his pain. Bloody tendons were in his grip, in his mind, screaming. The bastard who did this a crippled fuck burst satisfaction inside his fading head. But Sampson couldn't grab anything. He couldn't lift his head.

"What do you dream?" asked the doctor at that hospital in Germany.

"I don't dream."

"What do you think?"

"I want to go back. I want to find who did it."

"And you think you really can?"

"I don't really care. I'll find relatives. I'll find someone close enough."

"This isn't how the military operates, Sergeant Roy. In war people die. Your friends died, but you cannot seek revenge on the innocent."

"Who's innocent there? Women and children aren't even innocent!"

"Yes, yes they are, Sergeant Roy. They are not responsible for their actions. You know that. They are under a lot of pressure if they wish to stay alive. Their lives are more important to them than yours."

"We're there for them!"

"I know. I know, Sergeant Roy. But war is messy. It doesn't even make sense most of the time, does it?"

"Just point and shoot! That's all the sense I need!"

"That's not enough sense for us, Sergeant Roy. You have to understand why we're sending you home."

"You want killers, right? I'm a killer!"

"Yes. But your instability has us worried you'll kill more than the enemy, even more than the women and children of the enemy. It has us worried you'll kill your fellow soldiers. Get some help when you get home."

*   *   *   *

Grouchy didn't think much of the blood, his own or others'. As he rested peacefully inside his Kennesaw home, something else from the sand filled his memories with sweetness. Even while his daughter made such a fuss or calmed him with the peaceful rising and falling of her tiny chest, those thoughts would only pause, then proceed.

In this war a woman could be left behind on the battlefield and not one born and raised in the country he fought in. Grouchy had a war wife. He called her his war wife, and she called him her war husband. They met in a Porta Potty every few nights. Grouchy had locked it, and no one had taken bolt cutters to use it for their own bodily needs.

Her name was Lilly. She was a hefty black woman. When she first stood naked in front of him, Grouchy saw that her heft was made of hard muscle. Lilly flew a Blackhawk. Their meeting was by accident. Grouchy had never believed he could make love to a black woman. He'd been told he shouldn't. But her eyes spoke of what was accumulating in his. No eyes looked at him that way, not over here.

It started when Grouchy wrote her innocent notes. She wrote back, but Lilly's notes back to him were off topic and graphic. She wrote what she missed in minute detail, details that sometimes took up three pages. Grouchy pictured him and Lilly together, intertwined, orgasmic, having fucks of the century. Looking at a picture of his wife, he tried to kill his wanting with the thoughts of his and Sheila's most desperate embrace before he went. But Lilly's details became promises of what she wanted to do to him, if only he would do the same to her. She said she needed it and knew he did too. She said she wanted to taste him. Taste every part of him. The war was all the permission they needed, she said. When she wrote these things, Grouchy always wrote back saying he was flattered but also married. Lilly told him she was married too.

Inside a storage room Grouchy and Lilly came face-to-face. They were alone for the first time. They looked at each other like a dessert tray. Their lust was a percolating battle. Grouchy and Lilly came at each other like battling lions and grunted like them too. They tore off each other's clothes while they gnawed on each other's body. They were nearly caught. A private's unsure face almost stopped the relief, but he left the room as soon as he saw tumbling bodies of different shades trying to swallow the other. After that scare, Grouchy found a recently cleaned Porta Potty and claimed it as their exclusive rendezvous.

"I love you," Lilly said into Grouchy's ear once as she thrust herself upon him. He could hear her through his groans and brutal movement, but he said nothing back.

"You heard me, didn't you?" Lilly said as they dressed in what limited room the plastic enclosure afforded them.

"Don't say things like that to me," Grouchy replied. "You know what this is."

"I can love you over here, can't I?"

"We're *married*, Lilly. We love those who are at home."

"I won't love you when I leave. But I love you now. I don't care if that bothers you."

Grouchy kissed her scar, the one on Lilly's stomach. It was from a caesarean. She had three boys. Her husband was leaving her; she was sure of it. But Grouchy couldn't comfort her. He told her he wouldn't leave his wife. Their lust was natural, he said. It caused him no shame. But he loved his wife. He'd only seen a picture of his daughter.

Lilly didn't even get to tell him good-bye. Her unit was somewhere else, up in the north, when he left. Grouchy wrote her a note and then ripped it up. He thought it best to just leave her with memories and no promise of anything more.

$$* \qquad * \qquad * \qquad *$$

"Please don't tell me you love me," Sampson said to Mary one day. She said it all the time. She wanted him to know. Whatever was in his head she could handle, she told herself. But that was a lie.

"Why, Sam?"

"I know why you doing it. I know I'm like some schoolboy who has no friends. I know you want to trick me into thinking I should."

"Trick you? I *love* you, Sam! I *hate* what you're doing to yourself!"

"It's the only way, though."

"Why?"

"It burns it all away. I have to fight fire with fire."

"You'll burn everything away, Sam! You're burning *me* away!"

"I hate to do it, but I can't get through it no other way."

CHAPTER 7

When Sampson left his tent during the day, he did so with greater paranoia. Anytime helicopters flew overhead he thought they were looking for him. Every little twig crack, every little bustle of unfamiliar noise, he was sure was the police, perhaps the SWAT team. Usually, however, it was just a squirrel.

Sampson had been sober two weeks. He had no choice. He couldn't be seen in public, for he was the embodiment of a derelict and would end up in cuffs. He bathed in the creek at night. Sometimes water snakes slithered over his feet, along with the fish. He thought of catching fish and eating them until he imagined their wriggling while they died. Sampson cried. Many times he cried. He thought maybe Grouchy was wrong, for he figured only the ones who wanted to live cried.

*   *   *   *

Ed Roy dragged Sampson with him to church every Sunday since Sampson was eleven until he turned sixteen. Ed made him wear a tie. Combed hair was another requirement, and he got smacked when he messed up his hair right after his father had styled it into the perfect part.

Quoting from the Bible was Ed Roy's favorite pastime. He took one everywhere he went. Each quote was different from the last. Sampson figured it was one his father had just memorized. He figured his father spoke them to convince others he wasn't the man they saw. Ed's eyes still burned, though. They burned brightest anytime he heard violence from the TV or radio, or from someone recounting him time in a war or just between men. In church his eyes were vacant, only alive when a recounting of some brutality 2,000 years ago shocked them into life.

"There is always a time to kill, Sam," his father once told him. "I have guns in the house for a reason. I won't be left without my children or my wife. Someone come to try and take anything away, they'll pay with their life."

Ed took him to the gun range when Sampson was old enough to shoot. He cackled with pleasure when Sampson became good enough to strike a fatal blow to the paper target or a deer with larger antlers than the last. Someday a war would come, Ed said to his son. He told him he better be ready to fight in that war. His honor was on the line. If he failed, he failed everyone: his mother, his father, himself, his country, his god.

Sampson told his friends he would be a solider. His friends and he played war on the front lawn. One of them was Grouchy. Grouchy played like it was a game, though, and Sampson played it for real. Sampson yelled at his soldiers. He put them in formation. He hit them if they didn't follow his commands. If Sampson weren't so popular, many of the kids would have deserted him. Eventually, Grouchy did desert and played war with kids who knew it was just a game.

The ROTC was Sampson's only reason to go to high school. Grouchy didn't see him much after that. In boot camp they spoke to each other again. Sampson remembered the nickname that only he called David, so called David "Grouchy" again. Grouchy told him not to, but Sampson did anyway—and smiled anytime Grouchy voiced his protest.

The rest of the soon-to-be-soldiers followed his lead and called David "Grouchy". But when they were far enough away from Sampson, they called him "David" or "Dave". David didn't like "Dave" either.

✳   ✳   ✳   ✳

"You thought I was crazy, didn't you?" Sampson said to Grouchy inside their tent just as dawn was approaching and Sampson was waking.

"I thought your dad was. I thought you just wanted to please him."

"My dad was crazy before he stopped drinking, but-"

"No. Your dad was crazy always, Sam."

"*No*, when he stopped drinking, Grouchy-"

"Just because you stop drinking doesn't make the reason you started go away. He was twisted, Sam. Half the reason I stopped playing war with you was to get away from him. He didn't watch us with a smile, Sam. He was watching to imagine all the death we were just pretending. He wished he could see it, Sam, and you know it."

Sampson wanted to think he didn't know that. His father might be the personification of bloodlust now, but that didn't mean he was tainted. Sampson told himself *he* was tainted, not his father.

✳   ✳   ✳   ✳

His mom was gentle, too gentle for Sampson's taste. He would always remember that barrel pressed against her head and the peaceful look on her face, wishing the last sound she heard was the trigger taking her away. She had no fight—like his dad had too much. Ed tried to smother his aggression with scripture. But Sampson's father preached scripture like he was cocking a barrel and pleading with anyone to shout, "Fire!"

Sifting through a closet at home to take what he wanted for the woods, Sampson saw too many photographs of his father and him hunting. It seemed their only companionship was through guns. They talked only about guns, war, fighting, revenge, America's honor, America's dominance, and the need to keep it so. They didn't converse in scripture; that was a monologue reserved for his father. There was no room for anyone else's interpretation. The words made little sense to Ed as they did to everyone else, but someday he was sure he'd understand, just as they would too—with his help, of course.

Sampson's sister was married now, married to a man who beat her. Sampson beat that man the first time he saw a mark on his sister that could only be from two fists. But his sister didn't appreciate Sampson's need for reprisal. She came to the house angry. Another bruise was on her face, and bruises were all over her body. Yet she was still angry with Sampson. She told her brother to mind his own life and she would mind hers. Before he went into the war in the sand, he made himself look at her bruises as if they were mosquito marks. What else could he do? She'd made her case. He would let her go to hell.

"Man and wife have to work it out," his father told him one day.

Sampson didn't know if his father ever laid a hand on his mother other than during the fight that ended with the shotgun barrel shoved against her head. He didn't think so. He never heard a noise. But his father beat her with words, words that Sampson tried to ignore. He made sure to tell his mom he loved her, though. He made sure to tell her every day.

*   *   *   *

"You ever visit your parents?" Sampson asked Grouchy as he slipped an already half-eaten ear of corn into his mouth.

"Mom's sick. It looks too sad."

"You keep saying this sad shit. *I'm* far more sad than any of them."

"I can *talk* to you, Sam. I can only watch them. I can't say shit. Well I can say *shit*, but they won't hear *shit*."

The truth was Grouchy visited everyone who still lived whom he wished he still lived beside. Often, he looked over his little girl's crib. He watched his wife rise with her crying. He watched her bear the burden of everything. A letter came for him from Lilly, and Grouchy watched Sheila open it. The letter recounted their times together. He watched his wife cry into her hands and then look to the ceiling and forgive him.

"Turn yourself in, Sam," Grouchy said. "Please turn yourself in."

"If I had any strength in my body, I would. I just don't want to see anyone. I don't want any help. I don't want to try anymore. I'm used up."

"You'll have a child soon, Sam. Do it for your child."

"You said it yourself; that child will only be mine biologically."

"Still … even if you never see your child, your child will hear about you, will know what you went through. If you can find your way out, your child will be proud of the blood in its veins. You've been through more than most men twice your age. If you can survive all of that, your child will know he or she can too."

"I have my father in my veins. I have meanness in my veins. I have my mother in my veins. I have submission in my veins. How do those mix, Grouchy? They mix by me burning out the first and becoming the last."

"Neither of them was born that way. They *became* that way, Sam. What do you want to become?"

"I want to become a part of these trees. I want to just stand still and feel the weather around me. I want to watch and never move. I want to be planted to a space of earth and stand by until the forces of this world cut me down."

"Hate to tell you this, Sam, but the world already has. The question is, will you stay down?"

CHAPTER 8

Grouchy wasn't very good at first base. He stumbled when he ran. He couldn't hit very well. Sampson hit hard and where they never expected. He'd been written up in the paper. The local sports section called him a future big league shortstop since T-ball.

Sampson's dexterity could be overwhelming. He could dive for a sharply hit ball, snatch it, and throw it home before the runner could even start kicking up dust on the third base line. Home runs were not his forte, but driving in runs was. No boy on any Little League field in Kennesaw matched his talent. No boy created such an atmosphere of expectation as when Sampson approached the plate.

There wasn't much yelling in the bleachers—only when Sampson made one of his great plays, or when someone ran out a great bunt, or when the big kid with all the peanuts lodged in his teeth hit a home run. But over the din of the cars along the streets and the chatter of parents, over the cracks of the bat and the umpire calling someone out, was Sampson's father, yelling. He yelled at his son, telling him what to do and expressing his unhappiness when he didn't do it, or didn't do it as told.

Ed Roy came to every one of Sampson's games drunk and boisterous, as if he were at a hole-in-the-wall bar and everyone should just accept his slobbery appearance as part of the scenery. He had yet to put that shotgun barrel to his wife's head. Alcohol was still a pleasure, not a crippling vice. Sampson's mother wasn't with him. She reserved what strength she had for refusing to go anywhere with Ed when he was drunk.

A few times Ed was asked to be quiet. Once he got into a fight with another father. It ended when Ed flashed his police badge and asked if the father wanted to go to jail.

Sampson never looked in the bleachers. He never wanted his father to come. He didn't mention the games at the dinner table, hoping just once his father wouldn't remember. But his father always knew, had his baseball hat on, had his bulging gut full of the hardest grain alcohol money could buy, and started lecturing his son about his technique as soon as he started the car.

No one ever told Ed what an embarrassment he was, certainly not Sampson. Sampson's friends never razzed him about his dad. They knew how dangerous that could be. And Sampson figured criticizing his father was more dangerous to him by ten. His father had yet to hit Sampson, beside with the quick back of his hand or a paddle to his bottom. But for some reason, even before the incident with the shotgun, Sampson felt his father was on the cusp of something he didn't want to tempt.

✳   ✳   ✳   ✳

The cross on top of Grouchy's mother's chest was starting to make an indentation. She barely moved from bed. She had cancer before Grouchy went to war but thought she had it beat. It came back strong after he died.

Grouchy stood there watching her chest rise with difficulty and fall just the same. He spoke to her, but she never showed any notice and never spoke back to him. The near-dead could see him. Many had. As the young and old alike walked in life and he walked beside them, they saw this man, this nearly translucent man, and knew what he was, though Grouchy offered them no words. He could only believe this meant his mother wasn't going to die, that her sickness was just a brief reoccurrence and would fade like all her others. But all her doctors thought differently.

His father stroked his mother's hair and Grouchy watched. As each strand of black and grey dislodged onto his father's fingers, Grouchy saw death nearing, not retreating like he hoped. His father held these strands until gravity brought them to the floor. He smelled his hand when he was away from her. He cried when it hit him she would soon be away from him forever.

Grouchy was sad, but happy too. His father would lose his mate, but Grouchy and his mom might see each other again, might walk hand in hand to their next destination, which lay beyond the cloud of shifting shapes and colors and beckons all when their time on earth has ended. It beckons all, but doesn't force their acceptance. His mom would be ready. He knew that. Grouchy wished he'd be ready then too.

*   *   *   *

Above, the planes made so much noise. Sampson was starting to look and act like a caveman. Anything industrial had him wincing and cowering. His primal fear was starting to spread. A primitive mind was starting to engage. When a noise disturbed him in the woods, he grunted. Sampson sniffed the woods for berries or anything else that smelled edible. He rarely guessed right and had acute diarrhea some days. His body begged him to just steal. Each time Grouchy tried persuading him to leave this kind of life, Sampson deflected him and grew surlier with each deflection.

"I don't want to *surrender*! *This* is how I want to live!"

"Do you think this is a war?"

"*All* of life is a war, Grouchy!"

"No, it isn't. Your dad wanted you to think that. But this has nothing to do with war, Sam. It has to do with happiness. *Are* you happy?"

"I'm as happy as I can be."

"Really? Can you remember lying beside Mary? Are you just as happy now as you were when you were sober and in love?"

*   *   *   *

Mary always smelled good. When she left the bed to start breakfast or use the bathroom, Sampson would bury his nose into her pillow because he couldn't stand to be without her scent if he could help it.

Her parents didn't like him. They were liberals. They smoked pot when they were young. They went to sit-ins and protested the war in Vietnam. When Sampson passed this information along to his father, he called them outright traitors and said he'd never go out of his way to meet them. He never did. Neither did his mom.

Sampson and Mary didn't talk about what could divide them. So, they didn't talk very much at all after a while. They didn't need to. What they had was under the surface, under the mind, a chemistry that kept them together. It would have ended sooner or later, however, and this belief comforted Sampson for a time. But those glorious days of living together as man and wife before he was sent to fight still filled Sampson with feelings of uncomfortable euphoria and grief.

In the evening Sampson sometimes saw Mary. When Grouchy wasn't around he sometimes talked to her too. But unlike Grouchy, Mary wasn't a ghost. She was his feeling of responsibility manifested in the one he most let down. Or who he thought he most let down. She held a baby in her arms. In his delusion, the baby looked like him when he was a baby.

"What's your name?" Sampson said to the baby in Mary's arms.

"It's Susan, honey," Mary said.

"Will Susan have a daddy?"

"All babies have daddies."

"Her daddy can't take care of her though."

"No, he can't. Her daddy didn't even know I was pregnant when I left him. It took you almost a week to know I was gone."

"I can't explain, Mary. I can't tell you why I failed you. I can't tell you why the bottom dropped out. But it did, and there is nothing in the world that can bring me back from down there."

"You could have gotten help. You never did."

"It's for the weak."

"What are you now?"

"Grouchy says I'm near-dead. I don't want to be *near*-anything anymore!" he yelled. "If I'm about to be dead, Lord, make me dead. If I can get out, give me sign. If I can be a normal man again, *help* me do it, goddamn it!"

*   *   *   *

School let out early one day. Pipes had burst inside a school bathroom and lined the halls with foul-smelling refuse. Sampson's father was away on a fishing trip somewhere, or that's what he said.

Alice and Sampson came through the door and heard a strange squeak. It bounced around like it was coming closer, but was only reverberating around the empty house. The two children: Alice, fourteen, and Sampson, twelve, followed the sound up the stairs and to their parent's bedroom. They saw a balding man on top of a woman. Their father had a full head of hair and was fat. This man was skinny. They gawked at the humping, wheezing body for almost thirty seconds before their mother's eyes opened and saw them standing there.

She screamed. The man leaped from her body and quickly dressed. Intense shame shot through their mother's grey green eyes.

"Don't you tell your daddy about this," she said to her children when she finally could speak. "He would kill me."

Somehow both Sampson and Alice understood. Somehow, even though they were young, they knew their mother was unhappy. Neither of them had seen the opposite sex naked yet. Neither of them knew much about love except what they heard in church since their father started dragging them there every Sunday. But they knew what their mommy and daddy had wasn't love.

Alice would reveal what she had seen to her father, but not until she was out of the house and in a loveless marriage of her own. Her father didn't seem fazed. His last dozen or so sexual partners didn't include his wife. They were hookers, and he didn't have to pay because he was a cop. Before Sampson was married his father bragged about cheating on his mother. He bragged about women he made up. Sampson wondered if he'd gone back to drinking, but his father swore he was speaking sober.

Sampson cheated on Mary with some men, but never women while he served. He never allowed them to penetrate him. He figured this made him less of an anomaly. The sex was always rough, like the first time he'd had sex. An uncle whom he hardly ever saw lured him into his guest room and did to Sampson what Sampson did to all those young queer boys in the army who were hiding their sexuality just like him. It was a secret among them that he was game. Sampson threatened every single one with castration if it didn't remain one.

✳   ✳   ✳   ✳

Counting on his fingers, Sampson tried to figure out how long he'd been in the woods. It was going on nine months, but he was losing so much perspective he thought it could have been five years.

Some fires from the sand brightened the woods he now sat in. Sampson imagined those fires again when he looked out his tent flap. He saw the fires coming closer. The fire should surround his body, he thought, and burn him away.

He saw so many bodies that way, especially children. Sometimes the fire had burned them so badly that it severed the head from the body. The smell was so sickly sweet it had an attraction that soon repelled him with great prejudice. He didn't let his men see him, but he threw up, telling himself he was just weak.

"The world is a test," his father would tell him. "Just a test. Every bad thing that happens is testing you. The real world is after here."

Sometimes Sampson wanted to make his dad promise that. He wanted a promise. He didn't want "belief". His father needed to tell him he *knew* it to be true. But Sampson knew that his father and truth had never much crossed paths.

CHAPTER 9

Sampson lay idle on the dusty ground for more than fifteen minutes. Insurgents had scrambled all communication. But, the insurgents had run out of ammunition. Everything was quiet, except the smoldering Humvee with its cackling flames and yawning, burning metal. Sampson was gone from his mind, somewhere in never-never land. One man had a long, sharp knife. The women and children watched the road. The man with the knife approached Sampson's body. A helicopter flew overhead. Another Humvee was deployed. The man took the cloth from his face. He started making a speech. If he didn't, Sampson would have been a headless body. Instead, the approaching Humvee riddled the would-be-killer with bullets.

*　　　*　　　*　　　*

Long before Grouchy was left without a leg, his wife, Sheila, filled her house with other wives who had been left behind. She invited the list from Kennesaw. It wasn't a very long list. She invited twenty, and ten came. Black and white, older and younger, and among the smiles was shy Mary's.

Mary was shy as a girl, and she stayed that way as an adult. The women seemed giddy and enthusiastic. Everyone was hugging and sharing intimate stories with women they'd never seen before and might never see again. They showed pictures of all their kids, crying as they did. Mary wished she had remembered her problem with crowds before she came. She stayed, though she wanted to walk out as soon as she walked in.

Sheila was sorry she reached out. She regretted her need to communicate with others who knew. She didn't know *them*. She didn't like *this*. Sheila displayed a toughness that said, "Don't cry to me." She reminded Mary of Sampson. Sheila had known Sampson, and Mary had met Grouchy. None of the other women had known either. When Mary said Sampson's name and Sheila said Grouchy's, the two women found an enclave and let the house be overrun by busy women who found enclaves of their own.

Sheila was pregnant, due any minute. Mary was jealous. Sheila was sure her husband would come home alive. Mary didn't have a faith, didn't believe in faith, so she didn't ever guess if hers would.

The two lonely wives saw each other often after that. But they needed each other more than they saw each other. Mary came to the hospital just after Sheila gave birth. She stayed in Sheila's house and helped her look after the baby. She left only when the bank called complaining of a missed mortgage payment. Mary held Sheila after they learned that Grouchy had lost his leg. Later, she confided in Shelia that she was leaving Sampson. Sheila told her to give Sampson more time, but Mary told her how he had called her Susan.

The two women continued e-mailing each other. They spoke of Mary's growing belly. They spoke of their loneliness. More than a dozen times, Mary had asked if Sheila had seen Sampson. No one had, and if they did they wouldn't know what they were seeing. Sheila suggested Mary come down to live with her and they could be young mothers together. Mary was getting tired of Ohio. She was remembering why she wanted to go to school out of state. Her small town was feeling just as stifling as before she left. She remembered that she left to change and came back to be the same. Then she remembered why she didn't want to be the same. As the due date got closer, Mary realized that caring for a baby with all her emotionally distant family was a life she didn't want, so she moved back to Kennesaw. She gave birth to a girl she named Cecilia.

*   *   *   *

"She's here, Sam," Grouchy told Sampson after he saw Mary and Sheila in his home, cuddling a baby who had Sampson's same eyes, the same brightness in his eyes before Sampson went into the sand. "You have a little girl. I know where she is. You can go to her."

"Go to her like this? Yeah, right!"

"Well, not like you are. But once you get some help, she's just a little ways a way."

"What's the girl's name?"

"Cecilia."

"Who's Cecilia?"

"After that song I think," said Grouchy. "I heard them talking about it."

"Them? Who's she got with her? My parents? She living with my parents?"

"She's living with my wife, Sam. They're really good friends. They're each other's help."

Mary got a job teaching elementary school. Her dream was to become an English professor, but she still had so much more schooling to complete. If money weren't an issue, she'd have dived in head first. However, Sampson's disability checks were in his name. They didn't have a joint checking account, and Mary didn't have the energy to explain she was the wife of a man who had gone away. The paperwork. The counselors at the VA. They all made this so hard, and a new child was hard enough.

Sheila drove a shuttle to and from the airport. She brought Elena, her and Grouchy's child, along. Sometimes Elena's cries caused complaints. But though her boss listened to the complaints and said he'd talk to her, he never once did— not about her child, at least.

$$*   *   *   *$$

Sampson began having terrific headaches. His restlessness and fear collided fiercely and always end in a draw, leaving him weathering the damage. Grouchy saw what was happening and let him be. He feared Sampson might suffer a stroke. He also feared Sampson might attempt to end his life. Sampson's body tossed and turned in those filthy clothes that he hadn't changed or washed in months. Some kind of skin rash or infection was imminent, Grouchy was sure. But he could do nothing about that. If Sampson's mind had already convinced him he was a man of the forest, if he was only humoring Grouchy with the possibility of coming back into a world that demanded less of his body but more of his mind, Grouchy wished for the infection to spread so Sampson could be free from both.

"How do I do it, Grouchy?" Sampson asked him one day.

"Just go to the street and wave down a cop. Tell him what you did. Tell him about your service. You're in *Kennesaw*, Sam, a very patriotic town."

"But ... what ... what will they do?"

"I don't know. You didn't hurt anybody. You still have the money. When you give it back they'll probably just hospitalize you for a little while."

"For a little while?"

"You want to get well, don't you?"

"I don't know if they care about that. They probably just want me trapped."

"You're trapped already, and the more you stay in this trap the harder it is to get out of it."

Sampson started down the mountain, but when he saw normal hikers, hikers with clean clothes and a look that showed a lack of disturbance, he couldn't move another step. He imagined his image looking like Bigfoot. The cops wouldn't believe him, or in Kennesaw they'd be disgusted that war had turned him inside out. It didn't matter that barely anybody really knew what he knew. The judgment would be in their eyes.

Frozen, Sampson just watched. He hoped to thaw. But only when he turned his head back to where his tent stood did things settle inside. Sampson waited nonetheless. He waited for his courage. Courage was all he had before. He'd faced imminent death more than once. Inside the country he patrolled, ninety percent of the population hated him fiercely and many had guns. But he still couldn't go down this mountain under daylight.

Sampson began to cry. He shook branches overhead. He wanted to plunge that knife in his back pocket into his throat. But he couldn't do that either. The trees now looked like bars. The wind was manufactured air conditioning. His clothes were his chains. His fear held the keys—and held them far from Sampson's reach.

Collapsing into the ground, Sampson felt numb. He looked at the top of the trees and saw the limitless sky. Finding a tall enough ladder to float on those clouds seemed the only solution. He thought he should have died on the ground in the sand. Sampson thought maybe he did die, but for some reason his soul had left a body and mind to remain.

Chapter 10

The mountainside held caves, which were inspected daily. It was a brutal and scary task. Grouchy crawled on his belly. He waded though the muck of dead animals. Some had been killed by other animals, but most had been butchered by men. Grouchy disarmed the mines he could see.

Grouchy and his crew started into each cave with small steps. Men had been blown up, killed, struck blind, and struck mad entering these caves. When they left each one, it was with the relief of men stepping from a grave they were ordered to dig.

Grouchy went alone into the recesses of the caves. He heard the click, as quiet as a dropped pebble, but it resounded much louder within his trained understanding. The click sounded just as Grouchy's feet passed a tripwire made to look like dead leaves. He knew exactly what it meant and stared at where it came from. Only a bad fuse would save him.

The explosion ripped into Grouchy's thigh and his leg was gone. He saw it rip away from his body. It shot into an inch-thick sheet of rock and splintered into a hundred pieces. It took him thirty seconds to scream. Blood poured and he screamed until he passed out.

Grouchy woke up in Germany. The doctors told him he was going home. He called Sheila and she cried into the phone while their baby cried in the background.

"I'm glad, Sheila. I'm still alive. I'll be fine."

Sheila was glad he was coming home, too, but she feared for his mental state. She'd seen the soldiers on TV. The broken ones, the bitter ones. Grouchy could be one them—catatonic, a boozer. She thought all his smiles would fade soon. He'd be mean, upset that he wasn't whole anymore. But he never woke screaming. Never once did Grouchy complain about that missing leg. He was home. He was alive. Sobriety was never an issue, and happiness wasn't either.

*   *   *   *

Sheila hurt. She had a friend to live with. Two babies and two mommies seemed the best solution, but it wasn't. The hurt came on stronger when she realized it could never be. Grouchy wanted to reach out and hold her. When Sheila cried into her pillow, he wanted to stroke her hair.

"Why did you have to fuck with me, God?" she would scream into her pillow. "Why didn't you just kill him over there? Why did you have to let him come home and seem so healthy? What did I do to deserve that, God?"

*   *   *   *

After falling asleep under those trees, Sampson had to search in the dark for his tent, and he fell and he hurt himself. His ankle twisted badly, painfully. It looked like putty and dangled as he tried to walk. Each movement brought a greater grimace. He was out of food. He had to descend the mountain sometime so he didn't starve. But instead, Sampson once again looked for food within an eye line from his tent and ate bullbrier berries all day long. The deer didn't even eat the bitter berries.

Three straight nights of painful diarrhea weakened Sampson. He had to drink something. He would have to steal food again, even though it hurt his ankle so bad to go down.

Each shoot of pain brought a tiny cry out of Sampson's throat. He weaved into traffic, but he didn't care. A police car stopped behind him and demanded through the single black speaker blaring from its roof that he turn around. The pain was too much for Sampson to care about being trapped by the government anymore.

"What's wrong with you?" asked the beefy cop, stepping out and looking at Sampson with disgust and annoyance.

"Hurt my ankle."

"Besides that?"

"I'm a veteran, sir. Please go lightly on me."

"What?"

"I held up a convenience store some time ago. I can't remember when. I have all the money." Sampson dug into his pocket to bring out the dirty bills.

The cop came forward slowly. His headlights shined into Sampson's eyes, which were twitching with pain. He looked ready to surrender. The cop tried to determine his sanity. Would this man stab him with a broken Coke bottle?

"You say you're a veteran," said the officer, stopping his approach once he smelled Sampson.

"Yes, sir. I was honorably discharged too. I fought my heart out. I saw many men die. I was ... hurt. Not like the rest. But I was hurt. I was. You can look it up."

"Well ... I appreciate that," said the officer, feeling certain Sampson was never in any war. "But we need to get you off the road. We need to have you looked at."

"I understand that, sir. Please give this money to that man. He was an asshole, but I suppose that don't mean I can steal from him."

"You hold on to that money for now. I'll check out your story once we get to the station."

$$* \quad * \quad * \quad *$$

Sampson sat at a desk, his hands twitching, his ankle constantly moving to try to ward off the pain. He rambled. The memories of the sand came through his throat. He told the officer everything—everything the officer needed to know and everything he didn't. When Sampson repeated himself, he increased the details to an even greater degree.

"It's bright in here," Sampson said.

"Really?" said the officer. "Seems a little dim to me."

"I haven't been under artificial light in some time."

"How much time?"

"Don't know. What year is it?"

"What *year* is it?" said the officer and stopped typing. "You don't know what *year* it is? You seem to know everything else."

"I've lost track of all of that. I kind of like that I did."

"Now, which store was this?"

"Clements Stop and Shop."

"Oh, OK. Now I remember. That was about a month ago."

"I think it had to be longer than that."

"No, it was just a month. Read it on the board. I heard he and his dipshit son was raving at anybody that would hear, like they won something. You say you're a veteran?"

"Yes, sir. I have a VA card right here. It has an appointment on it. My wife made it, though. I never went. I'm having problems with my brain."

"You don't say," said the officer, and then felt bad for saying it.

"Everything was fine until the three A's died," Sampson said, though his memories were telling him everything wasn't fine for much longer than that. "Did you know anybody in the war?"

"My dad was in World War II."

"No. The war in the sand."

"Not really. Some friend's sons. They're back already."

"Hurt?"

"No. None of them was hurt. They didn't see much combat."

"That's all I saw."

"OK. Well … this ain't anything we can square away here. We're gonna need to take you to the hospital."

✳   ✳   ✳   ✳

The hospital staff undressed Sampson. They tried not to seem disgusted, but they were. They saw growing fungus on his body, felty grey and crusted over from the increasing filth. It was the worst around his inner thigh, near his anus. With masks on, they scrubbed Sampson. He was frightened by the touch at first, and then it felt so good.

Sampson was put into a guarded ward. His ankle was bandaged. They said it would be fine. He lay next to an old man who gibbered nonsense until they injected him with some drugs. Fear crept back in. He didn't want to be that old man in forty years. He didn't want to be a ward of the state until his death. But the bed felt so nice. Soon after the old man stopped gibbering Sampson fell into a deep sleep.

"I'm here, Sam," Grouchy said out of the blackness. "Do you want me to stay around?"

"Only if you don't want to go, Grouchy."

"Not yet," Grouchy said, though it was more because of his unwillingness to leave his wife than help Sampson.

"How's your mother?"

"She's not good, Sam. But she'll be free soon. She'll walk into the cloud. I know it."

Sampson was shaved the next day. His hair was cut. They showed him a mirror, and he didn't know who was staring back. He saw crazed eyes that looked out of place inside the rest of the clean face. Anyone who knew him before would have understood this image, but none would have understood the man stumbling from the woods.

Sampson saw only the past. He saw himself, the self that existed so long ago. He saw a ghost. That man was dead. He was killed long before the woods.

Chapter 11

Sampson's naked toes touched carpet. A beautiful young woman sat opposite him. She had been the psychologist on duty since she graduated Georgia State some six months before. Her legs were so bronze they almost shined. One danced on a knee. Sampson wished she would spread each knee and tug away what hid her pussy.

"Tell me why you went into the woods," the psychologist said. She was sleek and young. Sampson was seduced, though that was hardly her intention. Any woman showing enough flesh at this distance from him would have invigorated him just the same.

Her breasts were not especially ample, but they were breasts, and Sampson stared at them. He was erect. The psychologist was uncomfortable. Sampson was young. Most of the patients she saw were old or unresponsive and imbibed with a libido that never worked. Sampson wanted her. He wanted *it*. The guard manning her door hardly looked attentive, so she scooted her chair back from the impression rising from underneath Sampson's gown.

"Mr. Roy? Can you hear me, Mr. Roy?" she said.

"Can I touch you?" Sampson responded.

"No, you can't, Mr. Roy. I'm here to help you."

"It would help me if I could touch you."

"No, it wouldn't. I'm not here to help you with that."

"I haven't touched a woman in so long."

"OK, Mr. Roy, but you won't be touching me."

"It might help me to remember what you asking."

"Really? Well, first try to remember when you last touched a woman, and when the memories come back you can start answering my questions."

∗   ∗   ∗   ∗

They were called tinderboxes, the men in units who seemed sufficiently bothered before they ever saw battle. It was on their file. But the commanders couldn't worry about who was or who wasn't one when the firing started.

Jason was one. He could be the light of day, or bring night early when he didn't speak and just stared at the distant sky, wishing he were one of the drifting clouds. He was prescribed medicine, at home and in the sand, but Jason didn't take any, ever. He said the pills made him feel numb. He said he'd rather feel the high highs and the low lows. The lows were getting lower all the time. Battle wasn't for guys like him. It shook what was already held so precariously in his brain.

A scorpion tattoo was emblazoned on the web of his left hand between his thumb and forefinger. Jason had few family and he never got any mail. There was no one for him to call back home. He considered the military his family, but the military really wasn't the place for him. He cried during the boring day. A swell of good feelings kept him up past curfew chattering, feelings that would disappear as soon as the sun came up.

Grouchy thought it was ketchup. Or, he wanted to think that. He thought Jason had fallen asleep eating a hamburger. But the bullet wound was oozing between his eyes.

No one showed any surprise. His death was an inevitability. Jason was the raining cloud, the weeping cloud that would run out of reasons. His fragility was evident in his speech, his eyes, his languid movements. Grouchy lent an ear, but he was the only one. He always advised Jason to take his medicine. Jason always promised him he would, but he never did.

Jason's commander had recommended he be shipped home on numerous occasions, or at least reassigned to a duty that would be easier for him. But since all his limbs worked and he hadn't tried to harm himself yet, the commander's superiors said he was just going through a phase. They had never met Jason and never would.

The commander said that Grouchy should write a personal letter to include with the official letter the military would bring when officers visited the closest relative's home. Grouchy didn't know who to write the letter to. Jason's mother and father had died almost a year after he was born. He was raised by a grandmother who was now in a home. Jason hadn't been able to communicate with her for more than five years. He had no siblings. He didn't have a wife or a girl-friend. Friendships were never easy for him, not even with the men he backed up in a fight. Jason was truly alone and had grown tired of it. Grouchy wrote the let-ter to the "Family of Jason Sean" and gave it to his commander.

*   *   *   *

Sheila and Mary put up safety barriers in the house when they decided to get a dog. The puppy was born to a family who couldn't take care of it. It was a pure-bred Golden Labrador that got into plenty of trouble. He'd knock over every-thing in his path. But he was still cute. Along with their in babies, it was an idyllic scene much of the time, though Sheila and Mary were certain that raising three new creatures was a good way to go completely crazy.

Sheila's boss, Tommy, invited himself over quite a bit. He had a new baby, too, and was a single parent now as well. His boy's mother died from complica-tions after giving birth. She held her son only once; the boy would only see his mother in pictures. Tommy couldn't hold him at all, at first. His boy had taken away his love. The baby was not a gift, not a replacement, not a miracle, not a blessing. Grief-stricken, Tommy raged at the injustice. For a month Tommy drank and raved and yelled at the ceiling just like Sheila yelled at God.

The anger had to lift. No matter that a life he wanted more was taken for a life he'd yet to know; he had a son. Tommy wondered if he should love the baby who killed her. In his stronger times, he told himself the baby didn't. The doctors did, or maybe fate did. Sometimes blame was not part of the answer. Sometimes there was no answer.

He felt part of a family when he came over to see Sheila and Mary and their babies. He felt utterly alone when he left. His son cried more and more often. Cuddling against the two women with softer flesh, cuddling against the babies he never wanted to leave made his son cry relentlessly when Tommy had to take him away. His son needed a mother. Tommy didn't love Sheila, but didn't know if that even mattered now.

*   *   *   *

Storms above the hospital brought back Sampson's memory of finding a home in the woods. He was quite drunk and planned on getting drunker. The tent was rolled up in his backpack. The rain came upon his head and he loved it, though it made him very sick. But seeking medical attention seemed contrary to his purpose. Sampson vomited on that leafy, mossy ground. But blissful solitude superseded the voices that told him to go home and get help.

Sampson was feeling crowded now. He hadn't literally seen Grouchy since the day he tried to go down the mountain. The other patients were getting on his nerves. He didn't think he was anywhere near as sick as they were, and he didn't want to have their sickness just to be taken care of. He asked how long they planned on keeping him. No one ever answered him.

The drugs the hospital gave Sampson made him feel as if he were underwater. He'd rather be drunk. The drugs made him want the taste of liquor on his tongue. He swore that the first time he was able, he would buy a pint of his favorite and empty it just as quickly.

*   *   *   *

Grouchy didn't like the way Tommy looked at his wife. He thought the dead didn't feel jealousy as the living did. But what he was feeling couldn't be called anything else.

"There's another man," he told Sampson one late night at the foot of Sampson's hospital bed.

"What do you expect, Grouchy? You not exactly available."

"I don't know if I can watch that."

"Don't you want her to be happy?"

"What if Mary found another man, Sam?"

"I'm alive, Grouchy. You told me to get well so I could win her back."

"But what if you can't?"

"I will! I have a daughter. *You* the one that told me to get help! Don't make me feel like it won't make a difference!"

An orderly opened the room's door. He asked Sampson who he was talking to. "I must have been talking in my sleep," Sampson said. Grouchy was gone when the orderly left. Sampson wanted him back. He whispered loudly for him to come back.

An administrator from the VA came to visit Sampson. She spoke in whispers to the psychologist Sampson wished he could touch and make love to. He was under sedation but could still hear every other word and could still feel so much want for either body—even a body like the administrator's, which was older and quite lumpy

"Do you have anywhere to go?" asked the administrator from the VA, who aroused him further with her unencumbered voice.

"Yes," Sampson said just because he wanted to be released.

"Can you give me the address?"

Sampson gave them his old home address. But the bank had taken that home back, and a new family had just moved in.

The hospital found him some street clothes that fit. They told him the owner of the convenience store wouldn't press charges as long as he never came back. And the owner wanted Sampson to know that he considered the $104 a gift to get him situated. The owner made the hospital promise they would tell Sampson that he supported the troops.

CHAPTER 12

The donated pants Sampson wore were one size too small. Ketchup stains lined the knees. The shirt, donated just like the pants, rested just above his navel. It was long-sleeved with red polka dots on a white silk-like fabric. His armpits were exposed through two large holes that dangled white synthetic strands and tickled his hairs.

The hospital called him a cab. Sampson waited in the lobby of the hospital, pacing back and forth, wondering where to go, what to do. He knew where Grouchy once lived. The address was in his mind. The trailhead of his favorite trail couldn't be but ten minutes away. A bar must be even closer. When the cab pulled up to the curb, Grouchy was already waiting for Sampson inside. He was sitting in the backseat looking at Sampson as Sampson looked at him.

"I don't know if you're well enough, Sam," Grouchy told him as the cab began to move.

"They said they had to release me."

"Do you really think you're ready?"

"I'm clean, aren't I?"

"You're still not clear, Sam."

"I'll get clear, Grouchy. Just a cab ride away. That's all and then I'll be clear."

"Where are you going?"

"To find courage."

"Sir," said the worried cab driver, "do you have any money?"

"Yeah, I have money," Sampson said, shaking the bills into the rearview mirror.

"Who are you talking to?"

"Just a ghost."

"A ghost?" the cabbie said and laughed.

"Yeah. Ain't you ever talked to a ghost?"

Time passed quicker once Sampson was drunk. He had the cabbie drop him off at a bar and drank half the money in his pocket. The first shot of Evan Williams tasted like the elixir of gods. The next shots were like good friends. The rest he confessed to. The other customers gawked as he talked to a shot glass and cried. Some of them laughed, others were bothered and said so aloud. Sampson cried, laughed, and drooled. The bartender asked him several times if he was OK. But Sampson couldn't hear him—only the voices in his head.

Sampson's second cab driver of the day idled for a while outside of Grouchy's old home. Sampson saw that puppy running on the front lawn and Sheila chasing after it. She had a baby in her arms. The baby was laughing and clothed in a sky-blue cotton outfit that Sampson imagined Sheila making herself. The cabbie told him he was spending a lot of money, and Sampson figured he was right; so he sucked in a breath and stepped on to the road after paying the cab driver with water-damaged money flaked with dried dirt.

Sheila looked up as Sampson neared her driveway. She froze. The puppy kept nipping at her heals, but she couldn't feel it. Her baby started crying, but she couldn't hear it.

Who was this man? Why was he coming at her that way? What's in those eyes? Is he drunk? Is he an ex-boyfriend mistaking me for an easy lay?

"H-hi," said Sampson. He tried to seem sober, but he wobbled on his feet.

"Where have you been, Sam?" Sheila said cautiously, though she felt somewhat relieved. She started walking towards him. The little hands of Elena started to reach for the puppy, and she cried again when he ran from her sight and into the backyard.

"I've been hiding."

"You know that Mary is here?"

"Yeah."

"How?"

"Grouchy told me."

"Grouchy?"

"David told me."

"David? David is dead, Sam."

"I know. He talks to me, though."

Sheila's curiosity turned back into caution. She didn't know what to do. A drunk, crazy man was in her driveway. But then she thought about Sampson's daughter, a daughter he'd never seen. Cecilia lay inside. Sheila's first decision, to ask him to leave, stopped just before it left her lips.

"Are you OK, Sam?" she asked.

"Hard to tell, I guess."

"It's not hard for me to tell."

Mary came to a window that was closed but free from the brown drapery that had been tied to each side. She looked on the scene with concern until she realized the man in the ill-fitting clothes was the husband she figured was dead. Dead in a ditch or in the actual woods. Dead by his own hand in a run-down motel where he gave a false name. Dead by an irate man stabbing him in the chest until his broken heart stopped beating.

Sampson saw Mary looking from the window. The shock on her face forced some sobriety into Sampson's veins. She was glued to the window, fascinated by the demise. But she was also afraid. Sampson wasn't dead, but looking at him, she wished he were and knew it wasn't an awful wish.

Sheila turned to see what Sampson was staring at, and then hurried inside when she saw Mary at the window. Elena's cries grew louder with every bounce of her mother's legs. Sampson watched the two women engage in animated, almost crazed conversation. When it was over, Sheila left Mary and Mary left Sampson's view, but she didn't come outside with Sheila as he expected.

"I want to see my baby," Sampson said.

"Not right now, Sam," Sheila replied.

"I want to see my baby!"

"This isn't a good time. You're in no condition."

"It's my baby!"

"Sam," said Grouchy, once again by his side. "I told you. Do you want to freak them out? Do you want to have no chance of getting back into her life?"

"But it's my baby!" Sampson said to the air where Grouchy stood.

Sheila looked at that space of nothing and finally became completely confident that Sampson's attempt was too soon.

"It's my baby," he repeated, turning back to Sheila with a grim tone and countenance.

"I'm sorry, Sam, but you're in no condition. This is the wrong way to try to see her for the first time."

"I was in a war!"

"I know you were."

"You have to understand what that did to me!"

"I do understand. But what it did to you was make you unstable. Would it make sense for us to let an unstable man see a newborn child?"

"So what do I do?"

"Sober up, for one."

✳   ✳   ✳   ✳

The concrete was hot. The sun bounced from it on to Sampson's clothes. He walked for blocks. Enough money was in his pocket for a cheap motel room and some more liquor.

Watching TV just made Sampson sad. He couldn't believe the war wasn't over. He wondered what they were waiting for. Other friends were probably dead, the friends he couldn't even say good-bye to, friends who only had an address he'd escaped from many months before.

Grouchy leaned against a cheap dresser next to the bolted-down TV.

"I wish you wouldn't have told Sheila I talk to you," he said.

"She doesn't believe me anyway."

"Well, don't say it again."

"I ain't gonna get close enough to say it again."

"Sam, call the VA. You need more help. A few days inside a hospital won't clear you up."

"I guess I gotta get a job."

"Call the VA for that too."

"I don't want to be no ward!"

"You need help," Grouchy replied patiently. "You keep spinning your wheels. You just sink further down, Sam. Buck up and do what your daddy never would. Try and cure yourself."

"At least my daddy could keep a job."

"Yeah, that sadistic fuck got the best job he could hope for."

"No, *I* did. I got to kill people for real. No investigation. No nothing."

"And look what all the bloodlust has done to you?"

"You saying I should be ashamed?"

"No, Sam. I'm saying you're not your daddy. I know you remember when you could have been."

*   *   *   *

The building was bombed from above. A child, half-blinded by particles of dust and confused by the blast that ricocheted his brain against his skull, stumbled out from the wreckage, where ten bodies lay.

"He's a booby trap!" one man in Sampson's unit cried. He ran to the boy, stuck his nine-millimeter Glock into his chest, and just about pressed his finger to fire.

"What the fuck you doing, soldier?" Sampson yelled, swatting the gun aside and staring down into the young soldier's face.

"He's a booby trap!"

"I don't see where they could have put all that. He's barely dressed, soldier!"

"We bombed it, didn't we? No one else is alive!"

"What is your point, soldier? Are we soldiers or goddamn barbarians!"

"We're trying to rid this place of the barbarians!"

"This boy don't look even near ten," said Sampson, pointing at a boy who wavered where he stood, dressed only in thin, overused underwear. The boy was punch—drunk from the explosion, foaming from the mouth and bleeding from his ears.

"He come from barbarians then!" the soldier screamed.

"Soldier!" Sampson said and slung his automatic weapon around to point it into the soldier's chest. "You tell me right now if you a soldier or a goddamn murderer. If you a fucking murderer, I'd rather booby trap *you* and send you into one of their bunkers."

"This is a war!" the soldier screamed back.

"That's right. But war ain't another word for massacre to me."

*   *   *   *

The motel room smelled of mold. The more Sampson drank, the more it irritated him. So he walked outside, found a spacious tree, and sat underneath it. Sleep gave him some peace until someone kicked his side.

"You gotta home?" asked the police officer as Sampson looked up to see mirrored sunglasses reflecting his just-awakened face.

"I was renting a room in there," Sampson said, pointing behind him with his thumb.

"So why are you out here?"

"It smells in there."

"Well, it smells worse in jail, so I suggest you get back in there."

"All right. Thank you, sir," Sampson replied and scrambled to his feet.

He approached his motel room door only to turn and lean weakly against a pole holding up part of the walkway's awning. He was completely drained from a day of chemical highs and emotional lows. His trembling hand began to reach his key towards the keyhole so he could stumble into a room that was air-conditioned and had a mattress to lie on. But the pole that flexed with his every breath felt as much comfort as he deserved.

It was dark now. Sampson could feel the woods calling him again. They were a ways a way, but he could walk there. He was wearing decent shoes. The hospital took his useless boots and threw them away. He was given bargain sneakers, cracked in some places but still sturdy.

"No, Sam," said Grouchy. "You can't do this again."

"What's the point?" Sampson started to cry. "I can't see my daughter. I can't see my wife."

"You aren't *ready* yet. Go back inside that room and in the morning call the VA."

"I belong in those woods."

"No, you belong in the world. I know the world looks real strange now because it's not the woods or the war, but you're not an animal, Sam. You're a man. You have to remember that again. And you will, sooner or later. But waiting until just before starvation kills you isn't the right way."

Chapter 13

Sheila and Mary needed a new couch. They found a black leather one on clearance. A young man from the store loaded it in his truck. He followed the two lovely ladies to their home. He fantasized about a threesome until they thanked him, tipped him, and said good-bye.

Mary and Sheila sat on the new leather, which seemed to squeak louder than when they sat on the couch in the store. But the squeaks were buffered by their babies' cries. The puppy's endless barking was more annoying. The leather was cool on such a hot day. It hugged their bodies and grabbed any naked flesh.

"I didn't tell any of his family, Sheila," Mary said with a steaming teacup in her hand. It was from a set of dainty rose-colored teacups her parents had sent her just a few days before.

"I know that. He said David told him."

"Yeah, so you said. But that's obviously not the answer. You know that's not how he knows."

"Well, then, how else, Mary? He don't know Tommy. He don't know nothing, not without someone telling him, and no one did where he was."

"You're telling me that you really think he's talking to your dead husband?"

Sheila shrugged. "Maybe ghosts are real."

"Then why hasn't David come talk to *you*, Sheila?"

"Hell if I know. I just said *maybe* they're real. I sure as hell can't figure out their methods."

Grouchy was with them. He was sitting beside Sheila. Though she couldn't feel it, and neither could he, his hand touched her hair. He tried to smell her, but he didn't really have a nose, so he smelled nothing. That wouldn't stop him from trying, though.

His mother had died a week earlier. Grouchy was at the funeral. So were his father, Teddy, Mary, Sheila, and their two children, clutched and squirming against their chests. When Grouchy's mother died, she walked directly towards the back of the line for the cloud, just like he knew she would. He could have called her name. She would have heard. But he didn't want her to rethink what she shouldn't. Grouchy thought he saw her turn around. Turning just before she was taken, she looked in the distance, maybe at him. He thought he saw a smile. But it was so far away. Everything was a blur at that distance. He chose to believe that she did anyway.

*   *   *   *

The secretary was a bit rude. Sampson didn't really know what to say except that he hadn't gotten over the war. She asked him about certain symptoms. Sampson supposed he had them, but didn't know. Whatever mental problems she listed, he figured he *must* have.

"You're not being very helpful, sir," she said.

"I told you, everything you say sounds about right."

"Well, we need to assign a caseworker to you, and each has different specialties."

"Listen, all I can tell you is that I just spent almost a year in the woods. So, *you* figure out what that's classified under."

"That's not classified under anything."

"I just want some help, goddamn it! I didn't go to some library to look up all my fucking symptoms. I spent a year in the woods! Close your eyes, pick a symptom, and help me the fuck out!"

The secretary sighed and said, "Do you have a number I can reach you at?"

"Yeah, but only for another four hours."

*   *   *   *

The doorbell rang at 10:00 AM. It was a Saturday. Mary and Sheila had drunk a bit the night before. Tommy had come over and drank with them. Sheila could feel more intent in his demeanor. His eyes, which were usually friendly but neutral, seemed to signal he was looking for more than just a friend. Mary could see it, too, but she didn't say anything. It was too soon. Everyone knew it was too soon.

Looking inside from the front lawn, Grouchy asked himself how long he planned to hold on. It was obvious something would happen, whether it was Tommy or another man. Sheila was a young woman, not even twenty-five. She wasn't so pathetic to live through Grouchy's memory forever. He knew this, but his want wasn't swayed. Desire still survived and beat madly inside his soul. He couldn't leave her, because that would leave him void of her. It didn't matter that she was forever void of him.

"I need a ride," Sampson said to Sheila when she opened the door.

Mary stayed inside the room she shared with her daughter. Part of her wanted to see Sampson, to look in his eyes, to feel his embrace. But every time Mary heard Sampson's tone echo from the front door and down the hallway, it reminded her of the tone she'd fallen in love with, which wasn't there anymore. It hadn't been since he returned.

"To where?" Sheila asked.

"To the VA. They said I could stay there a while. Don't make me walk, Sheila. I don't got any more money for a cab."

"What you said about David, Sam ..."

"He told me I shouldn't have told you."

"Well, what does he look like?"

Sampson shrugged and said, "He looks like Grouchy. He looks just like I remember him. But he has two legs again."

As they drove to the VA, Sampson held his tongue. He wanted to plead with Sheila to have Mary visit him with his daughter. But Grouchy was in the car, softly reminding Sampson to calm down anytime an emotional outburst welled up within him.

The VA put him in a room with a veteran from the Vietnam War. He was still suffering. The nightmares abated for some years, then came back. His wife had left him. His daughter was afraid of him being around her children. The vet looked eighty, but was really in his early sixties. Sampson wished his roommate were an empty bed.

"You could end up like me," the man said, smiling sadly. "Stay away from the bottle. Remember, the bottle only erases things for an hour or two. When you sleep it off, everything comes *right* back. I knew all of this. But the bottle was my best friend. You hear? The bottle is *never* your best friend, buddy. It's an evil bastard. It stabs way better than it soothes."

Sampson was inundated with questions from nurses, questions he already had answered on the phone, or tried to answer. He figured the woman he talked to from his motel bed just passed the buck to some other unfortunate worker. So he had to repeat himself when he would rather just sleep.

*   *   *   *

A tremble came to the ground and Sampson looked up. The Humvee heading the convoy was rocked. Sampson left his Humvee, along with his team. Shouting came from every other Humvee. Black smoke blanketed him. Sampson could sense a bullet with his name on it was aimed at his head.

Just before Grouchy was transferred from road duty and to cave duty, he was in Sampson's unit for a time. Sampson didn't know who he was near at this moment, but he heard the sharp whistle of a bullet and dived on the man he had no doubt it would hit. The bullet struck steel; the man he lay on was Grouchy. Grouchy didn't like Sampson much. They were only friends loosely. They never had an unkind word, but Grouchy always thought him a little too cocky.

"Are you OK?" Sampson said, not knowing who he was talking to.

"Yeah, Sam, thanks."

Sampson removed his sunglasses and focused on Grouchy's face. "Grouchy? Shit, when did you show up?"

"Just yesterday."

"You should have found me."

"Didn't know you were around," Grouchy lied.

*   *   *   *

The Vietnam vet was chuckling. Sampson looked over and saw someone at the foot of his bed. This man wore an old, dusty uniform. Sampson was confused and looked harder at the man. The man looked at him, then at Sampson's roommate. His roommate turned his head to Sampson and examined his eyes.

"You see him?" his roommate asked.

"Of course I see him."

"That's the Grim Reaper, pal."

"What?"

"Died next to me in the swamp. Been haunting me ever since."

"He what?"

"Yeah. No one has ever seen him but me. So that means you're as doomed as I am."

"I have my own. He didn't say I was doomed."

"He's just being nice."

"Yeah, he's just being nice," said the dirty, dusty, ghost who visited the Vietnam vet, with a smile that Sampson didn't like. "No one can see us who isn't headed our way."

"But you've been alive for over thirty years after it ended!" Sampson said to his roommate.

"Yeah, both of us are surprised."

"So, I'm not doomed."

"Doom can stay with you a mighty long time," the ghost said, with a menacing smile.

*   *   *   *

Mary liked the looks of the orange trees in Florida she saw in magazines. She thought maybe once she got her degree that's where she would head. Teaching in the day and lounging on the beach with her daughter after work was her dream. She would never worry about the brutal winters in Ohio and the very rare brutal winter days in Georgia again. But Mary's fantasy was ruined by the reality of who provided the sperm for this beautiful daughter she rocked in her arms.

"I need to see him, Sheila."

"Only when you're ready, Mary."

"It isn't right."

"*He* isn't right."

"No, he isn't. But he's trying."

"Showing up here drunk is trying?"

"Well … he showed up. He's trying. He isn't going to be right the second he starts trying."

*   *   *   *

Cows mooed outside Sampson's window. His roommate would open the window and tell them to shut up, but Sampson liked the sound. He felt their primitive need to survive and the limitations of the pen they were trapped in. They spoke to him. Sampson felt a kind of kinship, a kinship he didn't have with his roommate.

"Every night I'm on the patty again," the roommate told him. "Every night there they all go, these guys I was smoking a doobie with just a few hours before. One gets his head blown half off and he's down there, the murk sucking in his blood, you know?"

Sampson knew, but didn't want to hear it. He wanted rid of his thoughts, and they didn't need company. Mooing with the cows seemed ideal, or going back in the woods where birds and critters talked to him without wishing for any talk back. Sampson so wanted to go back in the woods, where history made no difference.

CHAPTER 14

Grouchy knew of the others, the ones, like himself, who trudged within the margins. A longing for something that could never be again saddened every sad face, and Grouchy understood. But this one, *this* one had a face that reveled in the sadness; the bleaker the better.

Avoiding him was not an option, for that other ghost was always there, always wearing a smile void of some teeth, always standing at the foot of the Vietnam vet's bed. His smile reminded Grouchy of a crocodile just before it grabs its prey.

Grouchy had yet to get angry as a dead man. He didn't think it possible. His emotions ran from sadness to envy. But this ghost tested Grouchy's breaking point. This man was bitter and mean. He talked to the bitter, mean Vietnam vet, who joked about hurting his wife and his kids while his ghost giddily encouraged every troubled detail.

"Why didn't you go?" Grouchy asked the ghost, interrupting a conversation the ghost was having with the old man. Sampson slept.

"Go where?" the ghost said. His smile was gone. His face was buckling for the trouble it always sought.

"The cloud."

"Mind your own business, pal."

"No, I won't. You've been hanging around this long? Why?"

"It's fun to watch stuff, that's why," the ghost said, turning so he could try to stare Grouchy down.

"Watch what?"

"Watch what? What, you don't got a lady? You're just hanging around for kicks, right? Tell me something, pal, is she married again? Or, let me guess, she's fucking every guy to forget about you."

"I don't know what you're talking about."

"Hmmm," the ghost said with a despicable smile planted back on his face. "Seems you might be watching but not paying any attention."

"Paying attention to *what*?" Grouchy said angrily.

"Oh, I'll tell you. See, I watch, like I know you do. And the whore *I* married isn't doing too well with the chemo these days." The ghost chuckled with a bitterness that could have turned Grouchy's stomach, if he had one.

"Yeah? Why is she a whore?"

"Not two years after, she's married again, that's why! My son and daughter calling this new guy 'Dad'! I ain't their dad. Never was! Too young to know any better. You think that's right? A dad that's just a picture."

"You *died*!"

"And?"

"They're supposed to be lonely forever? You want them lonely forever, is that it?"

"Well, *I* gotta be."

"No you don't!"

"If you're such the ambassador, buddy, tell me why are you still hanging around? I know you ain't from the cloud. No one comes back from the cloud."

"I'm going," Grouchy said turning back to Sampson's sleeping, twisting body.

"No, you aren't. But when you decide that for sure, come look me up. We can have fun together."

"Your ideas of fun and mine wouldn't match."

"Your idea of fun will change. Trust me on that."

＊   ＊   ＊   ＊

The hospital was old, the employees gloomy. Mary felt wrong being there, but still traveled up that rickety, grey elevator to Sampson's floor. Most of those inside were from the war in the sand. But Mary saw some old guys without any legs. She saw some old guys who wore the most basic type of rubber arms and hands, sometimes metal. They clasped at things like a machine. Mary would have thought the clicking of metal against metal *was* a machine if she didn't hear them breathing. She watched them in their dressing gowns looking up at her like she was a ray of light. Pride would have been the appropriate feeling, but Mary was hardly proud. She wanted to leave and never see them again.

Sampson was asleep when Mary entered his room. His roommate looked up at Mary and seemed delighted before he moistened his lips, before his glassy eyes showed lust for such silent prey. Mary looked away from him quickly, as his intentions seemed more akin to a rapist than a kindly old man, and shook her husband's quiet but fluttering legs.

"Sam ... Sam," she said and he started to open his eyes, sit up, and rub his eyes. He opened them fully to see his baby for the first time. Cecilia was swathed in pink in the same design he had seen Sheila's baby wearing. The same stitches looked coming loose. The same helpless form looked so beautiful. So beautiful, and this one was his. Sampson started to cry, though he was hardly awake.

"Hold it down!" said his roommate. "Jesus, what is this? Oprah?"

Mary glared at the man and he winked. He licked his lips once more.

"Can I ... can I hold her?" Sampson asked.

Mary lowered Cecilia into his arms. Her tiny arms twisted into the air. Her blue eyes looked into Sampson's, which were just as blue. Her tiny arms switched direction and headed for his nose, which she grabbed. She sent a delightful shock of electricity into Sampson's waking limbs.

"You're enjoying this, aren't you?" Sampson's roommate said to Grouchy, who stood beside Sampson's bed and would cry, too, if he could.

"Don't talk to me," Grouchy said.

"You think I don't know why you're hanging around? You got somebody, don't you? Just like Billy said. You got somebody just like Billy, don't you? You're gonna watch her, too, just like Billy. You'll get bitter like he did. Billy wasn't always like that. He grew bitter after he died. He was the sweetest boy before that, son. Maybe you think you're sweet now, too, but that's all gonna end. It's *gotta* end. Mark my words."

*   *   *   *

Captured insurgents were marched in front of Sampson's muddy face. Another crew had just been wiped out before his eyes. The two kids who ran around planting IEDs were staunch. They said nothing. There was an interpreter, too, so they couldn't feign any misunderstanding.

"Who do you work for?" Sampson demanded, and his demand was translated back to the kids, who might have been thirteen at the most.

They said nothing. One of them smiled.

"Don't you fucking smile at me! You in a lot of trouble!" Sampson said, and his words were translated.

The kid said something with another smile. It was translated back as, "Not as much trouble as you."

Sampson struck him. The kid's nose bled. His smile left him for a time, then returned. Sampson struck him again. More blood. The kid's smile looked more of a weapon than an expression. Sampson planted the butt of his automatic rifle into his head, and the boy went down. He blinked rapidly. That cryptic smile was gone, as were most of his senses.

"Goddamn it!" Sampson screamed at the kid on the ground. "You think this is the way? You think we'll just slink out of here? We're the United States! We finish the job!"

This was translated to the boy on the ground. But the boy's stoic partner answered. "We want to know what you think your job is."

*   *   *   *

Sampson woke up to sunlight and a sense of newness. That baby in his arms made him feel useful. His roommate laughed at his sense of optimism.

"Yeah, you think everything will be OK, don't you? It won't. I saw the look on her face. She's just doing what she thinks she should."

"No she isn't," Sampson said.

"Really? You willing to make a bet?"

"I don't have any money and neither do you."

"Fine, a friendly bet, then."

"You'd have to be friendly for that to work."

"Oh, buddy! I'm the best friend you'll ever have from this time to your end."

"Then I hope that end comes soon."

"Look, if she comes back you can have my desserts until one of us leaves."

"I want nothing meant for you."

"You already do, Sam. You have a ghost and that ghost will be hanging over your head forever."

"He's a guardian angel to me."

"If you really think that, then you're more worse off than I thought."

＊　　＊　　＊　　＊

"I don't know, Sheila," Mary said, sipping on some coffee, though her nerves were already quite aroused. "It just isn't the same."

"No, it isn't the same. Did you think it would be?"

"That's not my point. Something is gone. It's just gone."

"He's been through a lot, Mary. If you love him you have to hold on until he finds some sense of peace."

"What if I don't love him?"

"You don't love him because of this?"

"I don't know. I might have stopped loving him when he came back."

"Same scenario, Mary. He got like this over there."

"Well, it might have taken my love away."

"Is love just something easy to you? If it is then that ain't love. I don't know what it is, but it ain't love."

"I should feel something for him, Sheila, but I don't anymore."

Hearing her words, Grouchy didn't know if he should tell Sampson. He chose not to.

＊　　＊　　＊　　＊

Grouchy stood in front of Sampson's smiling face and wanted his present happiness to evolve into real hope. If hope could grow, then Sampson could deal with eventual disappointment. Even if he never could reach Mary again, he did have a child. Sampson held his child. Cecilia wasn't just an idea anymore. If he needed more of a reason than for himself to live, he could now live for her.

"Tell him the truth," Sampson's roommate said to Grouchy.

"The truth about what?"

"About that goddamn woman that came in. Tell him what she really thinks."

"I have no idea what she thinks."

"You're lying! You think setting him up for a fall is helping him? Shit, you are a god-awful idiot if you think you're helping him. He's building all his hopes on this! If the dream ain't real, then a future ain't either. Billy *always* tells me the truth."

"Billy spins whatever he tells you to keep you like you are," Grouchy said. "Where is Billy now?"

"Billy's doing what you do when you're not here. He's spying for me and for himself."

*   *   *   *

Sampson watched his roommate toss and turn as he suffered inside a nightmare. He almost felt sorry for him. But everything this man said to him was designed to make Sampson feel as hopeless as that man had become. Sampson wished death for him without any feeling of selfishness, for Sampson was sure the guy wished it for himself nightly.

Grouchy, however, worried that the man's intention to spread his bitterness would succeed without Sampson ever needing to think the Vietnam vet one of his friends. Mary hadn't come back. She didn't call like she said she would. Sampson told Grouchy he was sure there was a good reason. But the more days that passed, the more Sampson's hope suffered, just like that old man promised it would. And the old man was so happy to remind them of that.

A man walked into Sampson's room dressed younger than he was. His eyes smiled through tiny oval glasses. A pony tale of blondish brown jutted out from the back of his head. A golden earring dangled from his right lobe. He walked like a cowboy, though. He had the staunch shoulders of an ex-solider. Sampson decided he could like him, which was fortunate because this man was his caseworker.

His name was Robbie Dix. He invited Sampson to follow him. They came into a room with two plush couches covered with velvety purple, making Sampson wonder why the couches could be plush but he had to sleep on such a thin mattress.

"Let me tell you a little about myself, Mr. Roy. I fought in Vietnam. I still have shrapnel in my knees. I was a heroin addict for ten years after the war. I lost my wife and my children. My children have started speaking to me again after twenty years of nothing. I say these things so you understand that I understand, and whatever you tell me I will not judge you for."

"I'm sick of all the bullshit," Sampson said.

"What is the bullshit, Mr. Roy?"

"Call me Sam, please."

"OK."

"I'm sick of the news. I'm sick of all these people saying they support us. I don't even know what that means."

"What do you think it means?"

"I think it means they feel guilty. I think it means they got no idea, so they just say they support us and that makes all the shit they see on TV all right. It makes them think that just by saying it some magic happens in our heads."

"The Vietnam vets didn't have it so good, Sam."

"Do I look like a Vietnam vet to you? I got no idea what you went through. I never said I did. But I know what *I'm* going through. I got a wife that's showed up once but probably won't show up again. I got a kid I don't know if I'll *ever* see again. And I got the news blaring that everyone supports us, but it means *nothing*. All it means is bumper sticks and T-shirts. It's commerce built on guilt. It's like holy water to these people. They know they sacrificed nothing and we sacrificed everything for this shit."

"Do you feel used?"

"I feel used by everybody. My government. The people in my city. In my state. In my country. The fuckers that blew up my friends. The world that puts up my image to show everyone who the bad guy is. I was just a soldier. Just a solider. I got orders and did as I was told. I'm an ant, and the queen is in the White House being jerked off by folks who think I'm just a graphic in a video game."

CHAPTER 15

Alice was a shy girl. She wasn't at all like her brother. Alice was older by two years and not very social. She made friends painfully and painfully kept them too. But as puberty set in, she didn't want a friend; she wanted a boy. All her boys punched the air like her father. They were loud and rude and didn't care about anyone's opinions but their own. Sampson didn't much like them. Neither did his father.

Alice had heard. Somehow the news traveled. Perhaps Sheila told Tommy, and Tommy told someone who Sampson once knew, and that person brought her the word. Alice didn't say how. She just said she heard.

Sampson was shocked, then bothered, when Alice walked into his room. He was only comforted by the fact that his roommate was asleep, which meant his mouth was too.

"How are you, Sam?" his sister asked him.

Alice looked much older than she was. Sampson looked for bruises, but he couldn't see any. Maybe the makeup she had on covered them. Maybe she'd become proficient in that area.

"Well, you see, don't you?"

"Where you been all this time?"

"The woods."

"The woods, all this time?"

"Yeah. I'm thinking of going back."

Alice didn't have much to say. She just looked at Sampson and tried to see her brother. This man looked like him. He sounded like him. But the words and expressions came out wrong. His eyes were the same color, but looked injected with an unfamiliarity that made them seem stolen. Alice felt she was with a stranger. It gave her a kind of satisfaction. If her brother weren't her brother anymore, there was no more reason to worry about his future. But he was, so she worried.

Sampson wanted to know if his parents knew, and Alice said they did. He told her to tell them to stay away.

"They want to see you, Sam."

"I just told you, Alice, I don't want to see them."

"But why?"

"I just *don't*, OK? I don't even want to see you."

"I didn't make you like this, Sam."

"No, but when I see you, I see what I was. That man is dead. Not sure if I like it or not, but since I don't know, it's just confusing when I have to think about it."

*   *   *   *

Sorting through his past filled most of Sampson's time. He would sometimes reach for the phone to call Sheila's house but bring his hand right back when he feared rejection.

Sampson wanted the confidence back. He wanted the ladies' man back. But wanting both of those was like looking at a mountaintop and desiring its summit even though oxygen was hard to come by where he stood in the valley.

Grouchy hadn't been around for a while. Even though the fear of him ending up like the bitter ghost of Billy was a constant thought, he kept watching Sheila and Tommy.

He couldn't help himself. If it were just she and Mary, he could skip a few days. But he couldn't skip when Tommy started to frequently visit. His frequent visits turned into daily visits.

It started with hugs that lasted longer than usual. Tommy kissed Sheila's cheek once. They fell asleep together on the couch. Their babies slept in the same crib sometimes.

Mary was watching them too. She desired something, but not from Sampson. She felt guilty because she had lied. The week within which she promised to return passed without her coming. Two weeks passed and she hadn't even called. She reached for the phone, then pulled back her hand. What would she say? She wasn't coming. She couldn't tell him that. Why call him just to lie again?

Sometimes Mary dreamed of Sampson. She dreamed of him like he was before, and in the brief seconds just after waking she was sure the war was just her imagination. Then the day would become sharper. Sampson's body wasn't beside her. Cecilia's crib was in front of her. Life wasn't a nightmare, but it wasn't a dream.

*   *   *   *

"I don't know, Sam," Grouchy told him. "I haven't heard them talking about you."

"What do they talk about?"

"Nothing really."

"What goes on?"

"That guy, he comes over. He's there a lot."

"Yeah. They screwed yet?"

"Jesus, Sam! Why you gotta talk so crudely?"

"What do you want me to say? 'Make love'?"

"They haven't done either."

*   *   *   *

Sheila thought of Grouchy and the possibility of his watching when that inevitability came closer. Sheila, like Tommy, didn't feel a great attraction. She just needed something. A tender embrace from a lover seemed so far away, but Tommy was hurting for the same reason she was, so it didn't have to be. But when a polite kiss turned into an open mouth, she pushed on his chest.

"I'm sorry," he said.

"I'm sorry, too, Tommy."

"How long do we wait?"

"Don't know. Wish there was a law or something we could go by."

Grouchy was there when Sheila spoke to him. She asked him to allow her this. She desired some sort of sign and asked for it while speaking to the ceiling. Grouchy wanted to tell Sampson to tell her he said it was OK. But it wasn't OK. She was his. He hated how selfish he felt when his feelings of decency deserted him. But Grouchy wasn't ready to be completely decent. He wasn't ready for the cloud, so he wasn't ready to let go of his woman either. *Maybe,* he thought, *if we didn't have a kid.* But *they* didn't. *She* did.

✳   ✳   ✳   ✳

Sheila visited Sampson with Cecilia in her arms. He was happy to see his daughter but feared hearing the reason why Cecilia's mother couldn't accompany her.

"She's been real busy, Sam," she said.

"Don't lie to me, Sheila. I'm her husband. She's only seen me once in nearly a year and you going to give me the busy crap?"

"You tell her!" said his roommate.

"Shut up, asshole!" Sampson said, turning to him. "I might be damaged, but I can still kick your ass and I'm just about to prove it!"

His roommate responded by turning his head angrily towards the window and said no more.

"It's hard for her, Sam."

"Yeah, like it isn't hard for me?"

"No, Sam, but …"

"No. No, Sheila. You tell her that if she's any kind of woman, she can explain it herself. I ain't no monster. I have no violence on my mind. I already know what she's going to say, but *she* needs to say it to me. I appreciate you bringing my daughter, but if my wife is ready to let go of me, it ain't gonna be by messenger."

"I want you to remember, Sam, you let go of her first."

"I'm a damaged man, Sheila. I am not myself. If I was, I never would have done that."

✳   ✳   ✳   ✳

Too much stirring in his bed convinced Sampson he'd received all the help he could inside the VA hospital. He always spoke honestly with his caseworker, Robbie Dix, but it didn't make him any less antsy for something else. Maybe the woods. Maybe life in another city. He didn't know.

Since he wasn't thought a danger to himself, the hospital gave him no guff. They were running out of beds anyway. They'd been warning Sampson's roommate he would be discharged the second they became overcrowded. But his roommate had no intention of leaving until he was physically escorted away.

"You remember, Sam … women are not the answer," said his roommate.

"What is?"

"There is none."

"So why don't you just jump out the window?"

"Because," Sampson's roommate replied and smiled his usual poison, "I like to prolong the pain."

Sampson was given cab fare and the cab took him to a bar. But he had no money. He ordered drink after drink and when he passed out, he was tapped.

"IIIII'm a veteran," Sampson slurred.

"Of what?" the surly bartender asked.

"The war in the sand."

"Yeah? And that means what?"

"I got no money."

"You gotta be *kidding* me! You rang up a tab of nearly $60, dickhead!"

"I'm a veteran. You can call the VA."

"Get the hell out of here!" But Sampson couldn't quite move. So the bartender deposited him in the bushes, where he slept until the sun came up.

CHAPTER 16

Sampson woke on a street he knew. One straight walk. One turn. Turn again at the stop. Another straight walk. He was there.

It was a weekday, but Sampson didn't know what day it was. Sheila's house was empty, save for the puppy. Sampson listened for a creak from any critter after he knocked and leaned in. He heard nothing, so he went to the backyard and opened the unlocked porch door. Inside the house, just beyond the sliding glass door, the puppy lay nestled on newspapers within an interlocking wooden fence. A mess of brown poop sat in a fairly large pile. The puppy began to pat its paws against the fence and yapped, but Sampson fell asleep again with the help of the roof's shade.

Some shoves woke him. He felt the hard tile and thought he was in jail until the falling sun gleamed some of its last rays on to his head. Turning on to his back, he saw Mary holding Cecilia. Mary looked nervous and angry. The tip of her nose was twitching. Her eyes darted around Sampson's. Sampson wanted to ask where he was, but Mary preceded him with her own question.

"What are you doing here, Sam?"

"Here?"

"At Sheila's."

"Oh," Sampson said. An explanation was on his tongue before he remembered he had a more pressing question for her. "Why didn't you come back like you said you would?"

"Is that why you're here?"

"I have no idea."

"Are you drunk?"

"Not anymore."

"You left the hospital to get drunk?"

"I did," Sampson said without shame.

"Are you going back?"

"No. Too crowded in there."

"Well, then ..." Mary sputtered. "Where will you stay, Sam? You can't stay here."

"And why not?"

"We have children here. You're not well."

"I know I'm not well, Mary. But the vows said that didn't matter. You remember the vows, right? I remember promising that I'd take care of you, and I remember you saying you'd take care of me if I need it. Well, I was healthy when we got married. But I ain't healthy now. This a time I need my wife's help. This a time for you to help me, Mary."

"I can't, Sam. OK? I wish I could. But I guess if what you're saying is right, I wasn't prepared to get married. I'm not prepared for this either."

"So you just gonna throw me to the wolves?"

"Don't yell!" Mary yelled as Cecilia started to cry. "I'm going inside."

"Goddamn it, Mary! Maybe I was a piece of shit! Maybe I only thought of myself when I came back, but can't you forgive me considering what I've been through?"

"I've forgiven you, Sam," she said turning to him halfway. "I just don't love you anymore."

Sheila had just stepped through the front door of the house when Mary left Sampson on the porch crying his heart out. Sheila retrieved Sampson and hurried him into the house. Though his sobs were now muffled, his previous cries still brought some neighbors into the street. Mary barricaded herself and Cecilia in her room. Cecilia continued to cry. Sampson's and her cries matched sometimes, the pitch and warble of two helpless beings.

"You need money?" Sheila asked impatiently, but mostly with worry.

"Yeah! So I can buy a fucking gun!"

"Oh, Sam, come on, Sam ... she ... Sam ..."

"What are you going to say, Sheila? Huh? I mean, what can you say after she said that to me?"

"I guess there's nothing I can really say, Sam. I'm not trying to take it away. I mean ... I couldn't if I tried."

"OK, then, get me a gun. I know Grouchy had a few around. Just give me one of them pistols. I'll go in the back. You can say you didn't know."

"You shut up, Sam! OK? Shut up! You're alive, Sam! You know what that means? David isn't alive. A lot of people who went over there aren't. You have a *daughter*. You have a goddamn life. You can fall in love again. David can't."

"Grouchy watches you, Sheila."

"Shut up, Sam!" urged Grouchy, who stood to Sheila's left.

"You shut up! It's bad enough *I've* been betrayed."

"Betrayed?" Sheila said. "Does he think I'm betraying him?"

"Yes!"

"No! Sam, *don't!*" Grouchy insisted. "*Don't*, goddamn it!"

"Well, why are you here then, Grouchy? It ain't just for me. Don't even try and say it's just for me. You're keeping watch, so I'm gonna tell her like it is."

"It *isn't* like that!"

"How … um, how am I betraying him?" Sheila asked nervously.

"He sees that guy. Tommy, right? He sees you two together. Don't know what you do together. He won't say. He tells me you haven't screwed. You gonna screw him, Sheila? Right in front of your *husband?*"

"How do you know his name?"

"Sheila! Can't you figure out by now that I'm not making Grouchy up? I might be a little crazy, but I'm not lying. He's still around. He can see you at anytime."

"Oh, Sam," Grouchy said, wincing and showing as much disappointment as a ghost can. "Do you know what you're doing to her?"

"I … don't know how you know his name, but … I'm alive, too, Sam. I'm lonely. Don't I have the right to try and be happy?"

"You ask yourself that, Sheila. Grouchy lost that right. And you just gonna flaunt it in his face by taking up with another man? You tell *me* if that's a good enough reason to make yourself happy."

✳   ✳   ✳   ✳

Sheila got on the phone to the VA hospital. The secretary confirmed that Sampson had been discharged. When she asked if he could be readmitted, the secretary said he had left on his own volition and could only be forcefully admitted to a psychiatric hospital and only by order of a judge. Sheila couldn't keep him inside her house, but she couldn't kick him to the street either. Not like he was.

Only one man came to mind who was physically stronger than Sampson and who'd been in the military as well, though never in a war. That man was Tommy. Tommy said he'd watch Sampson until he settled down. When Sampson heard who'd be his next caretaker, he chuckled.

"Want to convince me to convince Grouchy to reconsider?"

"Reconsider what, Sam?" Sheila said.

"Reconsider his blessing of course."

"I'm not talking anymore on this subject. You're a sick man. So I have to suppose you want everyone to suffer along with you."

*   *   *   *

Healing in Germany, with nothing to preoccupy him except his mind, Grouchy inevitably reexamined his choices in life—choices he started examining just after the wedding and just before he went to war. War made the exercise too draining. After the explosion rendered his services unnecessary, he had nothing to do, nothing to worry about, so his unresolved worries became worries of the present.

Did he love Sheila, or just love the idea of a family? His family was established. Did that mean he couldn't ask the question anymore? He didn't know, so he kept asking.

When Grouchy got off the plane in Atlanta, just the sight of his baby and the woman who gave birth to his child, told him, "Those questions are pointless. You've chosen this life. You wanted this life. So enjoy this life."

But now, Grouchy wanted to ask those questions again. However, this time his choices were gone. No matter the answer, he could take no action. He could watch, but that was all. He could want, but that was all.

Tommy was friendly. He wanted to help Sheila and help out a fellow vet. He didn't emphasize his service, however, for he'd never seen anyone die in combat. He'd never been in combat. He had never feared for his own life. In his late thirties he finally settled down. Before he found a love he never wanted rid of, he used to be quite the womanizer. Before Francine became the only person he would ever want to touch again, Tommy touched every woman who let him. He had a son to show for his commitment and a desire for just one lover again.

"It's not much, but it's a room," he said, showing Sampson the extra room in his house. His late wife had decorated the room for visitors. It had an economical, Victorian style. Only Tommy had slept in the room, and that was after his wife died.

Sampson didn't say a word to Tommy when they were introduced. Tommy asked Sampson questions, but Sampson wouldn't reply. Tommy remembered that his grandfather, who served in World War II, was quiet almost always. That grandfather had seen some bad stuff, and it changed him. Tommy's mom told him to never take it personally. So he didn't take Sampson's silent treatment personally either.

"You want to fuck her, don't you?" Sampson said, sitting on the blue, ruffled bedspread. Those were Sampson's first words to Tommy.

"What?"

"Sheila ... you want to fuck her, right?"

Tommy pondered how to answer such a question. It was certainly crude. But telling this guy that would only make matters worse. So he sighed and said, "I like her. We're both lonely."

"Oh, so that makes it right?"

"Makes what right, Sam?"

"Cheating. It makes her cheating right. Is that what you saying?"

"Who is she cheating on, Sam?"

"Her husband!"

Sampson said it with such ire that Tommy became slightly afraid. Tommy wasn't afraid of much. He was over six feet tall and quite hefty. Bar fights were common stress relievers for him when he was young, and he once tackled a guy with a gun to the ground. But Sampson was different. There was something sinister about his sickness. Almost as if it could overtake him if he didn't watch out.

"You do know he died, right?" Tommy said.

"Yeah, I know that."

"OK, so ... is she supposed to grieve forever?"

"*He* is!"

"Oh? He is? Well ... he shouldn't."

Tommy backed out of the room. Once he closed the door to give Sampson his privacy, Grouchy appeared at the back of that door. Grouchy looked ready to attack. And if he could attack, he would have. He looked as bothered as anyone could. His eyes were no longer translucent; they were radiating. His mouth was clinched tightly, and the shame it forced on Sampson lowered Sampson's head. Still, no intensity from someone else could hold any real power over the anger he was tired of keeping to himself.

"What are you trying to accomplish, Sam?" Grouchy asked him.

"Do you think I know?"

"No, I don't. So stop doing it. You want me around? Stop doing it."

"You can leave anytime, Grouchy. I don't want to hold up no one's life."

"Except your own, of course."

"Yeah, I got no choice in that matter."

"Right. It's easier to think that, isn't it?"

✳   ✳   ✳   ✳

Sheila faced a blank wall. Tears filled her eyes. Her daughter was behind her, in her crib, resting peacefully. But Sheila didn't feel peace. Watching Elena, with no worry in her little head, didn't diminish her own worries at all. Sampson had to be telling the truth. David was talking to him and watching her. She couldn't exactly explain that to Tommy, though. A strange sense of guilt forced loyalty upon her. It wasn't reasonable, but it was still greater than any loyalty she had for Tommy. How would she say that? She would guarantee herself a life without any man if every eligible one knew she was afraid of the man who died.

Sheila looked eighteen. She still had a nice body. In grocery stores, men of every type—every shape, race, and age—would often stop in their tracks when they encountered her, especially when she was bending over. Her appeal had been with her since she entered puberty. She could have married Larry Westmoreland. He owned three funeral parlors and drove a Porsche. But David had kind eyes and not a mean bone in his body.

"Don't listen to him, Sheila," Grouchy said behind her, though he knew she couldn't hear. "I ... want to leave. I think I do, at least. I don't want you unhappy. I don't want you lonely. I guess ... if we didn't have a child, it would be easier for me. I have this pride still. I just don't want my kid calling someone else 'Dad.' I know it's stupid. But I can't get rid of it. I'm trying, though. I'll try harder. I promise."

"David," Sheila said to that wall. "I don't know if Sam is saying what you've told him to say. It doesn't sound like you. But, whatever, I want you to know ... I don't love Tommy like I loved you. I don't think I ever can. But ... he's a good man, David. Elena needs a father. His boy needs a mother. I don't want to do this alone. Please, don't make me."

CHAPTER 17

Angry rants pelted the other side of Tommy's wall. The shouting woke him up. *Something terrible must be happening,* he thought, before he thought of his gun. But he recognized Sampson's voice before reaching for his shotgun.

Sampson was pacing naked when Tommy opened his guest room's door. Sampson's blue eyes looked more black now as he stared at the white carpet, clenching his fists and just muttering now.

"Buddy," Tommy said in a bothered whine, "do you want me to take you somewhere?"

"Take me *where?*"

"I don't know. Do you think you need to go back to the hospital?"

"What *for?*"

"Because it's three in the morning and you're yelling at my floor, Sam."

"Fucking women! You hear me? I sacrificed for my country. I come back fucked up and she leaves me. I try and get well and she says she doesn't love me."

"Maybe because you're not well, yet."

"How can I get well without her?" Sampson said and began to cry.

Tommy was touched, but didn't know exactly what to do. Looking at Sampson, Tommy thought he might as well be looking at an injured lion. It was mighty once. He truly wished for it to be mighty again. But Tommy pulling the thorn out of his paw just might garner a slash to his throat.

Tommy stepped toward Sampson, but he stopped when Sampson raised his head and glared at him. Tommy raised his hands in defense and cautiously smiled. He had a feeling something very bad was about to happen.

"Sam, I have a baby here, you know. If you're dangerous, I will tell you right now I will not hesitate to subdue you."

"I ain't gonna hurt no kid, goddamn it!" Sampson said in disgust. "I ain't gonna hurt anyone!"

Through all the ruckus up to this point, Tommy's son was silent. But he started to cry now. While still monitoring Sampson's unpredictable demeanor, Tommy slowly started to back out of the room to hold his son and tell him everything was all right, despite the fact that he didn't really know.

"Go to sleep, Sam. OK? Go to sleep or let me take you somewhere. But this won't do."

Sampson sat on the bed. He was erect, which Tommy hadn't noticed. Sampson hadn't either until his quivering appendage weighed his lap. He stood up, walked over to the door, closed and locked it, then sat back down. He put his hand around his penis and imagined that psychologist at the general hospital. The last memory of a nipple put the taste back into his mouth. He could feel himself inside a tight body. He could see the psychologist's hazel eyes rolling into the back of her head.

*   *   *   *

"Start thinking about what comes out of your mouth," Sheila said to Mary. "Think about who you're dealing with before you say such shit."

"I said what I was feeling, Sheila. It wasn't shit to me."

"I don't care *what* it is! *Don't* say those things to him."

"It just came out!" Mary said defensively.

"Yes, that's obvious. Sam is sick, Mary, and he's a long way from being well."

"Do you want me to lie to him? Do you want us to take him in?"

"This isn't a black-and-white deal, Mary. He needs to be taken care of, and the ones that should be doing it lay it all on us. He gets fucked up on our dime, but it's still on us. Why they come back and the government just lets them roam around, being all fucked up in the head like they are, I don't know."

"They don't know either."

"Yeah, well they should. The more this goes on, the more I think they don't give a shit."

*   *   *   *

Gregory Helton lived south of Kennesaw, in La Grange, Georgia. He suffered a nearly fatal brain injury when a bullet struck him in the sand. His mother had raised him alone since he was two. She had a job at the Kroger Supermarket. She filled out the paperwork to get the proper benefits for her son, but more paperwork came in the mail every week, and it was all at least an inch thick. She couldn't work, take care of Gregory, and solicit the government all at the same time. She tried. But the government made her try and try some more.

Gregory's breathing had been getting worse. The signals in his head to his lungs and his heart were frayed and sometimes stopped his breathing for a few seconds at a time. The machines that were supposed to help him breathe were so old their condition was never quite right. Gregory's mother called and men came out, but what they fixed always broke again within the week. She asked for replacements, but that required another inch thick of documents, and then another and another. After every sudden scare, Gregory was hospitalized for the shortest amount of time allowed. He needed another operation, and if it couldn't be scheduled soon, he would just stop breathing and die. All the medical professionals his mother saw told her otherwise. But even with just a high school education, Gregory's mother knew they were either lying to her or just plain wrong.

"Listen to me, Gregory," said Grouchy, who had never known him in life. "I know somewhere within you you can understand me. Listen. If you go soon, walk to the cloud. You'll see it. You'll see a line waiting to be let in. I know you might want to stay around. I know you might want to comfort your mother. But you can't. Go into the cloud. You'll see her another time. It's best for you and her if you move on."

Two days later Gregory died. His mother came home and saw him slumped forward. The beeps of the machines surrounding him continued. His mother held his cold hand and thanked God for releasing him. Only for the day, Gregory watched his mother. She cried. She called the hospital. She watched as Gregory was taken from her forever. After that day, Gregory heeded Grouchy's advice and headed for the line.

*   *   *   *

It was limited, but at least it was alcohol. Tommy had two twelve-packs of beer. Sampson would have preferred hard liquor, but as much as he searched, he could find none. He had no money or any idea of the direction to get any. When Tommy left for work, taking his infant son with him, Sampson left the guest room and opened the refrigerator. He told himself he would just have a few. A few turned into all twenty-four.

He was surprised it affected him so. Usually he had to drink a full bottle of something much harder before he succumbed, but one minute he was watching TV and the next Tommy was above him. Sampson smelled piss. It was his own. Tommy looked at Sampson like he was the most pathetic animal caught in a trap it had set itself. Sampson tried to speak, but only nonsense left his mouth.

"You need to go back," Tommy said, nodding his head.

"Huh?" Sampson found enough steadiness to sit upright on the newly piss-stained couch.

"I can't do this, Sam. I want to help you out. I want to help out Sheila, but-"

"You want to fffffuck, Sheila," Sampson slurred and looked at the wet spot all over his crotch.

"Whatever you say, Sam. You need to go back. I'm taking you back."

Tommy looked for a change of clothes that might fit. None did, but they were clean. He maneuvered Sampson out of his front door and almost to the passenger side of his truck before Sampson collapsed and started to laugh.

"I'm not going back," Sampson said laughing. "It's a warehouse! It's just a fffffffucking warehouse!"

"They're professionals, Sam," Tommy said, helping him up. "I'm not. I run a shuttle service. Just a shuttle service, that's how professional I am."

Tommy stood Sampson up. For the first time Sampson noticed the woods just beyond Tommy's house. His energy began to focus on them and his freedom from all this mess. He emphasized his drunkenness until Tommy released him, and then Sampson began to run. Tommy just watched at first. He was sure Sampson would fall, but he didn't. Into those woods Sampson went, blending in like a deer. Tommy went in after him and looked, but couldn't find Sampson.

"Sam!" Tommy called. "Sam! Come on! I'm trying to help you! Come on Sam, show yourself!"

Sampson heard Tommy from he had hidden behind a canopy of limbs where he had also thrown up. When Sampson was sure Tommy had gone, he lay down in a soft piece of ground until the alcohol fizzled in his veins.

Half-exhausted from looking and half-wired with worry, Tommy waited at Sheila's door. Mary answered. As usual she didn't say much. Tommy had wondered since he'd met her how the hell she and Sheila ever got along. He assumed that they did only because of their predicaments. If they'd met any other way,

Tommy assumed Mary and Sheila would never have had more than two conversations, let alone become roommates.

Mary was pretty but bookish. Sheila was pretty and liked soap operas. They were both smart, but Mary seemed sheltered, delicate. Sheila wasn't a ruffian, but there was a toughness in her eyes that branded her a survivor. Mary seemed to just float along like a small stick on a fast flowing river.

"He just took off, Sheila," Tommy said.

"So ... should we call the cops?"

"I don't know what we should do. Why the hell isn't Mary in on this, Sheila? Why are we talking in whispers? It's *her* husband."

"Don't worry about Mary. She can't be a mother and a wife to someone like Sam at the same time."

∗   ∗   ∗   ∗

Happy children surrounded the ice cream truck. The older, white-haired, slow-moving driver barked at them to get in line. Sampson hadn't had an ice cream in a long time. He was hungry. He hadn't eaten since the VA hospital offered him an orange.

Sampson didn't want to look creepy, so he pretended to be looking for his cat. He called a different name each time for his own amusement, and none of the kids noticed because they could only stare at the tall caps of soft white ice cream printed just above the ordering window.

But when the old man slowly began to drive away, Sampson started to run after the singing vehicle, yelling, "Wait!"

The truck squeaked to a stop. The driver looked out the opposite window in annoyance at an out-of-breath Sampson.

"Yeah?" said the truck driver

"I don't have any money," Sampson said panting.

"Yeah?"

"Can you spare an ice cream for a vet?"

"A vet? A veterinarian?"

"No. I was in the war."

"Oh, yeah? Well, I gotta pay my mortgage."

"Listen, whatever you can spare. I'm *really* hungry."

"Well ... why the hell not," the driver muttered and left his steering wheel before making his way to the ice creams nestled in a freezer he had just locked.

Sampson waited at that window just like one of the eager children the driver had just left. The old man produced a slimy package containing a green Popsicle. It wasn't what Sampson had in mind, but he thanked the driver nonetheless.

Sampson made his way to a bar that he hadn't stiffed lately. They didn't ask for a credit card when he ordered. He sat alone in a booth and had twelve bourbons before he passed out.

"No money. No money," he said when he was stirred.

Sampson could feel someone big picking him up. He was sure he would once again be thrown outside inhospitably. He was thrown, but on a hard floor instead. He didn't care, and sleep soon returned.

CHAPTER 18

Sampson's hands stuck against grime. The dusty backroom was black and empty, from what he could tell. The only light Sampson noticed was barely shining underneath the back door.

He yanked the door's cold metal handle continuously, but it was locked. He searched for a turning deadbolt, but could only trace the lines of a keyhole. The door that led back into the main building was locked too. Sampson jerked that handle as well and kicked at the wood, but he couldn't free himself no matter how hard he tried.

He started to scream. If Sampson were still drunk he would have tried to ram the concrete walls. His screaming made him hoarse and tired, and he soon slumped helplessly to the floor.

Maybe this is hell, he thought. *I guess I'm in hell.*

The sound of keys against the back door brought Sampson to his feet. In walked a short, older man with an overcompensating in belly. He wore a naturally dyed calfskin jacket complete with tassels. He looked ridiculous. This rotund, small man started fishing for the light switch that had eluded Sampson's fingers.

"Oh!" said the man, grinning with selfish pleasure when the light shone on Sampson's teetering frame. "The deadbeat is up!"

"Where the fuck am I?"

"At the bar you got your fill at, son, of course. Don't you remember? Drank nearly half a bottle of whiskey but don't got the cash. Well, well." The man grinned wider and put a hand on each generous hip. "*But,* I got a lot of dishes ready to be washed. Enrique had to split. He ain't legal, you see. That has to happen sometimes. Anyway, point is, he left a mess of dishes for you."

"Then we square?"

"Sure, what else can I do? I could call the cops, but hell, I figure this was your drunk tank for the night."

*   *   *   *

There wasn't enough time. His buddy said as much into the radio.

"We move him and he's dead for sure!" said Lionel's buddy, someone who necessitated a bond while they fought.

The radio cackled with the same instructions.

"I'm telling you!" said Lionel's buddy. "He's hanging all over the place. His guts ... they ... Jesus, we need someone here. We need someone here *now*!"

"Lionel," Grouchy said, and Lionel looked into his nearly translucent eyes. "Your sister is OK."

"She is?"

"Wait! He's talking. Lionel! Hey Lionel!"

"Yes," Grouchy continued. "She'll make it. She'll be fine. You don't need to hang around. She'll be fine. Go into the cloud, Lionel. Don't make the mistake I did. It's harder the longer you wait."

"Lionel! Listen, I'm telling you!" Lionel's buddy shouted into the radio. "Lionel! Goddamnit! I think ... I think he's dead. He's dead, Sarge. He's dead."

*   *   *   *

"Good work!" the fat man who owned the bar said while looking at the clean dishes and mugs, as if Christ's own glory had given them shine.

"Well, I just wanted to get it done, and now I want to leave," Sampson sighed.

"You telling me you ain't interested in the job, then?"

"You never said nothing about a job. What kind of job you talking about?"

"Well, like I said, Enrique had to split. We need a dishwasher."

"Really?" said Sampson and rubbed the back of his neck with the rag in his hand. "I don't know how good I'd be to you in that department, tell you the truth."

"Looks like you'll be plenty good," said the fat man, motioning to that same pile of impressive work. "You got a place to stay?"

"I ... actually, don't."

"Well, you can stay in the backroom. There's a bathroom back there. You can wash up in the sink. I'll give you five dollars an hour, under the table. Ain't gonna make you fill out no forms or nothing. Don't need to tell no one your name if you don't feel like it."

"Five dollars?" Sampson said with a grin.

"OK, five dollars an hour and you can get a bottle at the end of the night. I mean a fifth, son, of whatever you want. Just *one*, though," the owner said. He noticed Sampson's face change from uninterested to practically convinced. "That offer more tempting, isn't it? *Gotta* be tempting, seeing how much of a tab you wrung up all by yourself."

"Can I take part of the pay in advance?"

"*No*, after your shift," the owner said sternly and turned his body in preparation to leave the kitchen. "And don't try and mess with me. I'll make sure the bartenders know only when we close up you get that bottle. Any messes you make while you fucked up, you gotta clean up."

＊　　　＊　　　＊　　　＊

Orange trees and more orange trees. In every dream, or every dream Mary could remember, they were the background, or the foreground, or every single part of the ground. She would be walking in a grove. The sun was shining. There was a breeze, and Cecilia was always in her arms. A man was always by Mary's side. He was clean-shaven and smelled nice. He wasn't Sampson. Didn't look a thing like him.

"Am I a bad woman?" Mary asked Sheila two days after Sampson had vanished again without a clue. "Is it wrong for me to feel this way?"

"No, Mary," Sheila said, holding Mary's hand as she cried. "But … it's how you did it. We're dealing with a different man from who we once knew. I mean, I didn't know him too well. But … I know he isn't that guy I once knew, that's for sure. This Sam can't take the truth right now."

"I'm afraid he'll do something to himself."

"The cops know, Mary. We can't do anything else."

"I should never have said what I said. Not like that, at least."

"No, Mary. You're right. But what's done is done."

*   *   *   *

Hitting the floor at night, Sampson almost felt the impact. But he was plenty sauced. When he needed to go to the bathroom, he had to stumble in the dark towards the closet-sized privy in the backroom's east corner. Sampson fell many times. He knocked over many cans that rested on those spindly, steel shelves. He always found the bathroom, eventually. Sampson relieved himself and inevitably fell asleep on the floor in there. The owner found him there almost every morning.

"Gonna get you a pillow," the owner said laughing while he helped Sampson up. "Want some McDonald's?"

Sampson ate the Egg McMuffin after taking out the slice of ham. He drank the orange juice the owner had bought him as well. He spent his days resting off his drinking. He spent his nights washing dishes and then taking that bottle of Evan Williams to find God while the devil sharpened its stick.

He didn't talk to anybody while he worked. Most of them didn't speak English anyway back there in the kitchen. Sampson and they were in the same space, but their worlds just didn't interact.

Sampson thought of Grouchy. He wondered where he was. He regretted making Grouchy angry, and he wondered if that had caused Grouchy to never want to see him again.

Grouchy sensed his wondering. He was still angry, but starved for a task as well. One morning before the owner arrived, he called Sampson's name. Sampson stopped snoring and woke up on that cold, dirty bathroom floor that mostly smelled of his face.

"I don't think I'm doing you much good, Sam," Grouchy said once Sampson could find focus.

"I'm not listening, am I?"

"I don't know if you can right now. If God himself told you what to do, you'd probably ignore that too."

"There ain't no God. Far as I'm concerned, you're him."

"Well, then, you've just proven my point, haven't you?"

"Ain't you gonna give me some advice, at least, Grouchy? Ain't you gonna tell me what Sheila and them are doing?"

"First off, my advice is going in deaf ears. Or mostly deaf ears, at least. Second, I don't know what they're doing. That little bullshit show you put on makes me ashamed to watch. But … for some reason, I still can't leave."

Grouchy left Sampson's view as soon as the bar owner started calling Sampson's name. Sampson felt a great longing. He almost wanted Grouchy back more than Mary.

CHAPTER 19

"I want to be with you, Sheila," Tommy said. "I want to see if we can be a family. I've known you for a long time now. I know we never thought … But life brings surprises sometimes."

Sheila wondered if Grouchy heard Tommy. She wondered if he was monitoring the conversation and watching her face for her reaction. Sheila wanted to reciprocate. She wanted to tell him that maybe they should try. But she was imagining not only Tommy waiting for an answer, but Grouchy as well. It was in her mind. She wouldn't look to the space she imagined Grouchy inhabited. For too many seconds she just stared, and Tommy's expectant face started to lose shape.

"Sheila … I'm really going out on a limb here," he said.

"I know you are, Tommy."

"So what do you say?"

"I say … I can't say anything right now. It just don't feel right, right now. I don't want to hold you up, Tommy. If you need someone, you should look."

"I'm not thinking too many people out there have been what we've been through."

"Well, then … you're gonna need to wait if you want me. These things don't happen in some negotiation. They just happen."

"Well … *can* it happen, Sheila?"

"Anything can happen. Matter of time and place, far as I'm concerned."

When Tommy left, Sheila still felt an invisible presence she didn't understand. Grouchy had turned into a character he never was. Sheila saw him in a light he would be ashamed to resemble. To her, he was like some judging entity now. She felt callous eyes upon her, some wrathful warning surrounding her. Every thought she had about wishing for a union with Tommy was followed by fear, for she imagined those thoughts passing by unseen eyes threatening reprisal.

Sheila couldn't help but touch herself sometimes. At night, even with her baby in her crib, which made her feel guilty, she touched herself. She bit on the pillow as climax approached. Pleasure by her own hand never interested Sheila much, but pleasure was hard to come by these days.

She thought she saw Grouchy smiling after one particularly powerful orgasm. It signified, to her, that he was saying this is how it would be from now on. She could imagine anything she'd like, but could never, *ever* act on it. Sheila had been in this emotional prison since Grouchy had died, and the realization made her cry.

"It isn't fair, David. It *just isn't* fair."

Grouchy didn't hear. He didn't lie to Sampson. Since she had taken Sampson to Tommy's house, Grouchy had avoided Sheila and all aspects of her life. He was looking for lost souls soon to die. All the lost souls that had died looked awful, vengeful, pathetic, and trapped in a purgatory of their own frustrated emotions. He wanted to help those that hadn't died make the right choice when they did. This was better than letting frustration cripple him into outright ugliness.

＊　　　＊　　　＊　　　＊

"You see what friends are made of, don't you?" said Billy, the Vietnam vet's ghost, to Sampson one early morning as Sampson tried to sleep on the dirty bathroom floor of the bar's backroom.

Sampson didn't recognize him at first. He thought Billy was a burglar and got up to try to defend himself, though his wits were still quite dim. He reached for a bottle on the counter, but fell back down to the floor.

"What do you want?" Sampson demanded.

"Calm down, Sam," Billy said with his slick smile that highlighted his few teeth. "You don't remember me? Look at the uniform. You remember me now?"

"Huh? Oh … you the … oh, yeah, the Vietnam vet. The one who died by the old man … in the swamp or something."

"That's right. Fucker died two nights ago, and what does he do? He gets in line, Sam. He *gets* in line. I've been hanging around for him since '69 and he leaves me high and dry, Sam. High *and* dry!"

"That don't matter a thing to me, Billy. Go find someone else to haunt. I got a guy haunting me."

"There ain't a limit, Sam."

"I don't want you, is what I'm saying."

"Afraid I don't care. You'll either end up enjoying my company or you won't. You know what I been through, Sam. We need each other, don't we?"

"I *have* Grouchy!"

"Ah …," Billy smiled again. "No you don't. I heard him. He's done with you, Sam. You've been a great disappointment to that goody-goody. I don't ask for nothing but what you want to give. I'm easier that way. I think you'll grow to like it."

"He ain't done with me," Sampson said angrily. "Grouchy wouldn't just leave me alone."

"No? Well … neither will I, Sam."

Sampson heard insults and threats almost every night from the other bar workers. Succumbing to a liquor-induced stupor was his salvation. The environment was thick with unhappiness from people who didn't know how to escape it. The fat man who owned the bar was rude to every employee. He was rude to every customer. And the customers liked it, because they could be rude back. They could finally be rude to someone who wouldn't fire or divorce them.

One night Sampson woke from a stupor within an hour. Laughter from inside the bar perked up his ears. He didn't hear laughter from others much, just his own, usually, and the distant, bitter laughing of others. The laughter he was hearing now wasn't bitter. It was flirtatious and sleazy.

Soon, Sampson heard keys and the stumbling of bodies from the bar into his area. The fat man and a waitress Sampson had only fleeting glances of while he worked were stumbling. He heard clothes start to come off, a belt buckle and the snap of a bra before a body's collapse within a dark space just beyond the shaft of light the bar itself provided.

"Frank!" the waitress said. "Jesus, Frank."

"Get up, Sam," said Billy, standing within the bar's shaft of light, which reached just beyond the backroom's front door. "She needs some attention."

"What?" Sampson replied.

"Who's there?" the waitress asked.

"Get up, Sam, she's horny. When's the last time you fucked, huh?"

"Who's there?" the waitress said again, laughing.

The waitress found the light switch. Sampson saw that Frank, the owner, was passed out facedown on the floor, snoring. He was too drunk too fuck. Too drunk to stand. Too drunk to stay awake. The promise of easy sex had no sway over the liquor in his brain.

"Oh, hi," said the waitress, completely nude and not ashamed of it.

"Get *up*, Sam," Billy said.

Sampson didn't need any prodding once he saw her. He was drunk and without any sexual touch from someone else in a very long time. He said nothing. He just approached her while starting to undo his pants. The waitress giggled and took Sampson's penis in her hands when it came out.

"You don't smell too good," she said, but still put him inside her mouth.

He wanted inside her lower body, however, and took her head away. He pulled her to the ground and entered from behind. She gave no resistance. It was very rough. Sampson pounded her body like it was to blame. He grunted and she grunted back. When he sped up, she screamed, "Do it! Do it!" Looking back at Sampson, her eyes were fierce and desirous. She liked it this way.

Sampson climaxed inside her, so his sperm oozed out of her as she stood.

The waitress looked over Sampson and giggled. He was still feeling the lust. He wanted her back on the ground. The penis that stabbed with delight was still rigid and needing direction.

"This is no place for you to stay," she said. She told Sampson to get dressed and then grabbed his hand.

∗   ∗   ∗   ∗

Something was wrong. Cecilia looked slightly yellow. Mary took her to a pediatrician. It was a mild form of jaundice, the pediatrician said. But he didn't seem too worried. He said it would clear up on its own. This didn't make Mary any less worried, however. She always hated how her parents were so careful with everything she did, but it didn't stop her from turning into them.

Sheila was becoming annoyed. Mary didn't even like Cecilia and Elena in the same crib, even for just a minute. Sheila thought Mary was showing that superiority that folks like her had to start showing at some time. She figured that since Mary's career was taking off, now that she wasn't so afraid and alone, her upbringing was telling her that she was slumming living with Sheila. Elena's blur-collar blood just might rub off onto Cecilia's lily-white certain privilege.

This dream of two young mothers in a utopia of help and companionship was frayed. They didn't talk much anymore. Mary was too busy reading. She turned her nose up at everything Sheila watched on TV. Sheila was sure Mary was becoming who she really was, and who she really was was no friend to someone like Sheila.

"I think it's time I find my own place," Mary said one morning after a mostly silent breakfast.

"Figured," Sheila snorted.

"What does that mean?"

"Well … it's not like you're acting like you enjoy my company, Mary."

"I … I do," Mary said unconvincingly.

"One thing you ain't good at, Mary, is lying."

"I don't know … I guess there isn't what I used to think was there."

"Like with Sam, right?"

For a moment Mary thought it through. "Yeah, I guess. Like with Sam."

"Did you ever think for two seconds it would happen that way? Did you ever think you and him were from totally different worlds? It ain't like the movies. Those things rarely last."

"I loved him, Sheila. I did. I wouldn't have married him if I didn't. Since I was thirteen, I promised myself I wouldn't let a man touch me like him. Not until I got married. I was a prude, I know. I was from the forties or something. But all my friends gave it up to anyone, Sheila, and it didn't make them happy. I didn't want to chase anything. I didn't *want* to be *them*. I told him … I said if we do this we have to get married. And the next day we did. And then … when he came back-"

"It got complicated."

"Don't make me out like that, Sheila. I tried. I really did. I was heartbroken. But when he came back he wasn't Sam anymore. You said it yourself. Who I fell in love with was dead. Am I supposed to live with a corpse just so people think I'm strong?"

*   *   *   *

Sampson woke up with the waitress' smell all over his body. A strange, sweaty taste was on his lips. He was in a small bed in an apartment that overlooked a shabby back parking lot. He remembered fragments of their night, but only fragments.

Sampson's penis was sore. He was sure it was making up for lost time.

The waitress wasn't in the bed. When Sampson rose, she wasn't even in the one-bedroom apartment. A note was on the bathroom mirror. It read:

Food is in the fridge. Help yourself.
—Carly

CHAPTER 20

Her head hit hard, but it was her throat that rattled. Her car had catapulted into this ditch. She was miles from any help. With a jittery hand, she tried to dial her cell phone. But her mind fluttered with confusion. She dropped the phone to the floor just after she managed to dial a nine then a one.

Grouchy knew her in life. They went to high school together. Maybe even Sampson dated her. Grouchy wished he had the courage to ask her out, but he rarely had the courage to say hi.

She was the mother of two boys. Their father was in the sand and would be sent home after the army told him the news.

"Do you remember me, Gloria?" Grouchy said to her.

"No," she whispered. "I need help."

"I can't help you. I'm not alive. You'll be leaving your life soon too."

"I'm a mother."

"I know."

"They're alone," she said as her voice fell to petering whispers.

"Go into the cloud, Gloria. Please listen to me."

"But they're alone."

"Go into the cloud."

When Gloria left her body, she brushed past Grouchy like the days of old. She might as well have been wearing her cheerleading outfit and joking with some friends. But she was alone. She was alone and older but still confident that she should still be a mother to her two boys. Grouchy shouted about the cloud, but she ignored him and took the desolate road to what was once her home.

*   *   *   *

Sampson heard a clatter of keys at the apartment door. He had made himself three peanut butter and jelly sandwiches. But there wasn't any booze in the house. Sampson looked at the front door as if it were a liquor store door, and when it opened his vice would be sticking to the body that came through.

Carly was smiling. Her dyed, black, shoulder-length hair shimmered with powerful chemicals. She held a brown package in her left hand. The impression inside looked just like a fifth of Evan Williams to Sampson.

"Evan Williams, right?" Carly said, and he nodded.

"You ever gonna talk? Ain't heard you say one word since I took you. As far as I know you're a caveman."

"Look like one, don't I?"

"So you *can* speak. Let me tell you, you can also fuck real well, you smelly caveman."

"Haven't had the pleasure in some time."

"You're fired, by the way."

"I'm fired from what?"

"The bar, dummy. Frank said he didn't like you taking his girl."

"You were his girl?"

"Three nights a week I was. For an extra $500 he got to put his slimy hands on me. He got to put that small pecker in me too. I always made him use a condom, though. So don't worry. You didn't catch nothin' from him."

"That's good to hear."

"Let's get drunk."

*   *   *   *

If he could quit his job, he would. But Tommy had a son to support. He had house payments and truck payments. It hurt him to see Sheila every day. Every workday after he suggested a future together, she wouldn't look him in the eyes. Sheila would just grunt answers to all of Tommy's small questions. Humming to herself, she discouraged any substantial conversation and left his range of voice as soon as she was able. Tommy came home feeling so low he wouldn't look himself in the mirror. He woke up every morning thinking he'd just quit his job until he remembered a child made him responsible for more than himself.

If Tommy quit, he would be lucky to get half the pay he was making now. He didn't have much education. The army didn't do too much for his resume. He entered it as a private and left with the same designation. Before his job at the shuttle service, he was a bouncer and a guy who parked cars. A former staff sergeant who'd lapsed back into capitalism looked him up when he was thinking of starting the shuttle service. He always liked Tommy and offered a job as soon as he started the business.

"Your mommy is looking down on you," he said to his son, Tommy Junior. But mentioning that woman always brought tears to his eyes.

Her death seemed the most odd thing. She gave birth fairly quickly. She radiated with joy as she held Tommy Junior. But then quickly afterwards huge bruises on her body indicated the massive internal bleeding the birth produced and she was in ICU for two weeks before she had the stroke that killed her.

Tommy couldn't even look at Tommy Junior for two weeks after she died. Tommy's friends were his boy's parents until responsibility replaced his grief. Now, however, responsibility was starting to share priority with a need that couldn't be ignored. Tommy feared destroying himself if he tried to pretend he wasn't lonely.

Only Sheila would do. Other women just didn't know. He was sure they were out there, but he wasn't the type to search the Web to find commonality of grief. Sheila had the grief and a baby, just like he did. It seemed only logical they should get together. Tommy knew she thought so too. He couldn't figure why she had suddenly started to resist him when things were progressing in a slow but certain manner. The sex didn't matter. That could wait. Tommy just wanted a commitment to try.

Sometimes when Sheila came in to work, Tommy would stare at her down-turned eyes. He could feel them wanting to look up. He could feel her wanting to explain something she couldn't explain before. But Sheila would just take her assignments and walk out. She would just take her check and walk out. Each time she did, a tremor of pain shivered from Tommy's heart, into his stomach, and all over his body.

*   *   *   *

Sampson rolled off of Carly after another round of brutal, drunken sex. She told him to choke her while he was on top of her. He found the request odd, but he put his hands around her throat.

Carly said, "Tighter!" and Sampson squeezed tighter. She said, "Tighter!" again, but he wouldn't squeeze anymore.

That's when the names started. Carly called him "Scumbag" and "Asshole". She smacked him while she pumped on top of him. Sampson didn't think he liked it until he felt the orgasm rushing to be released.

"Why didn't he fire you?" Sampson said as Carly handed him a cigarette.

"I'm the only one in the place people like."

"So, are you going to fuck him anymore?"

"I don't know," Carly said and looked at Sampson sideways. "An extra $500 comes in handy. I don't even know your name!"

"It's Sam."

"Yeah, OK. I like your way, Sam. I knew I would. When I saw you I saw another dirty animal. Frank's a dirty animal, but he's an old animal. He's pathetic, really. Always came within two minutes flat. Grabbed my tits like he needed a drink. I need a buck like you around. Figure you don't mind the arrangement."

Sampson didn't like the sound of "arrangement." But Carly gave him a bottle. She got drunk easy, so two-thirds of it was always his. He had a mattress to lie on. He had free food in the fridge. Carly wasn't great looking, but she wasn't bad either. She had some extra fat around her thighs. Her breasts sagged a bit. She held him tight, though. She took away the lust that was making him crazier, excessively so.

*   *   *   *

The apartment was small, but Mary liked the view of the courtyard. There wasn't any central air. Just one window unit in the bedroom. It was within her price range. Mary could afford it along with day care.

Tommy helped Mary move. Sheila asked him to. Tommy didn't ask Sheila the many questions he wanted to ask. He couldn't. Even though she helped in the move and was with him throughout the day, she found ways to stay out of his way. The setting didn't suit those types of questions anyway. Sheila sometimes looked him in the eyes, but only accidentally and too briefly for him to speak with her. Sheila bought him a case of beer for his trouble. Tommy wanted to ask if she would drink with him. But once she handed him the beer, she turned around and walked away as quickly as wouldn't seem unnatural.

While driving past them, Sheila saw Sampson walking with a dark-haired companion. Sheila reached for her cell phone to call Mary, but as she was about to press the last digit, she knew it wouldn't elicit the interest she figured it should. Sheila wanted to call Tommy. Then she realized their conversations of late were so rudimentary that this might elicit deeper questions that she didn't want to answer. So she closed the phone and put it back on her passenger seat.

Sampson was walking into a liquor store with a girl whom Sheila immediately labeled as trash. She was sure he would knock her up. She was sure he would beat her up. His new lover would beat him up too. Sheila could tell. One look in a person's eyes, and Sheila knew what they were capable of.

She wondered if they shared a bottle and then their bodies. How long would it take the drunken honeymoon buzz to turn into slaps and hard fists? Trash did that sort of thing. That woman was trash, and Sampson had become trash because trash would have anyone. Sheila wondered if his name would be in the papers as a fugitive who had stabbed his lady friend to death.

Mary was edging out of Sheila's life, but seeing what Sampson had become made Sheila hoping with her greatest sincerity that Cecilia would call someone else "Daddy" someday.

Chapter 21

This man had been lingering around the margins for years. He was old when he died. He had wrinkled skin. A bitter countenance and bitter eyes completed the ensemble. But that didn't mean he lived that way. All of them looked bitter, for the most part. Grouchy wondered how long it would take him to look the same.

"Tell me something," said this long-dead ghost to Grouchy. "Do you think you're some kind of savior? Do you think you're making *any* difference?"

"I'm trying. It's worked with everyone but one."

"You got lucky with those others."

"I wouldn't call it luck."

"Really?" said the ghost condescendingly. "I've been here for over twenty years, buddy. I know the way this works, and we don't help it work."

"Why haven't you left?"

"None of your business why."

"I just want to understand."

"Understand *what*?"

"No offense," Grouchy replied, "but I don't want to be you."

"Then ... you see the line? Get in it."

"Of course I see it, but it feels wrong. I mean, I have a duty. Look, I know you think I'm just giving you an excuse. But I have. I've found a duty. I'm helping. I know I am."

"You've only *convinced* yourself of that, pal. You ain't helping *shit!* You know that feeling, that feeling that says it's wrong to get in the line. It don't go away. This is what I'm trying to tell you. If you can't say good-bye to everything you've ever known, you won't get in line. You might at first tell yourself you're doing something for somebody, somewhere. Everybody does. But when they realize it ain't true, they're too weak to do anything about it. If you don't use the strength you got now, you'll erode into someone like me. You want to avoid the resemblance of someone like me? March. It's easier said than done, but march anyway."

"I will … after my duty ends."

"After your duty ends? Man, people are gonna die until there ain't no people anymore. So what you're saying is that your duty will never end. That's what you're telling me. It's a crutch, fella. Just look out for yourself. You understand me? Let those that are going figure it out for themselves."

"No. They don't know. They don't know what they're doing."

"And neither do you."

*   *   *   *

It was lonely without her. Elena's cries increased now that Mary and Cecilia had gone. Sheila didn't think babies could form that kind of connection with other babies, but Elena's cries were certainly getting worse, and she wasn't sick.

Sheila had never given Grouchy's clothes away. They still hung in the closet, and now that she felt he was watching her every move, she was too timid to pack them up in boxes. But one day, a day she had off from work, she did. Sheila felt a swell of rebellion and bitterness. She told Grouchy he was dead. She couldn't see him anymore. Maybe he could see her, but she couldn't see him, and someone could use these clothes and the damn hangers they hung on.

She packed them all, even the clothes that reminded her of a trip they had taken together. Grouchy had an Atlanta Falcon's jersey. When she fingered the sleeve, she could feel that long, jagged rip. Sheila remembered how he'd gotten it. Grouchy didn't show off much, because he didn't have good balance. But he tried anyway.

They were climbing down the backside of Little Kennesaw Mountain. It was a steep trail that was full of precarious rocks. Grouchy kidded Sheila about her tiny steps until she pointed out that his were just as tiny. So he sped up and soon tripped on one of those cresting rocks within the middle of a trail. He rolled down off the trail a good twelve feet before he stopped. He looked dazed. His nose was bleeding but not broken. The look made Sheila laugh, because she could see Grouchy wasn't hurt badly. He just looked around stupidly and wiped his nose. He rose slowly. Embarrassed, he got back on the trail, walking ahead of

Sheila and sulking all the way back to the car while she tried to contain a laughter that couldn't be contained.

She left all of Grouchy's clothes at Goodwill. As Sheila pulled away, she stared at the building through her rearview mirror as though she were leaving behind much more than clothes. She was also leaving behind his smell and stretches made with arms that were luscious before they were buried.

"You'll never completely leave my life, David," she said into that mirror.

*   *   *   *

Try as he might, Sampson couldn't leave Carly's apartment. Carly was treating him exactly as she labeled him. He was her buck. He was just a tool for getting off. If Carly kissed him it was with a bite. If she held him, it was with him inside and her urging him to fuck her harder. He better be hard for her when she came home. If Sampson weren't, she would grab at his cock and tell him to leave if it couldn't stand up.

"You like living on the street, so go back to living on the street," Carly said less than a week after Samson became her apportioned lover.

"I didn't always live on the street."

"I know that! I know you weren't born out of your mother's dirty cunt on to the street!"

"Don't talk to me that way!"

"It's *my* apartment, loser. You don't like the way I talk, then *get* out!"

"I had a fine house before! I made mortgage payments and all that. I was in the war. I got messed up over there. That's why I ain't got no home!"

"What? You have nightmares or something? You've been here a week. I haven't noticed any trouble."

"Because we're always drunk! I don't dream when I'm drunk."

"I figure … I feed you. You got a bed to sleep on. You get free booze. Least you can do is let me get mine. It's only *fair*! There are shelters around if that's what you're looking for."

Carly would bait him. She wanted him to hurt her. During sex and outside of sex she only wanted turmoil. At any moment, without any provocation, she'd try to see what Sampson was made of, if he was anything at all besides her glorified dildo. He couldn't take the war, she'd say. Only weak losers couldn't take the war. Sampson answered back madly, of course, and that's when she asked if he wanted to hurt her. Carly would tell Sampson to hurt her. He'd go into the bathroom to calm down, but Carly pounded on the door as he ran the bath water to drown out her growing baiting. She wanted Sampson to use his fists so that she could use her own. He'd never hurt a woman, not with any violence of any kind. And he didn't want to start now.

He looked for money, but Carly never left any around. He'd leave and vow to never come back, but then feel the itch for enough alcohol to soothe his confused mind. He'd return before her shift was even half over. She faithfully bought him a bottle. They emptied it together, Sampson always taking the lion's share. Then he was the machine Carly hopped on and screamed at before an orgasm made her soft for just a few seconds. Sex was now a chore for him to stay alive. And then one day she came home without a bottle and told Sampson that he made her pregnant.

*　　　*　　　*　　　*

"I'm … I'm married," Mary told the man showering her with attention. "But … well, we're separated."

"Are you getting a divorce?"

"I … want to. I haven't had the money to get it together. Well, maybe I have, but I don't know … I guess I haven't had the energy."

"So … are you telling me you're not available?"

"No, I'm not telling you that. We've been separated for over a year. I've barely seen him in that time. He actually has some … well, some mental problems. He was in the war."

"Oh, really?"

"Yeah. He … actually lived in the woods a little bit after he came back."

"The woods?"

"Yeah, the woods. We don't know where he is. We tried to help him, but he ran away. We don't know where he is."

"Who's we?"

"My … well, my friend. Her husband died. He was in the war too."

"OK … Um, since you said you were available, I … would really like to take you to lunch sometime."

"I think … I could do that. But, just so you know, I have a daughter. She's still just a baby."

"I love kids."

"Good. I like guys who do."

*   *   *   *

Thinking wasn't an option. Sampson could either run or stay. He could either pretend to want this child made through rough, meaningless sex, or get back on the trail of dubious destination.

"I'm keeping it, if that's what you're wondering," Carly told Sampson after she informed him of the pregnancy.

"Why do you want to?"

"Because I *want* to! I need something like this."

"Something like this?"

"Maybe it'll give me some order."

"Or maybe you'll screw it up."

"Yeah, maybe. I guess it'll be my own little experiment, won't it?"

"I already have a kid."

"So? I don't. Go back to your goddamn kid if that's what you want to do. Mine never has to see you."

*   *   *   *

Sheila saw that Tommy was alone in the office. It wasn't usually this way. Usually drivers came in and out, and she and Tommy weren't ever alone. So she waited in her car until they wouldn't be. It was her day off. She just wanted to get her check. But she waited until someone else could accompany her inside, so she wouldn't have to hum so damn much.

Elena struggled beside her. She seemed to be losing patience with her mother's lack of ability to say what she needed to say.

"Just tell him," Elena seemed to be saying. "Just tell him why you're scared. If he's the man for you he'll understand."

"I can't, Elena," Sheila said to her out loud. "God, if he is the man for me, he won't want to be the man for me anymore after he hears I'm scared of some ghost."

"So you're going to just be held captive by this ghost? David will be a ghost forever, you know."

"Don't call him David! He's your dad!"

"You realize I'm not actually speaking. This is all in your head. I have about two or three years before I can form whole sentences."

"Yes, I know that."

"So just get it over with."

Someone pulled up, so Sheila left the car with Elena clutched to her chest. When she came inside, Tommy's eyes, dulled by boredom, brightened.

"Hi, Sheila," he said.

"Hey, Tommy," Sheila replied with her eyes turned down once more.

The other driver left the building. He had forgotten something. Elena's struggles returned, as did her voice inside Sheila's head.

"Say something."

"You been doing OK?" Sheila asked without looking up.

"Yeah … OK, I guess," Tommy replied.

"Why 'I guess'?"

"Well, why do you think?"

The driver came back inside. He handed Tommy his mileage sheet and left with his assignments.

"Do you have my check?" Sheila asked.

"Are you going to answer my question, Sheila? Did I … did I offend you or something? Did I suggest something totally out of line?"

"This isn't the time or place, Tommy."

"OK, fine. You tell me the time and place, and I'll be there."

"I … don't know it yet."

"I deserve an answer at least. Did I do something, Sheila? Tell me *something*. Please just tell me why."

"I'll call you, Tommy."

"You promise?"

"Yeah."

"When?"

"I don't know, Tommy. But I'll call you," Sheila said, sifting through the multiple checks on his desk. She found hers and left while Tommy was still trying to stutter a response.

✳   ✳   ✳   ✳

Time was a fast engine. Sampson thought he would barricade himself inside the bathroom for just a little while. But dawn was approaching. He'd been sitting on the toilet for over five hours. Billy stood in front of him the whole time, giving Sampson suggestions that sounded perfectly reasonable to a disgusting, dead man. But each one was more terrible than the last to a living man like Sampson, who didn't want to be bad.

"Put a knife to her throat and get her ATM number. When she gives it to you, slit it."

"God, you are a fucking psychopath," Sampson said, shaking his head.

"Only now. Wish I had the guts when I was alive."

"If you did, you'd of been dead a lot quicker."

"Who are you talking to, Sam?" Carly asked. She sounded sleepy, but her voice was still tinged with an ire that could grow in seconds.

"No one!"

"You finally going crazy on me? One night without a bottle and you going crazy?"

Sampson didn't answer.

"Do it now, Sam," Billy said. "She's sleepy. She won't even put up a fight."

"What do I do after?" Sampson tried to whisper.

"What, Sam?" Carly said.

"Just go back in the woods," Billy replied. "You seemed to like it there. I'd like to go there with you."

"I'd like you to go back to hell, where you belong!" Sampson said, and Carly started knocking fiercely.

"You knew what you were doing!" she yelled. "You knew you were wearing no rubber. You know how babies are made. *You* can go to hell, Sam! You can get the hell out of my house and go to hell!"

Sampson stood from the toilet seat and jerked open the bathroom door. He looked into Carly's suddenly stimulated eyes and said, "I wasn't talking to you!"

"Then *who*, Sam? Unless the cockroaches know English you were talking to me!"

"I *will* leave!"

"Good! Guess I'm not in much mood to fuck anymore anyway. You ain't nothing to me now. Hope the kid won't look like your ugly ass."

"Why are you so bitter? What did I do to you?"

"You're a man. You don't need to do nothing to make me bitter when I look at your face."

✳   ✳   ✳   ✳

The silence in the empty barrack made Harry glad he was alone. He didn't mean for it to happen. It just went off. He was glad no one saw. The gun shot into his gut. If he could move for help he would have, but every move sliced through his damaged body so harshly he couldn't. He had no strength to cry out.

Harry called silently for his brother to take him away. Grouchy saw Harry's dead brother by Harry's side when he arrived.

"Go to the cloud, Harry," Grouchy said.

Harry's brother looked at Grouchy with a feeling of intrusion.

"This is *my* brother. Who the hell are *you*?"

"You both should be going to the cloud."

"I'll decide what we do, OK? Why don't you get the *fuck* out of here?"

"You see, Harry? Do you see? Do you want to be like him?"

"Go away!" Harry said as loud as he could, which wasn't very loud. "Who is this, Chuck?"

"I don't know," Chuck said. "One of those self-appointed angels, I guess." He turned to Grouchy. "We'll do what we want to do! Go away."

"You should go! Go to the cloud!" Grouchy pleaded.

"Jesus! If it's so great, buddy, why ain't you already there?"

"I don't know."

"Yeah, and I don't either."

"There's nothing here for you anymore," Grouchy said. "You can't love who you see. They can't see you back."

"I don't feel dead when I see them," Chuck said. "And Harry won't either. Us, our family, our kids, we'll all go together. Find someone else to preach to."

CHAPTER 22

The headaches were one of the reasons, as were the soreness and guilt. So Tommy stopped drinking so much alone. When his wife died, he couldn't help himself. His grief was so brutal against his tender psyche; being shunned from Sheila's thoughts hurt him just the same.

He allowed himself only three beers a night, usually. Tonight he was on his sixth. He had been drinking this much every night since he realized the promise Sheila made to call him was made just to escape the conversation. Tommy picked up the phone to call her, but stopped dialing every time. When Tommy Junior cried, his father went into the bathroom to mask his breath with mouthwash so the baby wouldn't associate booze with love.

"I know, Tommy, I know," Tommy said, picking him up. "I want a woman's touch too. I want you to know what having a momma is like. I'm trying."

✳   ✳   ✳   ✳

The morning light shined on Sampson's face. He'd found a quiet patch of woods. It wasn't too large, though, so he'd covered himself with branches in case a cop came by. He was still angry and disturbed when he woke. Without liquor in his veins, he wasn't easy to predict. With liquor in his veins, he was even less predictable. Once again, where to go was the great quandary. He imagined he could find a Dumpster and find something that could be called breakfast. He would then find another clueless bar, and when it opened, he would con them out of an armful of drinks. Shelter was another quandary; so was running water. But if worse came to worse, Sampson knew a jail cell had both.

The people along the road looked at him oddly. He still had leaves and particles of twigs in his hair. He was unbalanced, almost stepping into traffic with every other crooked step. Sampson's body was crying for the daily numbing it wasn't granted the last two nights. It made him twitch with anticipation; the people along the road knew they weren't seeing a man walking to work. They were seeing a man who didn't work and slept where he fell. Kennesaw didn't hold too many homeless. They existed but were mostly invisible, and they always turned heads when they stepped from the shadows where they were expected to stay.

Sampson smelled something cooking from an IHOP just down the street and to his left. He imagined they must have thrown something away and sought out its open Dumpster. The manager came out yelling at him: "SKEDADDLE!" Sampson did, but not before grabbing an old cartoon of milk and thawing biscuits that had long outlasted their freshness date.

✳   ✳   ✳   ✳

Carly was thirsty for something too. She might not have been the Olympic drinker Sampson was, but she was still an alcoholic, just like him. After she took the pregnancy test, she swore off booze. It lit in her head that she was doing the right thing. A righteous feeling made her steps light, but the second morning, after a second night of nothing, brought a surprise: the expectation of what her body had come to expect. And, just like Sampson, her body rudely questioned why it wasn't getting its share.

The toilet seat shimmied with her shivering. She gave herself reasons why it was OK to have a taste. But nothing was in the house. It was too early for any liquor store to be open. A grocery store, yes.

A beer? Just a beer? Maybe a few beers? Couldn't hurt the baby none.

Carly was excited. Her body trembled with expectation as she drove to the supermarket. Walking though the automatic doors and into the ice-cold temperatures of the store receded that thrill and brought on impatience. She clutched the first pack she saw, got in line, her limbs jerking her around. She wanted the taste then and there. Somehow Carly bought the beer unopened from the cashier, who had tons of judgment in her eyes. Somehow she avoided calling that cashier a bitch. She broke open a can in the parking lot and sighed with relief just after the Molson emptied down her throat. When a cop pulled up, she turned the ignition.

*   *   *   *

The bar was about to open. Sampson read the hours and then came back to sit on the bus bench enclosed in graffiti-stamped plastic. He didn't care if this one called the law. It would put him behind bars, maybe long enough to drain his addiction. Why did he want that? He didn't know. It just seemed the proper thing to want.

Sampson's head lolled from side to side. People waiting for the bus got up from the bench to avoid his smell. This caused him no offense. His head sank to his chest and then rose again. A small car entered the Applebee's parking lot across the street. A tall guy got out. A small woman got out of the passenger side. She looked like Mary.

Mary ... how much I mistreated you. You were the only one decent enough. You were above me in everyway.

Wait a minute ... that is Mary! That is definitely *Mary.*

Who the fuck *is that guy?*

Sampson snapped to attention. He got up and crossed the street. Horns honked as he darted through the traffic. Injury or death seemed a powerless expression at the moment. Sampson parted cars like Moses and entered the restaurant. The servers looked uncomfortable when they saw this unclean, unshaven man. He turned away from their discomfort and looked in all directions. Finally, he looked at the table that hadn't noticed his smell and shabby dress and dirty skin.

Mary was smiling. She was smiling and happy. This man was someone she liked, someone she imagined she could love. This man went to college, a respectable college, where he majored in math. He taught where she taught. He desired a higher degree, just like Mary desired one for herself. And this man didn't drink. Maybe all her feelings for a salt-of-the-earth man like Sampson had finally been exhausted, Mary thought. Maybe she was growing up.

Her smile twisted into something fearful when two long, dirty arms thrust themselves between the happy couple. Mary saw Sampson's menacing face looking at her date, who tried to retreat from his granny glasses.

"She's a married woman!" Sampson screamed.

Mary's date looked for help from the staff. Some came over, but Sampson told them to shut up. They did once they backed off.

"She's my wife!"

The date looked at Mary. She didn't want to acknowledge this, but the truth was in her stuttering, self-conscious eyes.

"Mary?" said the man.

"It's true, Wil."

"Wil?" Sampson yelled. "What a fagot-fucking name!"

"Sam! Jesus, Sam! We're *hardly* married," Mary said.

Sampson grabbed Wil by the collar, and Wil struggled to get loose. As Sampson hurled back an arm, it was caught. He felt something sizzle his side. Soon he was on the floor twisting with agony. Mary looked at him with some tenderness, but mostly a fear reverting into embarrassment. A Taser used by one the servers put Sampson on that floor flaked with crumbs, and as he tried to get up, he was Tasered again.

"I was in the war! Doesn't *anybody* care? Doesn't *anybody* care?"

"Sam, you need more help," Mary pleaded. "You need more help!"

"I was in the war! I killed for this country! I saw so many things I'll never forget for this country!"

The police came in, and every guest of the restaurant watched with hyper-curiosity as they dragged Sampson out screaming obscenities and calling Mary names that made even the muscular cops wince.

"I was in the fucking war!" Sampson said in the back of the cruiser he was squeezed into, his leg almost breaking as he struggled.

"Good. Now you're going to jail," one of the cops said, as Sampson purposely pissed himself to give them more grief.

That night it began. Sampson screamed. He shuddered. When he could fall asleep, he would wake up soon after covered in layers of sticky sweat that had the consistency and smell of maple syrup. Guards came in to tell Sampson to shut up. He promised them anything just so long as he could get a drink.

Sampson couldn't eat his food. His body constantly shook. He opened his mouth to wretch out dirty air that he wished was the knot in his belly that couldn't be satiated by anything but liquor—the harder the better.

Fear of certain death troubled him constantly. His heart beat in his chest so loudly he was sure everyone could hear it. Everyone laughed at him and taunted him when he wasn't within the worst stages of detoxification. The other locked-up losers inside said they had some booze, and in desperation Sampson believed them until they laughed in his face after handing him a cup of dirty toilet water. Sampson drank it anyway, just in case.

Minutes ticked so slowly that Sampson didn't know how long he'd been trapped in the jail cell and the cell of his angry body. He moved like an old man until the nighttime, when he became a screaming imbecile. The others in the community cell were getting so sick of him that they kicked his side, but it didn't shut him up.

One of the guards who yelled at Sampson to shut up came in and dragged him out.

"You have a visitor! Now try and keep it together!"

"I need something. G-G-G-Give me something."

"You gettin' what you need. You'll leave here a healthy man."

Sampson's shaking body inched itself into the visitor's room. The room had many long brown tables and benches made of steel bolted to the concrete floor. Four guards were inside. They yelled when any visitor touched an inmate, or when an inmate tried to do the same.

Mary was inside. She looked at Sampson with pity. Just pity. It was the pity of seeing a broken animal or hearing of an old man being abandoned at a racetrack. Sampson tried to sneer, but his twitches didn't allow any solid expression of contempt.

"What … d-d-d-do you wh-wh-wh-wh-ant?" Sampson asked. He hugged himself. The cool air in the visitor's room felt like an artic chill on his sweaty skin.

"I want you to sign this," Mary said, sliding forward the divorce papers.

Sampson could barely read the words, he was so afflicted. But he figured out its gist.

"D-D-Divorce?"

"Yes, Sam. It's time. Wil will drop the charges if you sign. Applebee's said they won't prosecute either. They just don't want you coming back."

"You g-g-g-gonna marry him?"

"That was our first date, Sam. Thanks to you I'm not sure if there will be a second."

"G-G-Gooood!" Sampson said, and as the *d* left his mouth an arc of spit leaped from his teeth on to Mary's nose.

"Sign it," she said.

"What about, Vi-Vi-Visi-Visi-Vi-Vi-Visitation?"

"Visitation? Are you crazy? Sam, you're shaking from the DTs. You live on the street. You can't visit our daughter now. When you're better we'll talk about it."

"It's my kid too!" he managed to say without a stutter.

"I want to be fair, Sam. But you have to get help. I won't take her away from you. I won't tell her you're dead or anything like that. You want to visit her, get sober. Get well. Sign this."

"NO!"

"Then he'll press charges. Sign it!"

"I got another kid coming anyway," Sampson shrugged.

"Really?" Mary didn't believe him.

"Yeah," he snorted. "I don't need you. Y-Y-Y-You think I n-n-n-n-need yoooou?!"

Sampson's jittery hand took the pen, and with a guard watching closely, he signed the paper in jerks.

"You a cold-hearted bitch, Mary. A c-c-c-coooooold-hearted *bitch*!"

"Someday you'll understand," Mary said, wincing.

"Y-Y-Y-Yeah. I have the c-c-c-capacity to understand. You d-d-d-don't!"

"Good-bye, Sam," she said, getting up. Sampson was expected to get up, too, but his bones felt so stiff they seemed welded to the bench.

Chapter 23

Tommy knew it was wrong. He knew it was strange and desperate and wrong. But he did it anyway. It was his fifth night of doing it. Just in case. Tommy had to know. Did Sheila really just need time? Or was her time spent with someone else?

His next-door neighbors took care of Tommy Junior while Tommy engaged in his nightly mission. They had a two-year-old daughter who liked playing with baby dolls. Playing with a real baby made her ecstatic until she smelled the stink from his full diaper.

The official excuse Tommy made to his neighbors was that he had to work late. After he picked up Tommy Junior from day care, he went home, changed and got into the small rental car he had rented just for his purposes. Tommy's neighbors were suspicious, but Tommy had always done right by them. Whatever he was doing wrong didn't give them too much concern.

He'd park at an angle in front of Sheila's house where Sheila couldn't see. It was as boring as any stakeout. Sheila would come home and never leave. But that didn't mean there wasn't someone else.

Three nights, four nights don't mean there ain't someone else. The night I don't show up is the night he *does*, he reasoned to himself

Would he do this every night? He didn't know. Tommy would have to tire himself of this dream before it stopped.

On night five, just the look of something different thrilled the part of Tommy more interested in finding excitement than worrying about the disappointment after its high. Someone came over whom Tommy had never seen before. Sheila greeted her at the door like she'd never seen her before either. Tommy guessed she was a babysitter. He guessed Sheila was going on a date, and when Sheila got into her car, Tommy started his. He followed closely.

Sheila pulled into a bar. She just needed a break. Being hit on was the last thing she wanted, but she did want to drink. Just a bit. Sheila just wanted to sit somewhere and drink in another atmosphere besides home. Her plaguing thoughts wanted to bounce off walls she didn't own in exchange for the different perspective those walls might give.

Tommy continued driving when she turned. He passed back and passed back again and pulled into the lot when he got tired of passing. The mirror behind the bar faced the street. Sheila sat at the bar with her back to the window. Two empty stools sat on both sides of the stool she sat on. Sheila wasn't looking in the bar's mirror, so Tommy slinked inside and found a booth where he could watch her—and whoever—in the dark and hopefully not start the fight he was imagining inside his head.

Since she was the prettiest image within miles, Sheila wasn't sitting alone for very long. When someone sat next to her, she sighed. She could feel his eyes on her face. His eyes examined her youthful body and imagined getting some more drinks inside her so he could touch every part of it with every part of himself.

"Hi," said the man with amorous intention, and Sheila reluctantly turned to him.

Tommy watched. He liked it that Sheila looked put-upon. He watched to make sure this guy didn't take things too far. He watched to make sure the man handled her rejection well. If not, Tommy would handle him away from her. The temptation was present to do it right now, but his more studious side urged patience.

"Hey," Sheila said hoarsely and then looked back at her drink.

"What are you drinking?"

"Jack and Coke."

"Is that the most girly drink you could think of?" the guy said and laughed.

Sheila laughed briefly back, but only to be polite.

"I always wondered about those drinks. I never figured many girls really liked them."

"Yeah," Sheila said lazily and sighed again.

"You want to be alone?"

"Yeah, I actually do."

"A pretty girl at a bar by herself creates a buzz, you know."

"I know. But I thought I'd give it a try anyway."

"I think you're playing hard to get. That's it, right? Hard to get? I get it. You want me to try harder."

"No, not really."

"Yeah, I get it. I get it. You'll talk to the guy who really tries. My last girlfriend told me that was my problem. She told me I didn't really try. Well, I want to try. Believe me, I want to try—with *you* especially."

"I think you might be overcompensating."

"Can I buy you another drink?"

"I'm not even half finished with this one."

"Can I buy you one when you're through?"

"Listen," Sheila said, turning back to him. Her lack of interest was starting to weigh down her eyes. "Even if I was interested when you first came up, I wouldn't be now. I'm serious. I want to be alone."

When Tommy heard this, he rose from the black booth he'd been spying from and slowly started around the bar. Sheila was granting her pursuer just a little more patience, so she didn't notice Tommy.

The pursuer started to filibuster Sheila's sincerest wishes. "I know I'm no Brad Pitt. OK? I know you probably think you deserve the looks of someone like him. But I'm a good guy. I treat the ladies right in *every* way. You understand, right? That's what you're looking for, right?"

"I told you I wasn't."

"Look, it ain't right for some woman to just show up and act like she don't want no attention," the pursuer finished saying with frustration as Tommy sidled next to Sheila and said, "Hey, Sheila."

She knew who it was before she turned and felt such a relief that it didn't enter her mind why he was at the same bar she was, a bar she knew he didn't frequent.

"I'm here with him," Sheila said to the pursuer, who looked at Tommy's size and moved slowly away without saying another word.

Only when the pursuer went back to a table to suck on a straw and peruse his other choices did Sheila start to wonder. Why was Tommy at this bar at the same time as she? This bar wasn't close to his house. It wasn't special enough to travel for. And it was 11:30 PM. Tommy didn't stay up past nine unless it was New Years'.

"What ... what are you doing here?" Sheila asked. Her eyes searched Tommy's for a lie before he had a chance to answer with one.

"I saw your car and thought I'd pop in."

"You saw my car?"

"Yeah."

"I parked in the back."

"Yeah. I saw you pull in."

"Oh," Sheila said, and though she still wondered she let it go. The truth was, even if Tommy had been stalking her like she guessed, he saved her from a scene. He was the protector, the man she always saw him as. He was by her side when she needed him most, and her perpetual need for him finally seemed satisfied.

"Can we talk now?" Tommy asked.

"Now? Here?"

"Here's as good as any place."

"Not for me, Tommy."

"Sheila." His sigh was desperate. His eyes turned desperate. Sheila felt pained just looking at them because she knew the torture he was going through. She was going through it too. "I don't care where. You tell me where. I'll go anywhere to do it. I just want to do it. I just want to know."

"Yeah," Sheila said, turning back to a drink that looked to be holding too much for her taste at the moment.

"I just want to know," Tommy said again.

"You should know," Sheila answered him quietly.

"Then tell me," Tommy said just as quietly while leaning towards her.

"Let's leave."

"OK."

"Meet me at my house."

"OK," Tommy said excitedly and looked flushed with the knowledge that his lonely days were over.

Tommy tried to pay for her drink, but Sheila wouldn't let him. Both of their stools scraped as they got up. Tommy waited for Sheila to approach the chipped wooden frame of the bar's door and then opened it for her. They parted ways with a quick wave, and Tommy got into his car at the front of the bar as Sheila got into her car at the back. Sheila drove up the ramp before Tommy started his rental. He wondered if she'd notice his rental and ask about it. He wondered if she'd figure he'd been stalking her. Though, Tommy usually didn't call it that. He usually thought of it as a "necessary investigation."

Her form was dark and in shadows as Tommy started up her driveway. Once he parked he could see Sheila's eyes drifting over the silver compact car, which wasn't his style at all.

"New car?" Sheila said, still examining the car. Tommy could see the wheels turning in her head that questioned the choice.

"No. My truck's in the shop."

"Oh."

The surprised babysitter stood up from the couch when Sheila and Tommy walked in. Sheila had hired her for four hours. Why, she didn't know. Sheila figured she should have known she couldn't sit in a damn bar by herself for four hours and not be so harassed she'd want to leave. So, though Sheila had been gone for less than one hour, she paid the babysitter for all four.

"You want a beer?" Sheila asked Tommy. He said yes.

She grabbed the last two beers from the refrigerator and handed one to Tommy. Sheila sat on the loveseat, which was the same color of the black leather couch Tommy sat opposite on.

"You're gonna think I'm crazy," Sheila said.

"Why?"

"It's because of David."

"Well, I figured that."

"No. It's because I think he's still watching me."

"Oh." Tommy lifted his eyes as he considered what she said.

"You see? You think I'm crazy."

"I don't," Tommy said, and the look in his eyes convinced Sheila he didn't. "I don't. Who knows what happens when you die. My parents always said so-and-so is looking down on you, so I don't see why that's crazy."

"No. I don't think he's looking *down* on me, Tommy. I think he's in the room *with* me."

Grouchy was in the room with her. He'd been in every room she was in for more than a week now. He watched her battle her loneliness with tears and extra love for Elena. When he saw how much pain she was in, he wanted to cry out that she could do whatever she wanted to do. But now, as that potential came closer, he tried conjuring powers that didn't exist to become a living man again so he could kick Tommy out of his house.

"I still don't think that's crazy, Sheila."

"Do you ever think Francine is with you?"

"I ... don't, honestly. I don't. But that's just me. I don't even think she's watching me. I tell Tommy Junior she is. I know he don't know what I'm saying. But I still tell him that. Expect I will forever. It's just something you say, I suppose."

"Yeah. I guess you gotta say something."

Sheila noticed that Tommy didn't know where to place his beer. He didn't want to leave an impression on her coffee table, so Sheila got up to find a coaster.

Instead, she found herself taking the beer, putting it down on that coffee table, and leaning into Tommy for a deep kiss.

It took Tommy by surprise. At first his head went back, but Sheila followed it and opened her mouth, and slowly their tongues began to circle each other.

"Make love to me, Tommy," Sheila said into his ear, her voice shaking from a fear of her own request.

"Are you sure?"

"Yes. Yes, I'm sure."

Sheila stood up. Tommy looked at her to make sure she was sure. She was waiting for him with her hand out, waiting for his. Their hands locked into each other's, and Tommy rose while still looking into her eyes, uncertain of something he hadn't done since a month before his wife gave birth.

Leading him into her bedroom where Elena lay asleep, Sheila put her finger to her lips. She let go of Tommy's hand and started to slowly undress. So Tommy did as well.

Grouchy was at the foot of the bed as they embraced beside it. He watched Tommy's body, six inches taller and one hundred pounds heavier from his own, press into Sheila's body. The awkward movements of nervous new lovers, who were about to touch a body they'd never touched before, started before Grouchy could turn away.

It was a tender, almost immature adventure. Sheila and Tommy both knew what they were doing, but it was still a foreign act against the shape of an unknown body. They said they were sorry a few times. Tommy was gentle with his movements. Sheila kissed his face. Tommy closed his eyes.

When Grouchy turned, he faced Elena in her crib and thought he should be angry she was seeing this. But Elena was just a baby. She wasn't even conscious. She was sleeping, and there were no screams or pounding of a headboard into a wall that threatened to wake her up. The only audible noise was a rustle of sheets and some soft voices.

"You'll tell all your friends who your daddy is," Grouchy said to Elena's resting body. Her hair was light brown, like his. "And it won't be me. But you deserve one. And it can't be me."

Somehow, even with all the odd movements and almost unfamiliar touches, the act was pleasurable, tender. Slow, but certain, just like how they'd come to be together in this bed.

The new couple lay silent next to each other after Tommy returned from the bathroom. They didn't smile. They just wondered. Each wondered what they should say. The act seemed necessary. It wasn't brought on by passion. It wasn't even brought on by love. It was brought on by a loneliness that both knew only the other could help erase.

"Where's Tommy Junior?" Sheila said.

"He's with the neighbors."

"So, you knew you were going out?"

"Yeah, I had to. Got sick of looking at my four walls."

"Me too."

"I've been sick of wanting, Sheila. Seems to me I could get to think that's all I could ever do. Just want."

"I understand."

"I want Tommy Junior to have a mother."

"I know. I want Elena to have a father."

"I want Tommy Junior to know about his mother, but I don't want him wondering what one is like."

"We'll try, Tommy. If I fail you, just know I tried."

"If we both try, Sheila, we ain't gonna fail."

CHAPTER 24

A rose-color stain was on Sampson's cheek. It would disappear just to reappear somewhere else, like under his eye. Sampson's body no longer just wanted to tremble. It needed to brand him for stopping the medicine.

He hardly felt cured. His guts felt ripped apart. Sobriety had thrown him about, and Sampson wanted to guzzle something down his throat to snap the cockiness it so brazenly flaunted.

Sampson hitchhiked away from the county jail into Kennesaw. He walked over five miles to get back to Carly's place. He doubted Carly missed him, but he didn't care. When Carly said she needed "this," this child, it was an appropriate need for him, too, as he endured an unwilling, torturous detoxification inside jail. A second chance at fatherhood became Sampson's greatest wish when he and Mary stopped being husband and wife, legally and for good.

Sampson climbed the apartment stairs like a man who had run four marathons in a row without a sip of water. If Carly didn't want him, Sampson hoped she'd show him some rare kindness and allow him a bed for just a few hours. He weakly knocked upon Carly's door. He heard something moving inside, then something pressing into the door, then Carly's voice. "What do you want?"

Well, so much for finding kindness.

"Let me in," Sampson said.

"Why?"

"I want to try, Carly."

"I don't want no part of you. Where you been for the past week? You been fooling with your wife?"

"Don't have a wife anymore."

"Yeah, seems about right. Who'd want to be your wife?"

"We're gonna have a kid, Carly."

"*I'm* gonna have a kid! Nothing growing in *your* belly, Sam."

"Come on, Carly."

"You're just strung out. You'll use me like you did before and then take off."

"Use you? Use *you*? Jesus, Carly, that's how you got that kid. You were using me just as much as I was using you!"

Carly opened the door. Sampson could smell booze on her breath, hard booze. He thought about criticizing her for being so careless with their embryo before he realized he was hardly a shining example of clean living.

"I know what you're thinking," Carly said. "You're thinking I shouldn't drink, right?"

"Generally, women that are pregnant shouldn't. Especially not the firewater I'm smelling."

"Yeah, I know. I'm quitting. Just a little more. I'm done after today."

"So ... you got some?"

"Oh!" Carly said and laughed harshly. "You back to get some, huh? You back for some booze. You back for what you stayed here for in the first place, huh?"

"I'm just asking if you have some."

Carly grabbed Sampson's soiled shirt and pulled him in. She stared at him brutally after she locked the door, looking him up and down, just like Sampson would do to subordinates in the field who disgusted him. He figured he felt just like they did: nervous and shamed.

"Why ain't you married anymore?" she asked.

"She divorced me."

"Of course she did! Who wouldn't? You're just a mess of scrambled brains. You're just a loser now. You went there to become some hero, but you're just a goddamn loser. Ain't that right?"

"You don't talk to me like that when you haven't walked-"

"Don't talk to you like that? Hell, it's my house. You're here begging for some booze and you think you get a free ride?"

"Why are you like this, Carly?"

"Why are *you* like this?"

"The war, damn it! The *fucking* war!"

"Some of us go through our own wars, too, Sam, but nobody gives us pity 'cause it ain't on the news every night. There ain't no guns involved, but I got just as many bullet holes in me as almost hit you."

"Look … if you have something, Carly … I mean …"

"I mean, *what*?"

"What do you want from me?"

"I want some *emotion*!"

"*What,* Carly?"

"When I say something that makes you mad, I want to see you be mad. Don't ask me why I'm like I am. You just get mad at me with your fucking body, not your mouth!"

"What the *hell* are you talking about?"

"Don't ask me any more questions! *Show* me what you feel!"

"How?"

"Well, let me show you once more, moron—you're a *loser*, Sam! You can't fuck worth a shit, either! I ain't seen men slobber like that since they was in grade school! What are you doing with that tiny cock? What hole does it want? It don't know, and when it does it jitters around like a fucking jumping bean!"

"Yeah, right, Carly. That's why-"

"You know you won't ever be worth a shit again, don't you? You won't be worth a shit ever *again*! You'll never see your kid again. You'll never see the kid I have in me *ever*. Why would I let you? You're a smelly, homeless, fucking loser I just wanted to give a few rides to!"

"*Carly!*"

"Don't Carly me. What would you do if a man said that shit?"

"Damn it, Carly! … I'd … I'd knock him out. I'm about to knock *you* out, tell you the truth. I just got back-"

"Knock me out! Come on! What are you made of? What *are* you made of?"

"I ain't made of no man that strikes a woman."

"But I'm a bitch, Sampson. Aren't I? Come on. *Aren't* I?"

"You sure are some-"

"Shut up! Shut up! What can I say to you? What? Can I call you a faggot?"

"Go ahead."

"Yeah, you probably are one, seeing as I'm constipated most every morning."

"Well … don't let me-"

"Shut up! I don't let you *shit*! You do what *I* want! What's that like for some man back from the war, huh? Taking shit from some skank! How you like that? You like being bossed around by some skank your father probably fucked?"

"Now *stop* that."

"Oh, Daddy, huh? Daddy bad to Mommy? Is that it? Mommy a good little woman, but Daddy a big, bad man?"

"Shut up, Carly," Sampson said, showing greater nerve.

"Daddy fuck you up the ass, Sampson? Daddy do that to you?"

"Shut up, Carly. I mean it. I mean it."

"He did, huh? He fuck your sister that same way too?"

"No! He didn't do that to *anyone!*"

"Not even Mommy?" Carly stuck her thumb in her mouth and, mimicking a baby's voice, said, "Mommy have to get it somewhere else?"

"Not my family. OK? Not anything about my family."

"What are you made of, you fucking *loser*? I just insulted every single one of them! Did you protect our country like you just protected them? Is that why you're so disgusting now?"

"Stop it!"

"*Make* me!"

Sampson struck her. His fist landed right under Carly's right eye. Backpedaling, she started to feel the bruise, and then she started to cry. Carly looked at Sampson like she wasn't expecting it. She was crazy. He knew it. But he figured he was crazy too.

Carly hit Sampson back on the chin. It was a good punch, too, better than half the men he'd ever brawled with. He was more impressed than angry. But *her* anger was staring him in the face, warning of more blows to come, before she planted tight, hard lips on to his and dragged him into the bedroom.

*   *   *   *

Cecilia would resemble him. Mary knew it. Her daughter had her ex-husband's eyes already and they wouldn't change, as some babies' do. Her blue eyes were so beautiful and tender, but Mary imagined a time they could be as mischievous as his were. They could be as sad and happy too. Whatever emotion Cecilia held inside would broadcast through those eyes like the most high-powered projector on an outdoor movie screen. Just like her father.

Mary was sorry Cecilia would be estranged from her dad. Cecilia and Sampson wouldn't ever live in the same house, not with her, at least. Cecilia would probably become a huge rebel at some point and pretend to prefer a father who drank and found all sorts of self-destruction to fill up his time rather than a mother who had dedicated her life to her. Cecilia would probably tell her mother how "deep" Sampson was just because he was ruined. Destruction looks better to teenagers, Mary reasoned, because they've never built anything.

She knew to expect it. Mary knew to expect Cecilia becoming an unpredictable, emotional, maybe even unreasonable woman. A woman who could be so cuddly, then so distant, as Sampson could become within seconds. How distant he'd been every second he came home from the war.

Maybe if the man Mary could live her life with could come into her life soon, Cecilia would have no reason to rebel. She would have a father figure, someone healthy to look up to, someone who gave her love as much as she needed, someone who told Cecilia she was pretty every time she stood in front of the mirror wondering if she was. Someone who wasn't Sampson, but was like Sampson in all the right ways. But Mary thought that would have to start soon.

Mary told Wil she was sorry. Wil seemed to understand, but he'd yet to ask her out again. It was as if Mary had become trouble. Her mask was taken off. The woman who was once an innocent, stable, young professional was revealed to be a girl who wanted adventure at any cost, a girl who'd had so little in her life she didn't care if her pursuit of it ruined any chance for her to be truly happy. But she wasn't that girl, Mary told herself. Not anymore, at least, if ever. Sampson wasn't her ideal man when they met, but he wasn't who he was now. Maybe just temporarily he was understanding and seemed able to shoulder anything without it crumbling his psyche into a thousand pieces.

Mary picked up the phone determined to ask Wil straight out if his interest had been extinguished by the person she first shared her body with, someone who gave her a child she would die for. If so, it was his loss.

*   *   *   *

"I got your message," said Wil, sitting across from Mary in the teacher's lunchroom. "It was a pretty long one, wasn't it?" he laughed nervously.

"I had a lot to say, Wil," Mary answered without any laughter. "I didn't want to wait any longer."

"I … I'm sorry if that's how you read me. But … no, I … I haven't lost interest. It was just a bit of a jolt, is all. I mean, *you* asked me to take you home right after. *You* took off work the rest of the day. I don't know … I just didn't think it was a subject I should breach just yet."

"So what are you saying to me?"

"I'm saying … if *you'd* like to go out again … I mean … I would like to take you."

"You would really like to take me? Or you would just because you feel cornered? If you feel cornered, Wil, you don't have to. I mean it. I'm not looking for any pity dates. I'm not one of those girls."

"No, no pity," Wil said in a bit of a fluster. "I like you. I didn't imagine your husband was that far gone ... but, I like you."

"He's my ex-husband now."

"Oh ... really?"

*   *   *   *

Billy had returned. Sampson hadn't seen him since he recommended Sampson slash Carly's throat after securing her PIN number. He showed up at the foot of Carly's bed wearing that same broken smile. Sampson looked back at him with a scowl, wishing him gone before Carly finished her shower. The temptation to yell at what Carly saw as just a wall might lose him his roof. Sampson didn't want to lose this mattress for another nine months of the woods or another five days of a county jail cell. He liked the ceiling fan, too.

After Billy said hello in his usual slick way, Sampson yelled, but his voice was muffled by the beat of the shower.

"Where the fuck were you, Billy? Maybe, I mean *maybe,* I could have used you in jail. You just show up when nothing is happening. You just show up to cause trouble. *Grouchy* helped me try and deal with it."

"Yeah, you're right," Billy nodded. "You know I'm a son of a bitch, Sam. I sure ain't no David. I ain't the one trying to be fitted with angel's wings. But, like I said, I know you ain't no angel either. I know you ain't looking for that life beyond here. And beyond here is where you're heading. I mean, it's just true. You see me, right? You see so that means it's true."

"That old man lived *thirty* years!"

"He was one of the lucky ones! You're due soon. I know it."

"You don't know shit. If Grouchy didn't know shit, you don't either!"

"You want me gone, Sam? Stop living on the edge of life. Back away or come to the other side. You can't dance there forever, you know, without falling over."

"I don't *want* to live on the edge of life."

"You see? You don't even realize you're doing it on purpose. That's the best. Someone just *so* fucking clueless. That's the best for someone like me. Because you'll listen to me when you're most desperate, and I'll get to watch the train wreck."

*   *   *   *

Grouchy had run out of places to go. Tommy had moved in with Sheila. Her house was bigger. It had a bigger second bedroom that the babies could share as they grew, until enough money was available for a bigger house, where they could each have a room of their own.

Just to prove to himself that he could, Grouchy watched the beginning of this domestication. But all he did was confirm that he was in a world where he could accomplish nothing. All Grouchy was doing was letting the pain grow, and it would grow until he was a wandering, bitter soul like all the rest. But something wouldn't let him fully understand that and go where he should. It was like he was still empty. It was like he went to bed with a stomach still craving food.

So, Grouchy found himself at his father's. His father's age was progressing beyond the years of his life. His parents had Teddy and Grouchy late in life, so his father was a senior citizen. And, like senior husbands of senior wives who severed their strong, decades-long cord with their death, he was wishing for it himself.

His father looked out the window at the street most days, but his eyes didn't take anything in. It was as if he was preparing for death. Teddy called him some. Sheila invited him over for dinner a bit. But Grouchy's father wanted to be alone. Maybe he wanted them used to him being gone forever because he knew that certainty was nearing closer.

"David," his father said, turning to him. Grouchy wondered if he could really see him, or was just speaking to his memory. "That's you, isn't it?"

"Yeah, Dad."

"Your mother ... your mother, David ... she ... she told me she saw you sometimes. I thought it was her mind leaving her along with her body. I don't know ... maybe my mind is leaving too."

"She never said she saw me."

"She did, though. How you making out? What ... what happens after this?"

"There's a cloud, Dad. You'll see it. Go into it. Mom did. You'll see Mom if you go into the cloud."

"I will?"

"Actually, Dad ... honestly, I don't know. If I went you couldn't see me. You just disappear. That's all I know. There's a lot of us just hanging around out here that haven't disappeared. It isn't a happy place here. It's no place for you to be, Dad."

"Then go, David. Don't be unhappy anymore."

"I don't want to be, Dad. But I watch things, and I can't help watching them."

"Watch what?"

"Sheila mostly. She's found someone, Dad. I think she found someone for a long time."

"Does that hurt you?"

"It hurts me, but I know that's stupid and I know I shouldn't even be watching. I know I need to leave."

"Then leave."

"I'm going to try, Dad. Don't know when, but I will. When your time comes, don't hang around. That's my message to you."

"I won't, David. I want to be with your mother."

"Whatever reason you need … but … do it mostly for yourself."

*   *   *   *

Grouchy's father attended Elena's first birthday part. So did Tommy, Tommy Junior, Mary, Cecilia, and some other friends. Sheila saw much more hope inside his expression than she had seen from him since his wife died. He told Sheila about seeing Grouchy. Sheila asked what he said. Grouchy's father told her he understood.

"So I have his blessing?" Sheila asked.

"He just understands, Sheila. Be happy. That's all. Be happy. He wants it for you."

Sheila stood above Grouchy's father's freshly dug grave less than a month later. His last words to her grew louder in her head as his coffin was lowered into the ground. Sheila felt only gratitude—gratitude for knowing that the man who instilled her with a love she never thought she'd ever feel so powerfully again didn't think of her as a bad woman.

"Tell him I'm trying, Calvin," Sheila said. "Tell him I'll do my best."

CHAPTER 25

Carly was naked and still dripping with water. It was a hot day. The only air conditioning unit was in the living room. The bedroom was sweltering, but the breeze from the ceiling fan always cooled her wet skin and felt fine for a time.

After leaving the shower, Carly went into the kitchen. She grabbed an unopened bottle of Evan Williams from the freezer. The pubic hair that she used to keep shaved was starting grow. Sampson was glad. He never really enjoyed the looks of the smooth vagina he entered nightly. It felt to him like he was having sex with someone he shouldn't.

"This is the last one," Carly said, handing Sampson the bottle and lying beside him. "No more after this."

"OK," Sampson said, though he was certain he would sneak a taste for himself whenever he could.

"This is the last week of the apartment too."

"What?" Since the bourbon had yet to make it to his brain, Sampson worried.

"I'm not working anymore. I'm pregnant. You can work. You should work. I'm gonna moving in with my parents. Come with me if you want or don't. Whatever."

"Your parents?"

"Haven't seen them in years, Sam. Figure since I'm in the family way, I need my family again."

"Do they know about me?"

"Um ... *no!*" Carly laughed. "They don't even know about *me*. They probably think I'm dead. But when they see something they thought was an early ghost coming up their walk, they're gonna feel so glad. The site of you won't change that."

＊　　　＊　　　＊　　　＊

Curtains hid Sheila and Tommy's lovemaking from the road. They tried to stay silent while the babies slept, and they mostly succeeded. They were finally finding a rhythm to this most intimate act. These two bodies were feeling more natural with every new adventure they attempted. Sheila took birth control. She wasn't ready for another baby just yet. She thought she'd like three of her own. Tommy's philosophy was the more, the better. He would work two jobs if he had to. Tommy imagined a huge brood that would give him another huge brood to dote over when he was retired and spent his days drinking beer in his rocking chair.

They kept the new union from their coworkers. Sheila wanted another job anyway. Driving all the time made her much too tired and bored. She used to be a secretary and thought nothing could be more boring than that. She thought of working at a daycare to hone her mothering skills and keep the costs of daycare for her and Tommy's present and future kids at zero.

Tommy didn't know what he thought about all the pictures of Grouchy still around the house. He thought a time would come would they should be put away. But Tommy didn't know how to say that. This arrangement was much too new for him to make demands. He was living in Sheila's house, after all, and that was the man Sheila bought the house with. Her man. Tommy figured Sheila was only in the middle of the test drive to replace him.

Her last man, the man Tommy saw every day in pictures where he smiled or mocked anger, he never really knew. When Sheila started working for him, Grouchy was just about ready to go to war. Even as Elena grew bigger inside of her, Sheila continued to work. She didn't want to sit around all day thinking of what was happening to the father of what kicked and nudged inside her. The kicking and nudging was enough. Sheila wanted distraction from what it made her think. When Grouchy came back, Tommy saw his leg was missing and felt sorry for him. But it was hard to feel too sorry for him because Grouchy had such a beaming smile on his face most of the time.

Tommy thought of that smile. He was glad he would be the father to a girl who had the genes of the strong woman who lay beside him every night and the optimism of the man who wouldn't let something like a lost limb bring him down.

Sheila still cried, though. Sometimes everything seemed so perfect, and then she thought of the true love of her life and couldn't help but become overwhelmed with sadness. It only happened when she was alone, or when Tommy wasn't around at least. She felt she must be programmed for him to never see her grief.

Utter happiness surrounded her when Grouchy came back from the war. He was without his leg, but he had his senses, had no real nightmares, and was so satisfied he was alive that he couldn't help but radiate good feelings to everyone, everywhere he went. And then … she put him in the ground. Sheila was afraid, mostly. She was afraid of another high that would give her comfort, only to shatter and leave her with none.

✳   ✳   ✳   ✳

Sampson did most of the work. He packed up what they could inside Carly's small car. Carly didn't seem to mind leaving behind the broken couch, the broken recliner, and the broken bookcase, which held no books. She used it to hold her DVDs, which totaled five. She took those. She didn't inform the landlord she was leaving. She hadn't paid her rent for the past two months anyway. Eviction notes were piling up on the small coffee table, which Carly left behind as well.

Carly's mom and dad lived in Tucker, Georgia. She had a little brother who still might live there, but she didn't know. When she sixteen, Carly ran away and had never come back. Never phoned. Never thought about it. She had just turned twenty-four.

She grew more fidgety the closer they came to the LaVista exit off of I-285. Carly spoke aloud about turning around. Sampson didn't argue. He didn't want to live in the same house with Carly's parents either. The seeds of what Carly had become lived there, he assumed, and he didn't want to deal with three of them. But Sampson had nowhere else to go, and his need for responsibility still trumped the discomfort he had around Carly and the discomfort he felt sure to have around the relatives she made him live with.

When they pulled up, Sampson was surprised by the homestead. It was on a clean street and had a large front yard. The land held a long, one-story brick house with an expansive basement. Sampson saw a shiny, late-model SUV in the driveway. He looked at Carly, wondering if she was the black sheep. Was she the one fuck-up in a family of normals?

Carly didn't see his look, however, and she couldn't leave the driver's seat. She was too busy staring at the front window. Carly seemed to be trying to set in on fire with her eyes. *Something bad happened here,* Sampson thought.

She did get out eventually, and Sampson followed close behind—not *too* close behind. It was as though he had adopted Carly's fear and imagined a throng of Dobermans bursting through the front door when they came too close.

The front door was new and adorned with carved vines and roses. Carly knocked, then stepped back. She straightened her five-foot, seven-inch frame. Her neck was stiff, as though locked by a rigid brace. They heard the locks being unlocked, and the uncertain couple saw a small woman with graying hair in the doorway. The woman didn't recognize her daughter. She didn't like the looks of the man behind her. She was about to ask what they wanted when Carly's eyes introduced her. The shocked woman began to cry.

"C-Carly?" she said, and her arms opened before she rushed out to embrace her daughter.

"Hey, Mom," Carly said without any emotion. She fortified her emotional wall to avoid pummeling this small woman. "I'm pregnant, Mom."

"*Really?*" said her mother, becoming very excited and happy.

"Yeah. That's the father," Carly said, pointing behind her at Sampson with a quick gesture, signifying his insignificance to the fact.

"Oh … well, hello." Carly's mother hugged Sampson in a restrained manner.

A tall figure started towards the doorway slowly. Smoke curled from the nearly black cigar in his hand. His hair was mostly grey and crowded in on the brown strands trying desperately to hold on to what territory they still controlled. He walked out of the door slowly and looked over Carly like she wasn't wanted. But Carly looked back at her father with an expression that said, "Too bad!"

"Where you been?" said the tall man and put the cigar back in his mouth to puff out some hefty, billowing grey-white smoke.

"All over."

"So … like Alaska, for instance?"

"All over *Atlanta*, Dad."

"You practically killed your mother when you left. Did you know that?"

"Be quiet, Bob," said Carly's mother without much effort. "She's home now."

"You say you're pregnant?" said Carly's father.

"That's right."

"You married, you two?"

"No."

"You getting married? Not too interested if you ain't."

"Interested in what, Dad?" Carly said sharply. "Interested in *what?*"

"Bob, *be* quiet!" said his wife turning to him intently. "She needs a place to stay and she's pregnant. She can stay here. We have *plenty* of room."

"Does Aaron still live here?" Carly asked her mother.

"He lives in Atlanta now. He's a manager at a Kroger."

Carly's father helped with what little furniture they brought: the small twin bed, a lamp, and two chairs. Though Sampson smiled at him, Carly's father, when he did look at Sampson, only did so warily and said nothing. Sampson figured if they ever had to converse they could do so at another time. But he had no real need to ever talk to Carly's father if that's what he really wanted.

Bob led Sampson down to the room just off the basement. Carly's old room had become her mother's painting room. Aaron's room had become an extra storage space and was too cluttered to straighten out in any reasonable amount of time.

"'Spect this'll do," Bob said, his first direct words to Sampson.

"Yes, sir. Should do fine."

"What do you do for a living?" Bob asked, chewing on a cigar that had outlasted its tobacco.

"Um … I'm between things."

"Sure you are," Bob sniffed and left Sampson alone in the windowless room while Carly was being fed upstairs.

✳   ✳   ✳   ✳

Wil took her home. Though Mary always seemed to have something to do when Sheila wanted a free babysitter, Sheila readily agreed to watch Cecilia while Mary was on her date. Mary poured Wil some wine, and though he didn't usually drink, Wil drank the full glass in sips. She came close to him and he kissed her. Wil moved his hand down to her thigh and started between her legs.

"No," said Mary, pushing it away. "I'm not that easy."

"S-Sorry."

"I've only been with one man, Wil. You have to understand, when I make love I only do it if I feel there is a lifelong connection."

"Lifelong connection?" asked Wil nervously and almost laughed. He was thinking, *Who still does that these days?*

"Yes. A lifelong connection, Wil."

CHAPTER 26

Despite what Carly had decreed that last bottle of Evan Williams wasn't their last. So the brutal reaction against no alcohol started inside Carly her first night back in her old home.

The DTs already had their fill of Sampson's body until another good spell of drinking, then quitting, could tempt them back. But Carly was just getting introduced to her first dose and already felt severed at the legs and punched in the head. She felt sucked of all her oxygen and hopeful of death. Sweat lined every inch of her flesh, and she shook. Her trembling might stop, but then what? She didn't want to guess.

The sweat came on like a thick, scratchy blanket. And Carly wanted rid of it. She stripped herself of the clothes that were drenched in the same sickly sweetness that covered Sampson's body in jail. Carly dried herself off. Lying in the outline of sweat she left behind, she started to shiver. Her teeth clacked. Sampson tried to hold her, but Carly pushed him off. Sleeping was impossible for him as long as it remained impossible for her.

"This isn't wh-wh-wh-working," she said.

"Carly, you have to ride it out," Sampson said. "It gets better."

"No! This isn't w-w-w-w-w-wh-working. Take m-m-m-ma-ma-ma-my car. Get me a b-b-b-bottle."

"Carly, your parents aren't going to-"

"Did you hear what I said? Take my car and get me a goddamn bottle! My mom gave me some money. It's in ma-ma-ma-ma-my purse."

Sampson decided to stop the dialogue he was engaging in only for Carly's benefit. He knew Carly by now. She wouldn't change her mind. And ... he didn't want her to.

Fishing for the keys inside Carly's purse, Sampson saw a strange, small packet of something white and looked back at her to question if she was dabbling in more than just booze. But Carly was hugging herself too desperately for him to ask. She was groaning too loudly in her pillow for her to hear.

Sampson found Carly's wallet and took out a twenty-dollar bill. He left the room and then the house by the basement back door. The car they moved in was still parked on the side of the road, so Sampson figured neither of her parents would notice from their room in the back corner when he drove away.

"You got a car," said Billy, suddenly sitting in the passenger side. "You can sell it. You can get out of this shit."

"Shut up."

"Oh, so you want to be around when that thing is born? You *want* to be involved with this woman? You and I know that is pure bullshit."

"I need responsibility!"

"To a woman you couldn't give a shit about?"

"She's having my kid!"

"You already have a kid."

"Yeah, and that woman wants nothing to do with me."

"Neither does this one. If she dries out, which she won't, she'll see you as the same drag Mary does. But she won't. She won't dry out, Sam."

"Well, if she won't dry out, I won't be no drag, will I?"

"She already called you a loser, Sam," Billy whined. "And if she doesn't dry out, she's going to kill that thing before it can even come out."

Sampson didn't know one thing about Tucker. He drove around in mostly darkness until he saw an A&P shopping center partially lit up. A liquor store was beside it. It was open twenty-four hours a day, except on Sundays, and it wasn't a Sunday.

The clerk looked at Sampson's almost giddy energy with concern as he entered the store. He imagined another meth addict and had his finger near the call button just in case this one busted two bottles and tried to run away with five more, like the last one who came in in the middle of the night.

Twenty dollars only went so far, so Sampson approached the counter with the biggest bottle of Evan Williams it could buy. The clerk waited for some money to hit the counter. He stood rigid and ready for anything until Sampson took out that twenty-dollar bill and placed it just before the clerk's left hand.

"ID," said the clerk.

Sampson's eyes widened before he shook his head. He didn't bring his wallet. It didn't occur to him as he was racing out of the basement back door.

"I forgot it," Sampson sighed.

"I need ID."

"Come on! Look at me. I'm over twenty-one."

"It's the law, sir."

"Well, fuck the law, OK? I'm not a cop."

"Yeah, that's obvious."

"Good. Ring me up then."

"What's your birthday? Quick!"

"March third, nineteen eighty-two."

"Hmm," said the clerk, and was suddenly struck with a way to make himself some extra cash. "Tell you what … I'll give you a pint, but it's gotta be at the same price." He smiled.

"What? Fuck you!"

"Then you can't have it."

"Hell I can't!" Sampson said. He left the bill on the counter and took the bottle.

The clerk caressed the call button for a time, then realized the thrill of screaming police cars always ended in a downer in some way.

"OK, now, get a taste," said Billy, who'd been waiting for Sampson in the passenger seat.

"It's for Carly!"

"Yeah, I know. She's not going to drink the whole thing. Get a taste. Just a taste."

"No."

"Oh, Sam, *please*. You know you're going to. You *know* you are."

Sampson parked at the side of the lawn, where they had last left the car. He looked at the reflection of the streetlight coming off of the Evan Williams bottle. The streetlight highlighted the brown liquor so lusciously. Sampson twisted off the cap and didn't lower the bottle until he poured three ounces down his throat.

He felt soothed. So soothed.

Sampson picked it up again and emptied another few ounces.

He felt lifted. So lifted.

Staggering out of the car, Sampson almost fell and smashed the bottled into a million pieces. But he didn't and slowly found stability before he made his way past the driveway to the backyard fence and the basement below the lawn's ridge.

As Sampson approached the basement door he saw something glowing. Some smoke was mingling with the moonlight. Bob's tall frame stepped forward with a cigar in his mouth, and he reached out his hand.

"Give me that," he said.

"What?"

"You heard me. Give me that."

Sampson did. He was thinking maybe her father just wanted the house's cut of bourbon. But Bob gripped the bottle for just a second before shattering its glass against the house. He watched the broken bottle and its remaining bourbon fall on to the grass below.

"You want to stay here, you don't drink," Bob said, looking back at Sampson with eyes burning as brightly as the tip of the black cigar he was now holding in his hand.

"It … wasn't for me."

"Yeah? Well, then, that's worse. You think pregnant women should drink, son?"

"N-No."

"No is right! Far as I can tell, she wanted to shack up here to get a free ride until the thing is born. Well it ain't *gonna* be born if you and her just drink and drug it up like you been doing."

"I don't use drugs, sir."

"Hell you don't! I know the type."

"I don't, sir."

"Don't care. That poison is enough to kill what's growing. And another thing. *You* gonna work. I own a lawn care service. You gonna be on a crew. If you don't like that, I'll muscle you out of this house and deposit you in the woods where you belong."

How did he know? Sampson thought

"I'm waking you up tomorrow morning at seven. Don't fuck with me, son. I don't give a damn if you jacked her up. You ain't the one pregnant. *You* got no excuse to just ride on our dime."

Carly's father opened the basement door. He waited for Sampson's humbled, slouching shoulders to enter before he put his own feet on the carpet. Watching Sampson come to that closed room's door and prepare for the great disappointment and anger inside, he made like he was about to climb the stairs. But he came back down a step when Sampson's back disappeared into the room.

"Where is it?" he heard his daughter scream.

"Your dad … he-"

"Where is it?"

"Your dad, Carly! He-"

"You're drunk! You drank it! You drank it *all!* You *fucking* asshole!" Carly said, and Bob heard a lamp shatter that he imagined just barely missed Sampson's head. It made him smile.

*　　　*　　　*　　　*

Grouchy was in line. He was at the back of a long one. Young and old alike stood calmly. But Grouchy wasn't calm. If he still had a living body, he would probably feel nauseated. He felt a certain weakness. It seemed his footsteps forward were full of lead. But Grouchy remained. He vowed not to leave the line. He felt as ready as he ever would be.

He could feel a rush of bodies harassing those in back of him, and then they were at his side. Billy was among them. He was among some jaded, ugly faces that stared at Grouchy like he'd committed some gruesome crime against nature.

"This ain't the way it goes," said Billy, and for the first time since he had died, Grouchy could feel something like flesh on him. Grouchy seemed made of flesh again, but only when Billy and his friends touched him.

"You don't go and then decide to go! Not without a fight, at least." And with that, Billy pushed Grouchy out of line. Those in back of Grouchy were clueless. He had become a part of the invisible, but still walking, dead. The newly dead couldn't recognize these souls unless they chose to become one of them too.

Billy and his friends muzzled Grouchy's mouth and secured his legs and arms. Grouchy tried to struggle, but the five strong, desperate souls rushed him away from where his presence threatened their influence. No one could see what they did. Grouchy couldn't see anything, either, until they roughly deposited him to a colorless ground. Once they let him go, Grouchy lacked any physical feeling again.

"You go when you die, or you don't go at all!" Billy yelled at him as if this were a rule Grouchy should have known.

"I want to go!"

"I don't give a shit! You want to show us up?" Billy said and motioned to faces of old and young alike. The young faces were sharper, but the lack of any purpose wasn't any less intimidating in their eyes.

"What … what the hell are you talking about?"

"You can't leave. You *can't* leave. Try it again and we'll make it harder!" Billy said, and Grouchy was suddenly in a tiny, bleak and uncomfortably small room that the masters of the damned had built themselves. There seemed to be grey brick walls, sliming with greasy ooze, but they weren't there. They were the embodiment of the prisoner's true slavery to the masters. The masters tired of keeping their hate so unified, but they had to stay unified to keep this fantastical prison secure. The walls would come down when their attention was distracted by some fun on earth.

The other prisoners who had also infracted upon this law, groaned constantly. The echo of groaning could make a person crazy if he weren't already. They looked at Grouchy with bloodshot eyes while they groaned, a hollow bitterness creeping out to hit him with every deep breath. He told himself he wasn't one of them. He wouldn't be one of them.

"You lose conviction," one man finally said. He was in rags. He looked as if he were homeless in life. His grey hair was long and unkempt.

"What?" Grouchy replied.

"You lose conviction if you don't go just after you die. It goes away. Sometimes real quick, sometimes ... sometimes it takes some time, but it goes away. People like them, the bullies, they gain power because they hate. You can't fight them unless you find hate too. Or, unless you find success. If you feel useless and have no hate, you're trapped. You waited too long. You have to find success or hate, my friend. But if you find hate, you'll never go. The hate will keep you with us forever."

CHAPTER 27

Wil needed coffee, and the break room was never without. He entered through the windowless door. Mary was inside sitting at the darkest corner.

She was the only one in the break room besides Wil. He didn't see her, and Mary stared at him with such disappointment that if he turned around, the jolt of energy he was seeking would have been provided without any coffee touching his lips.

"So, you're that kind of guy?" Mary said, and the coffee spilled on to the counter as Wil jumped.

When Wil turned around, seeing Mary made him shy.

With his head down at his chest, trying to look as if he were inspecting some stain or strand, he said, "What?"

"You just wanted an easy lay, huh?"

"Mary," Wil sighed. He looked at her. The nerves Mary had stirred had left him. Now he was just weary again. He only wanted coffee, certainly not any hassle from *this* woman. "I don't know what century you're from-"

"What century I'm from?" Mary said and stood up. She emerged from the dark and stood just before the table. Her glasses magnified eyes that projected her feeling of insult. "Is that the century where women didn't spread their legs for every man who wanted it unless they were paid?"

"I'm … I'm not ready for that kind of commitment, Mary."

"Fine. So, you can't be with me until you are?"

"I just think-"

"You thought I was a lonely woman and would spread my love around just to think I wasn't, right?"

"No! No, I didn't think that, but-"

"But, you just want a *girl*friend. Nothing more until you find a *different girl*friend. You're not an animal, Wil."

"Well, Mary," Wil said with renewed confidence, "maybe I am. Maybe I just am."

*   *   *   *

The sun beat down on Sampson as he pushed the mower in rows. The sound of a high-powered mower or a motorcycle brought back the memories of the dirtiest parts of war. These sounds were hard to avoid unless Sampson was in the woods.

He had to bite his bottom lip to not cry out. The other members of the crew, who were all illegal immigrants from Central and South America, offered him cigarettes. They spoke very little English. Sampson smoked every one of their cigarettes, quickly and to the filter.

The leader of the crew was a pot-bellied Mexican named Edgar. Edgar spoke rapid Spanish to his fellow Hispanics and said nothing to Sampson. Anytime Sampson displeased him, Edgar merely motioned rapidly in some direction and Sampson did what he thought Edgar was suggesting, sometimes guessing wrong and watching another manic pantomime displayed until he got it right.

Bob showed up to one site when they were all taking a break. Sampson sat apart from the rest of the crew, and they didn't seem to take any offense. After he finished a sandwich, which a Mexican boy had brought but didn't want, Sampson fell asleep only to feel Bob kick his side when work started again.

"Don't think I got you this job to lounge around," Bob snapped. A black cigar jutted out of his mouth. Its long shape almost blocked out the sun.

"I just ... fell asleep."

"Well, get up! Get up now! They're working! Since you're white, I think they're afraid of you."

"Yeah, well, I don't," Sampson said and got back to the business of mowing. The drain of such work on his weak body caused him to collapse later on that basement bed. He drifted into never-never land until the next morning.

*   *   *   *

The dungeon walls came down eventually. Every reluctant soul left the room they had been banished to and wandered in different directions, if they so chose. Some just stayed in a space of colorless ground to avoid the hassle of abduction. Grouchy thought he would never leave. He thought that eternity would be spent with the groans and disappointments of the damned trying to convince him to join in and become so hopeless he could only cry for relief. He never allowed himself to be tempted, and all that resistance just made him angry.

Billy was sure to give him a warning glance when Grouchy went in his own direction. After Grouchy glanced back with a look of belligerence, Billy and a few of his goons followed him until they were sure he wasn't headed for the line. Grouchy knew he couldn't. His strength didn't match theirs. He wasn't sure how to make it so, unless he found a hate for them that rivaled their hate for everything else. But finding reason in the hate they found reason in would prevent his departure from this nebulous world just like the man inside the dungeon said.

Sheila seemed happy. Grouchy had to be happy for her, even if he didn't want to be. The bullies wanted him to find camaraderie in bitterness. They wanted Grouchy to loathe his inability to have what he wanted back and commiserate with them. Avoiding becoming them, however, still would not equal success.

Success would be standing in that line with enough strength to buffer another kidnapping. But that success would have to be preceded by a different success, a success that made this loafing seem worth it. Otherwise, no matter how much Grouchy wanted to continue to where his soul truly belonged, he would be plagued with the self-criticism that told him he had waited too long, the self-criticism that allowed the bullies to have their complete advantage over him.

"Sam," Grouchy said as Sampson sat alone on the foot of that basement bed. Sampson turned to Grouchy and was so happy to see him he cried. He was so weary, so wracked with a need to medicate himself that the relief of Grouchy's renewed counsel gave Sampson more pleasure than any chemical he could think to drench his body in.

"Where you been, Grouchy?"

"Been all over."

"Yeah? I know you probably could do much better with someone who would listen to you. Anyone with half a brain would."

"Didn't do too well at all, Sam. Seems I was kidding myself I could do any good at this state."

"So, leave, Grouchy. Move on. Really. Move on. I'm not worth staying for."

"Can't. You have to get better."

"Oh, God. I *want* to."

"No. You aren't hearing me. You *have* to. I can't go on unless you do."

"Who told you that?"

"No one. But I need that accomplishment. Just for myself, really. I want you to be well. But wanting won't do for me anymore. You *have* to get well. You have to help me, Sam. I'm trapped unless you can help me help you."

"You know if I could, I would."

"You're *going* to Sam. This is my eternal future we're talking about. I have to make sure you can't see me anymore. I have to make sure you're not going to self-destruct. When I do, I can move on. If I can't move on, I will become as bitter as Billy, and that truly is hell, Sam."

*   *   *   *

Mary came back with him to her apartment. Sheila was watching Cecilia for her once again. Having lots of kids around was becoming like a paradise to her. She had just recently gotten a job at a daycare center and realized she wouldn't mind having six or seven of her own.

Mary needed to get drunk to get it done. She needed to become another part of her personality, the part that blurred the core she had struggled to keep so pure. She wanted to know what it felt like, if she was indeed missing out by sticking to such rigid ideals.

Like she knew would happen, someone approached her. Mary was pretty. She was dainty. She had the looks of a teacher. But though Mary was the studious type, she attracted men of every sort. She was a woman, after all, a young, single woman in a bar who had no face tattoos or obvious fat. This man, Paul, seemed very nice. He seemed very smooth. Mary knew what he was doing, but she let him do it. For some reason Paul's place wasn't available.

Wife? Mary thought. She didn't see a wedding ring and wanted to ask, but didn't.

Mary and Paul sat on her couch, like she and Wil had. They drank some wine, like she and Wil had. Mary came close to Paul, like she had come to Wil. And Paul kissed her, like Wil had. His hand went to her breasts. Something inside Mary told her to stop this, but she silenced the voice.

Paul took off Mary's blouse, delicately. He put his mouth to her nipples, delicately. He took off her panties and entered her, delicately. But as the excitement grew, so did Paul's greed. He turned Mary around, and she had to hold on to the edge of the couch so her head didn't bounce with such ferocity that Paul would be having sex with an unconscious body. He probably wouldn't have cared.

He tried to enter a part of Mary she never allowed Sampson to. It hurt, and the screams of halt inside Mary's head became too great not to leave her mouth.

"No, Paul," she said weakly, but Paul still tried to force it inside. "No!" she said, but he wasn't listening. "I said *no!*" Mary was able to turn around and push him off.

"Get out!" she screamed. Paul's manhood was still erect and quivering for more.

"What?" he said.

"*Get* out!"

"OK, I won't do that," Paul panted, his eyes part begging, part suggesting it didn't matter what she wanted.

"No, I don't want to anymore."

"Are you *crazy?* You bring me here and you let me start but don't let me finish? That's *worse* than a cock-tease!"

"Get out!" Mary said once more, but Paul pushed her back down and tried to go where he had said he wouldn't.

She struggled, but Paul held her with a strength she didn't believe his lanky body possessed. He would do this. He didn't care what it meant. If she called the cops, so be it. His cock wanted dirty action.

This was rape now, but it wouldn't hold up in court. Mary saw the action in her head. She saw her ashamed body standing in front of the judgmental jury. The jury's eyes were leering and wanting to know why she drank alone with him in her apartment and didn't know this would happen.

No. This would stop now.

Mary grabbed a heavy book on the coffee table, swung it around, and smacked Paul's head. He fell backward. Only when he touched the bruise did he realize what he had almost tried to do. He could have thrown up. He could have slit his wrists ... and he still might.

Without looking at Mary, Paul dressed. Slowly, he left the apartment. His kept his eyes down. He was traumatized by his own actions.

Mary went into the bathroom and let the hot water beat down on her in the shower as she cried.

CHAPTER 28

Sampson worked long hours mowing lawns but was never paid. He did errands for Carly's mother and yard work for her as well. When Carly's mother asked him to, he also swept a vacuum cleaner and polished the furniture. The service station started thinking of him as one of their employees. Carly's mother often worried about different noises inside her car, and she sent Sampson whenever she did. He did the laundry. Carly's mother smiled at him, but it was a thin one. It was merely her way of being polite.

Carly received money on the sly from her mother. She used it to clandestinely buy her favorite white powder and go to liquor stores to buy a few of those tiny airplane bottles and empty them down her throat. She brought some home for Sampson. Carly stuck them under his pillow, and Sampson felt the impression when he first lie down. He tilted them back, however, inside the pitch of night because he didn't want to see the poison he was consuming just to feel somewhat normal.

He was on another mission for Carly's mother. *She at least smiles at me*, he thought. Carly's father never smiled it seemed. His daughter didn't either. The only time Carly showed much interest in Sampson is when she emptied the tiny packets of white powder up her nose and forced sex from a member that could barely stay erect. Sampson kept his eyes closed while his penis half dangled into whatever orifice Carly chose.

His latest mission was to the grocery store. Grouchy appeared in the passenger seat of Carly's car when Sampson finished stacking the trunk full of groceries. It had taken him an hour to find everything on the detailed list Carly's mother had composed.

"Do you love her, Sam?" Grouchy said.

"I … don't know."

"You don't love her. *I* know it."

"She's having my baby, Grouchy."

"It doesn't mean you can't be a good father, Sam. You don't have to be with the mother to be a good father."

"I want a family, Grouchy."

"You want a family when it means forcing the scenario?"

"I've been left already. I got one kid I'll never see, and I don't want that to happen again. OK? Figure if I try, it won't."

"Mary never said you'd never see Cecilia again, Sam. She just wants you to get well. When you get well, she won't keep you from visiting her."

"I don't know what the hell 'well' means to her."

"It means sober. It means stable. Get away from the temptation. Go back to the VA. You're just piling this shit, waiting for it to collapse on you, and when it does you know no one can save you. That is desperation, Sam. That is one step closer to really wanting it to happen."

"God, the speeches again," Billy whined from the backseat. Billy sneered in the rearview mirror at Grouchy, whose face had become an unreal flush of surprise after seeing the sight.

"You weren't satisfied with the ass-kicking we gave you before?" Billy said with an angry, urgent vigor. "You stay away from my claim."

"He *isn't* your claim!" said Grouchy, staring forward and away from the rearview mirror. "He's alive. You can't make a person who's still alive be in your crew, Billy. Put your energies elsewhere."

"My energies, asshole," said Billy, holding onto Grouchy's forehead and whispering into his ear, "my energies go where I want them to go, and my energies have usually served me pretty well. My advice to you is to save your advice for morons who'll take it, morons who won't get past me, but they'll still listen to you, David. Sam don't listen. He thinks he's a bad man for not listening. But that's because he's a bad man through and through."

"Were you bad through and through when you went, Billy? If you're gonna tell me yes, I already know you're a liar. The old man told me so," Grouchy said struggling against Billy's tightening grip.

"No one turns bad who don't want to be. Sam, he wants to be. And I'm gonna help him."

Grouchy saw his entire future becoming that haze he was walking through every day if he let Billy win this round. He tried to tell himself it was just one battle. But one battle would lead to two and three, and then every battle he would relinquish if he let this one get away. Every battle would diminish Grouchy's strength until he had no strength at all.

So he finally forced himself from Billy's hold and turned around to face him. Spitting as though he had saliva, he said, "You don't control things, Billy! You think you do, but you *don't*. You just control the weakest of the weak. Anyone can control them. Anyone can replace *you*."

Billy was surprised and his smile showed it. He spoke slowly, "Do you want to replace me, David?"

"Hell, no!"

"Well, too bad, because then you might have a chance. I run something, David. I am responsible for something. It's my reason. Don't you wish you had one?"

Grouchy cocked his arm back and smashed his fist into a nose that, though unreal, sounded just like its bones were breaking.

These two images, these two ghosts, bumped and grunted around Sampson's car like two real men. Every fabric that seemed ripped wasn't ripped. Every dent that sounded with a ping or a sudden yawn wasn't really pinging or yawning, and no damage was done.

The fight eventually became a one-sided affair. Billy put Grouchy into a headlock. Grouchy flailed his arms, signaling surrender. Billy smiled and started to loosen his grip when Grouchy struggled from the loop around his head and looked more dangerous than ever. Billy realized the headlock just gave Grouchy time to rest, and it stunned him. Grouchy hit him twice and stunned him some more.

"Georgie!" Billy cried out, and the old man who lay next to Sampson in the VA appeared next to Billy and joined in the fray.

"You told me he went to the cloud!" Sampson screamed.

"Well, I lied," Billy grunted. "This man is my ally forever."

Georgie and Billy double-teamed to thrust Grouchy in Carly's backseat. The thud of punches on virtual bodies was unreal, almost like an arcade wizard wracking up points on a boxing game. A sudden shove sent Grouchy through a backseat door, out of the car, and into the street, where Sampson could see Grouchy's form being run over brutally by every trailing car. Sampson didn't know what to think. He didn't understand if pain meant anything to a dead man. But what he saw looked plenty painful to him.

"I want you to leave me alone!" Sampson said to Billy as Georgie disappeared.

"No you don't, Sam. C'mon. Stop holding onto the ideal. If it doesn't fit you now, it never will. Let *me* be your guide. David will just bring you down. You can't do all he wants. You know that."

"I *will* do what he wants! Grouchy knows how I can be a better man."

"You can't be a better man," said Billy quietly. He moved close to Sampson's head and spoke into his cheek. "You belong with us, Sam. And when you finally fall off the cliff you've been dancing on the edge of, I'll catch you."

＊　　　＊　　　＊　　　＊

The groceries were for the first full family get-together in nearly nine years. Sampson tried to mask the experience he had just gone through, but he was preoccupied by the disturbance of three ghosts battling over his soul—and the one he was rooting for losing.

Sampson's eyes suddenly shifted to attention upon seeing Carly's brother, Aaron. He was a short guy, maybe five feet, five inches at most, and was balding. Aaron had feminine hands and shook Sampson's hand with the gentility of a female. Sampson knew immediately that Aaron was gay. It was in his walk, his mannerisms, and most of all his voice.

Aaron had beautiful, light blue eyes. They seemed the tender side of Sampson's bold blue ones. The two were introduced and then just looked at each other for some time without any words, only a mutual, silent attraction. They were looking a little too long for Carly's taste, and she turned her brother with a call to hug him like a long-lost relative whom she didn't really know or care for very much.

The dinner was cordial. It seemed to Sampson that most present were at least mildly uncomfortable about the addition of a family member they were certain they'd never see again. Maybe because of those feelings of discomfort or possibly just ritual, Carly once again got high that night and pounced on Sampson's sleeping body to wriggle that half-hard penis from his underwear.

"You have to stop, Carly," Sampson said with a bothered sigh.

"You don't want to fuck me anymore?" Carly cooed in his ear.

"I mean the drugs. I mean the drugs and the drinking. You don't really want this kid, do you?"

"My kid is strong. It can take some blow, just like me," Carly said and put a mouth to Sampson's penis to try to awaken more life from it.

Grouchy was in the room. He was looking into Sampson's eyes and shaking his head. Sampson had no choice at the moment, so he closed his eyes to avoid what he already knew. When Grouchy left the room, he saw Carly's father at the door, listening to the goings-on without his ever-present cigar in his mouth. Grouchy couldn't help but lower his eyes to see the bulge in Carly's father's pants getting tighter.

CHAPTER 29

Cecilia was just a baby. But when Mary cried, Cecilia's eyes grew contemplative and almost sincere. When Mary held her, she looked down on Cecilia and couldn't stop thinking about her little girl's future and crying. She cried almost everyday.

Her little girl would reach her hands up to touch Mary's tears, which only made Mary cry some more. She loved Cecilia so much. She wanted this little girl to feel secure. Both of her parents surrounded Mary her entire childhood, and for the most part it made her life easier. She had friends who had only a mother and tried to find a father figure in the many boys they allowed to use them.

Mary didn't talk to her parents much. They seemed full of slogans and pat answers for any problem. They seemed to lack any empathy. Her mother read the latest New Age books; to Mary, each one had a contradictory message from the last. Her mother spouted what she read as if it were infallible truth, but none of it gave Mary any comfort.

Mary was a fair-weathered friend—to everyone. When boredom or trouble set in that she couldn't handle, she just took herself out of the scenario. And, though Sheila knew this and was hurt by this, Mary called her crying. Mary had no one but her—*because* she was a fair-weathered friend. Sheila listened anyway.

With great emotion, Mary told her of the brutality of the man she thought was so tender before he treated her like his whore. Sheila listened patiently for Mary's need for something, someone who could complete a life that now seemed so full of holes.

"It takes time sometimes, Mary," Sheila said.

"Not with you!" Mary cried.

"Yeah, well, I was lucky. Well, no ... actually, I was unlucky and so was he. So we just squished together our bad luck to make some kind of life together."

"What do you think, Sheila? Am I too demanding? I mean, I know no one waits until they're married anymore. But ... I just can't ... I can't do what other people do."

"Mary, you gotta do what makes you happy. If you believe in your morals, then they're what you gotta live by. If that is how you find love ... If you need to wait to share yourself until you feel you'll be with that man forever, then that's how it has to be."

"I though it would never happen, Sheila. I really did. But it did. It happened so quickly with Sam. It just seemed so perfect. He wasn't my type. Not at all. But there was something inside him. I mean, maybe it was something I'd only see for a little while. But it was enough. Then, I didn't know what it meant really. I mean, I did, but I didn't know how much I'd miss it. Now, just the little bit of it that I got seems so far from me. When I was a kid, Sheila ... when I saw all the types of women I didn't want to be, I thought I would wait until I was thirty or forty. I didn't care that no one took me out. I could see a life alone. I really could. I didn't care the names they called me. It didn't matter then. It just didn't matter. But now, now ... I have a baby, Sheila. It's not like it used to be. It's hard to be alone now. And, I don't want Cecilia to feel my pain. I don't want her to get used to it."

"If you want it, you'll find it again," Sheila said. "If you are desperate for it, it will slip through your fingers. Please yourself first, Mary. Don't worry about anyone else pleasing you. That's how it works."

"Is that how it worked with you?"

"What I'm saying is it's the code you gotta live by, Mary. If love smacks into you, then it does."

*   *   *   *

A knock woke Sampson up. This was a rare free day for him, and it was truly free. There was no list of chores and errands for him to complete. It was raining hard so there were no lawns to mow. Sampson loved it when it rained. He wasn't paid anyway. He only agreed to work for Carly's father so the big man wouldn't kick him out. He wished for floods that would make mowing impossible for weeks. But Sampson knew the illegals who shared his job didn't feel the same.

Sampson was still half asleep, so he opened the door dressed only in his underwear. It was Aaron, and it surprised him out of the sleep that half paralyzed him. Aaron smiled at him, and he smiled wider when he saw that most of Sampson's body was exposed. His interest stirred Sampson's lust, a lust that was different for his lust for women. It was just as powerful, but different. It made Sampson feel dirty, dirtier than he felt when imagining the dirtiest sex with a body of full breasts and a vagina.

"No work today, huh?" Aaron said in his tiny, lisping voice. Sampson preferred that voice in men he found attractive. It made the sex more of an act between opposites that way.

"No," Sampson said stepping back and allowing Aaron to enter.

"Pretty depressing room, isn't it?" Aaron said as he came inside and looked around.

"Yeah."

"Not to me. Brought my boyfriends here. Brought them here before Mom and Dad ever suspected. Though I don't know how they couldn't. They're pretty good at shutting things out."

"They sure do that with Carly."

"No, Sam. They couldn't shut Carly out. Since she was twelve, she was just crazy. Too crazy to shut out."

"Why?"

Aaron shrugged. "Hell if I know why. Sometimes people are just crazy. There isn't always a reason."

"I think with Carly there's a reason."

"Really? Well, I can't explain it."

Aaron sat on the foot of the bed. He dangled his legs like a woman. He wrapped one leg tight into the other's knee. Aaron's eyes glistened at Sampson, and Sampson's growing interest pressed into his underwear.

"You're queer, aren't you?" Aaron asked.

"N-No. No, I'm not queer."

"Yes you are. Or, at least part of you is. I know queer when I see it. I've been honing that skill my whole life, Sam," Aaron said and laughed daintily.

"Maybe you just want me to be queer."

"Or maybe you just want to be straight."

"I'm straight all right, buddy. Straight as an arrow."

"I like straight arrows. It feels better that way."

"Listen," Sampson said and dismissively laughed, "your sister and me are having a kid."

"So she says. But you don't love her."

Sampson looked at the carpet and said nothing.

"No, you don't love her. Who could, Sam? Who could love someone like Carly?"

Sampson winced and looked at Aaron. "That's your *sister*, Aaron," he said.

"Yeah. And? You might have shacked up with her. You might have done it enough to bring what does come between a man and a woman who ain't thinking. I know what it's like. I've been lonely too, Sam. I've been with the wrong person too. All of them boys, mind you. Never once wanted to be with anyone who didn't have a dick."

Aaron got up and approached a body trying to seem unwilling. But Sampson didn't move his feet. He didn't retreat. Aaron's small but determined hands gripped his face and he kissed Sampson hard. Sampson liked it and liked it more when Aaron started to touch his naked stomach. Anxious rumblings permeated his guts, like that first time with Carly.

"What about your m-m-mother?" Sampson said nervously. What was about to happen shivered him to near convulsion. He didn't realize he missed it so much. He didn't realize that all those boys in the army were one reason he liked being a part of it so much. But he realized it now.

"She's out," Aaron whispered while slipping off the underwear Sampson slept in. "She's at a doctor's appointment with Carly."

"I d-d-didn't know about it."

"See how mutual your affections are?" Aaron said while starting to undo his button-down short-sleeve shirt.

*   *   *   *

Hell was in those eyes. They had ganged up on Grouchy again. The bullies didn't like that he'd resisted them again, so they had their way with him again. Grouchy was trapped in the dungeon again, surrounded by other trapped souls of little strength again. They were moaning and groaning like dying cattle.

Billy and his crew told Grouchy this time it was for good. They told him he was their prisoner forever. But it wasn't true. Grouchy already knew that the room had to be watched with their undisciplined hate. The walls would come down as soon as they became too restless and found someone new to strike with power that coalesced only when they used it in combination.

Grouchy began to truly hate them. Before, he just disliked Billy's presence in that same VA room with Sampson. Before, Grouchy sort of felt sorry for him.

When he was kidnapped, that feeling switched to fear. When Billy and he engaged in their battle in Carly's car, that fear drifted toward repugnance, and now it had settled into outright seething hatred, a hatred Grouchy had never known in life.

When the walls came down, Grouchy left with more resistance in his eyes than the last time the walls faded to set him free. Billy and his crew stared at him with the same threat they tried last time. This time Grouchy stared at them longer. He stared at them with a challenge that brought them forward, but Grouchy pushed them away. A few of the crew wanted to pursue, but Billy felt a strength in Grouchy he thought his crew couldn't combat, not at the moment, at least.

"Let him go," Billy said, and with Billy's command the few goons stopped following Grouchy's retreat. "We'll get him when he isn't feeling so tough."

$$* \qquad * \qquad * \qquad *$$

Sampson engaged Carly the night of the day he'd entered her brother and had the roughest, most cathartic sex he'd ever enjoyed. It made him feel guilty just afterwards. And though he felt guilty enough to start a session with Carly—he never had to start their encounters before—he wanted Aaron again. He wanted Aaron more than a woman. More than Carly, certainly. It was mainly the ease that prickled him with lust when he thought of Aaron, its lack of any strings. Sampson enjoyed men for this reason. Men knew what men wanted, and the mess of a relationship might come up between two homosexuals who had no bones about who they were, but it never would with a man who liked it both ways and wanted the world to think he liked it only the way he was expected. Sampson didn't think it would be a problem, at least. He didn't know. Every man he had sex with broadcast to the world his heterosexuality, no matter how little the world believed it. Aaron broadcast something totally opposite.

Grouchy sat next to Sampson as Carly departed for the bathroom with another packet of white powder. Grouchy knew what happened. He was trapped while it happened, but he saw Sampson and Aaron together. He saw them their whole time together. It made Grouchy wonder if this lust was a part of the real Sampson or just a part of the destruction Sampson seemed so powerless to avoid

"You want him more than her, don't you, Sam?" Grouchy said.

"Not in the way you thinking."

"What was all that talk about a family?"

"No one will know, Grouchy."

"You think a happy family can be built on you marrying one while still screwing the other?"

"I'm not thinking about it right now."

"That's the problem, Sam. You do a lot of thinking, and then you just stop thinking all together. Then, you do a lot of thinking again and get yourself in the mess you're in now."

"You a broken record, Grouchy. You know that?"

"Yeah, Sam, I do," Grouchy replied. "But I gotta make you memorize it somehow."

CHAPTER 30

Tommy and Sheila were married at a reception house, on the patio, while a Little League baseball game, which wasn't part of the service, was played underneath the deck. No blood relatives attended because none were left. Sheila was orphaned at thirteen when her mother and father both died in a motel fire. She had no siblings. Her parents had moved to Georgia from Texas to get away from their kin, so Sheila had never met any. Tommy was orphaned at twenty-one when his mother died of complications from diabetes. His father died when he was sixteen. Tommy's nearest grandparent died just before he was born. His uncles were all banished or dead.

Friends sat in the plastic white chairs as the ceremony commenced. Mary sat near the front, Cecilia clutched to her chest, crying through every spoken promise. Some strangers flashed Mary dirty looks because it seemed to them that Mary was unwilling to stop her. But Mary was powerless. The video would show Mary resembling a pasty mannequin throughout the ceremony. She was, in fact, squirming like her daughter, but on the inside. This scene was supposed to give her hope, she thought, but hope had no power over her envy.

Grouchy was feeling envious too. It burgeoned in his ghostly expression and couldn't be squelched, no matter how much he knew Sheila needed this union. He stood at the back and made himself watch the vows and the kisses and Elena hugging her new father, a man she would always know as her father, even when she was old enough to understand the man who was really, Daddy, was in the ground and would never come back.

"Stings, doesn't it?" Billy said. He had come alone. He figured the time for threats and violence had subsided for a while. The diplomatic touch just might persuade the likes of Grouchy to their side.

"No," Grouchy lied.

"Oh, David," Billy said with an evil chuckle that could never be mimicked away. "I know it does. There are ways. We have found ways to end the bliss."

"Why would I want to end her bliss?" Grouchy said, finally turning to face Billy's suddenly sober, grey, ugly exterior.

"Because she belongs to you. She can belong to you again, Grouchy. You just have to wait it out. You just have to be willing to be the bad guy for a while."

"A while? A while? No. I'm not an idiot, Billy. There's no death here. 'A while' to you means forever."

"Isn't that what you wanted, Grouchy? Forever? Weren't those the vows? Till death do you part? Well, you decided against death, didn't you? All you have to do now is help make her decide the same, and you'll have what you really want. It only takes some sacrifice on your part. Just a little."

Grouchy left Billy and the ceremony. He knew they shouldn't, but Billy's words felt too good to a soul that had started to embrace bitterness in order to get to the other side. But the other side would always be a million miles away if he truly did. Billy's bitterness was starting to make sense in world, where, in the end, it's all anyone has.

Sheila invited some men she thought Mary might appreciate. But her and Mary's understanding of each other was a long way from meeting in the middle. Sheila invited many religious men, but Mary wasn't religious. Sheila knew this, but figured only religious men would understand Mary's need for chastity until the night of the wedding.

These men were nice, but they lived in a plane Mary couldn't see herself ever being comfortable in. They were conservative, and while Sampson was, too, their conservatism seemed engrained in their bones, while Mary always felt Sampson was a parrot, only speaking what he had picked up from his parents and someday would change.

Sheila was too busy to monitor Mary's progress. But if she could see one man after the other lose interest and avoid the bar Mary was hitting pretty heavily, a crease of concern would line her face. She would believe Mary was always meant to be alone, and only had to forget that just once to have a lifelong connection in the form of a child.

*   *   *   *

Grayson was a sick man and lonely man. He was forty-five, and the nerves in his body were rapidly dying. But they were dying too slowly for Grayson's taste. Grayson had neuropathy. His wife had left him some five years before because he had become a drug abuser to mask the pain. His wife's purpose seemed only to serve as his drug courier or babysitter. She left when she was only thirty and was thankful she and Grayson had no children.

Billy started acting as Grayson's friend when all the rest had vanished. He was polite and listened to a man who had no living soul who would. Billy sought Grayson's confidence in order to instill an obligation that would add more menace to Billy's crew once Grayson's dying nerves took him away or he went by his own hand. Billy recommended that Grayson do it himself several times. Grayson had ignored those suggestions so far. However, Billy would never stop trying to convince him.

When Grayson could walk, he had to use a cane. He was set up with hospice, and the disability he lived on only afforded him a small apartment in a dying part of Marietta. It looked a shell of a neighborhood, just like he was a shell of a man. The gas stations on both corners were deserted. Ragged kids on bicycles roamed the streets as if they were hunting game. Grayson didn't want to die here.

He used to have such confidence. Grayson graduated at the top of his class and became a sought-after defense attorney. That was before Grayson turned thirty-five and his congenital condition set in with a vengeance. Cocaine and alcohol became his only retreat, and Grayson had been retreating or in chronic pain ever since.

Grayson didn't want to be in a hospital. He could have round-the-clock care. But he was too proud. He thought the woman that came over everyday was sufficient, though she really wasn't.

"What are you waiting for?" Billy asked. "It can get more and more painful, or you can do what you know is coming anyway."

Grayson sweat a lot. He didn't know why. It was the humidity, he guessed, in summer. In winter, Grayson thought his nurse put the central heat on too high.

The bathroom was like some holy shrine for which he needed a Sherpa to guide him in and out of because of how stiff he would become when rising from a fixed position. He'd become accustomed to the diapers he wore, though sometimes, when Grayson was lucid, he cried because he was so helpless at such a young age. His father could get around better than he could and he was seventy-five. Grayson couldn't blame anyone, though he wished he could find blame and choke it until it was dead. He used to show such gratitude to God, now Grayson thought his disease was revenge for some past wrong, a wrong he couldn't guess.

He scorned romance. When Grayson saw couples holding hands, he visibly sneered at them. He was a limping cloud of gloom everywhere he went. He had no patience for anybody, no gratitude, nothing in the way of civility. Billy loved it. Billy figured no cloud of gloom would resist the power to create more gloom when he became free from such a crippled body.

Billy would wait. A time would come when he could use Grayson and capture him all at the same time.

CHAPTER 31

It was such a hot day and it had been hot all week. The stretch of land Sampson and the crew mowed had barely grown. It used to be a cattle field, and it was almost brown.

Carly's father had a contract to mow the two acres of land whether it showed growth or none. The blades under the mowers threw up dust, mostly, which got into every mower's eyes. Sampson's tears battled the intrusion for a time before he had to use his sweat-drenched shirt to wipe his eyes and sting them at the same instant.

At quitting time, Carly's father hadn't shown. Sampson stood at the edge of that stretch of mostly churned-up dust waiting while the sun set. He was a long way from Tucker. He had no money for a bus, let alone a cab. Sampson didn't know where a bus stop was or where it would take him. He didn't even know where this road led. A small car started up the lonely road and stopped. Aaron was driving. Sampson's worry disappeared while his guts rumbled excitement.

"Dad told me where you were," Aaron said. "I was in the area, so I told him I'd pick you up. But I wasn't, Sam. I came all this way just for you." Aaron smiled.

He brought Sampson to a dead-end street that was shielded by overhanging branches and turned to Sampson and smiled again.

"Brought my boyfriends here a lot. Never had any trouble."

Sampson and Aaron got into the backseat, and Aaron offered of himself whatever Sampson wanted. Sampson wanted much, and Aaron acquiesced to it all. Sampson wanted so much that Aaron had to take off work the next day.

*   *   *   *

Carly's breathing was strange. It was rapid and sounded uncomfortable. Sampson maneuvered himself on top of her slowly, but she told him to speed up. Instead of yelling insults at him like their times in the apartment, Carly merely whispered them inside a house of relatives. It seemed sexier to Sampson in this way.

When they finished, Sampson asked Carly if anything was wrong. She replied that she was going through withdrawal. She said she had given up the coke. But alcohol was another matter. Carly had bought Sampson three tiny bottles that day and emptied six herself. When Sampson suggested rehab for both her and himself, Carly said her father would kick them out if he knew what she'd been doing.

"Sometimes I wish it could come later, Sam. I don't think I'm ready."

Sampson knew this. He didn't think Carly was either. He knew *he* most certainly wasn't.

But Carly's honesty moved Sampson. She never showed such vulnerability. Carly wouldn't have told him this weeks ago. She figured Sampson would tire of her and her family and move on. Now, Carly felt Sampson was with her until she decided she didn't want him. But she never would. Carly could only leave her family. All the men she ever had left her.

One morning before Carly's father took him to the crew Sampson had been working with for close to a month, he sat Sampson down at the kitchen table. The light of morning was merely a glow. Bob started every day with a cigar. He ended everyday with one too. He also had one for lunch and for supper.

"How'd you meet her?" he asked Sampson. The tone of his voice made Sampson think a camera was running secretly somewhere to record this interrogation.

"We worked at the same restaurant," Sampson said.

"Where do you come from?"

"Kennesaw."

"What's your history?"

"Was in the war, sir."

"In the war?"

"Yes, sir."

"What did you do after the war?"

"I got drunk a lot. I lived in the woods for nearly a year."

Bob's rigid glance changed. His eyes opened wider, and he looked at the ceiling as he blew out some smoke.

"It's making sense now. You're a screwup just like her."

"I'd appreciate you not referring to me that way, sir. Or her."

"Then explain to me why you stayed in the woods," Bob said, eyeing Sampson again.

"I needed time. I still need something, sir. I ain't cured."

"I never figured it. How does killing the enemy make someone sick?"

"It's not just the enemy that dies, sir. Sometimes even who we call the enemy ain't the enemy anyway."

Carly's father scoffed. "You know that going in."

"You ever been a soldier?"

"No. Never wanted to be."

"You gotta wear the boots, sir, to understand."

"Then why haven't they all come back to sleep in the damn woods? Huh? Tell me that."

"There is no real reason why or why not. They all come back with something, though. I came back cracked through. Maybe some come back understanding better. I don't know. I just came back understanding nothing. That's all I can tell you, sir."

$$* \qquad * \qquad * \qquad *$$

Sampson's legs were tired, as were his arms and head. But he was grateful the rain came on so strong that no lawns could be mowed from noon until the end of the day anywhere within the Atlanta area. Carly's father apparently didn't notice the rain or figured someone else could take Sampson home. And that's what happened. A man on the crew Sampson had become friendly with, who didn't understand most of his language, took Sampson home in his red 1982 Chevy truck whose muffler had gone and sounded like a machine gun. Sampson liked the guy even though he couldn't pronounce his name.

Rest was like a dream. Sampson imagined falling to that mattress and snoozing until his companion demanded sex from a body that could hardly satisfy. But before he opened his bedroom door, he heard two voices inside, and one was a man's. It was low and whispering, and Sampson figured Carly was doing to him what he did to Carly in his free time. He stood at the door and listened, and what he heard started a confusion that lapsed into anger and then a violent feeling of revulsion.

"Remember how much fun we had, Carly? Remember?" Sampson recognized Carly's father saying. "We can have fun again."

"I had no fun, Dad," Carly said weakly. "Don't, Dad, don't," she pleaded just as weakly.

"Oh, yes you did, sweetie. It was fun back then. I missed it when you left. I *know* you did too."

Sampson threw open the door to see Bob behind Carly with his hand wrapped around her body and on his daughter's crotch. He turned to Sampson in anger, as if Sampson had walked in on him with some other woman.

"What the fuck are you doing?" Sampson said, and the reality of the situation swept across Bob's face. Sampson saw a shame and humility he never imagined Carly's father would show.

"I was just ... I was just ... hugging her."

"No you weren't!" Sampson said and charged forward to push Bob to the floor.

Bob looked up at Sampson with bristling fear. Sampson stared back with murderous intent. He looked into Bob's face and saw the face of his own father and everything he was. Sampson clutched the lamp near his side and threw it at Bob's head. Now they had no lamps. Her father groaned after the impact and cowered in anticipation for more justified violence.

The basement stairs began to rumble. Carly's mother came in with anxious eyes. She looked to her husband and demanded to know what was happening.

"He was touching her! He was touching her down there!" cried Sampson, turning to Carly's mother and motioning to his own crotch.

Veronica, Carly's mother, looked stunned. Her face slacked and her eyes numbed, as though she was weary of hearing the same story so many times before. Veronica looked at her daughter, who had already started to cry. Carly was looking at the floor. She had become the little girl, transported back to the first of many episodes that dented her psyche and fueled her need to fight. She was just as confused, just as helpless.

"N-No, n-no, Carly. Right?" said her mother.

"Yes, Mom!" Carly said with her head raised and the rage those years had built up piercing through bloodshot eyes. "You *know* it, Mom! I told you then! I told you then! You never listened to me, Mom!"

"I was just hugging her," Carly's father cried with annoyance as he stood to his feet. His head was bleeding from the impact of the lamp, which now lay in two pieces.

"He was just hugging you, Carly, that's all," Veronica said, coming to Carly and trying to put an arm around her shoulder.

"No he wasn't! Goddamn it, Mom! No he wasn't!"

"You were just imagining things."

"I saw it!" Sampson said.

Veronica turned to him fiercely and said, "You were too! You both are so screwed up! You were just imaging things!"

Sampson was dumbfounded. But with the mystery of Carly now solved, he became filled with a kind of paternal protection and roared, "This is why she's like this! He put his hands all over her, and you just ignored it!"

"No! He wouldn't do that! He's a *good* man!" Carly's mother said.

"He's a fucking scumbag, and you are, too, for letting him!" Sampson grabbed Carly's hand and led her outside of the house through the basement door, up through the cascading rain, and into her car. Carly cried so violently that Sampson had to wrap her in his arms to put her in the passenger seat.

"We'll go to my parents," Sampson said desperately as they left the road. Carly had so many reasons to never come back home.

"No, Sam! No!" Carly continued to cry. "Not like this. I don't want to see anyone like this."

"Do you have any money?"

"Um ... a little."

"Enough for a motel?"

"Um ... I have a little. A little."

"We'll go to a motel. We'll get you cooled down. We'll go tomorrow or ... the next day. We'll get you cooled down first."

CHAPTER 32

Carly's eyes were opened. They were open for some hours before Sampson opened his.

As she woke in the middle of the day, she just looked at Sampson, sadly, and wondered the whole time. This was the calmest Carly had been since her father entered her room with the intentions she had run from just after turning sixteen, almost nine years before.

Just after they entered the motel room the afternoon before, Carly collapsed, sobbing, desperate, miserable, and somewhat deranged. She couldn't say a thing; she could only wail into Sampson's arms. He held her and brushed away the hair stuck on her face, which was drenched with tears.

When Sampson woke the next day and turned to her, Carly's face was just sad.

"So now you know," Carly said and continued looking at Sampson to see if he would now flinch after the last day and night stopped racing though his veins. She knew that when something that sudden happens, a person just reacts, and only later, after resting, can think.

"Yeah … I figured," Sampson said without flinching. "I figured it was something like that."

"I guess you want to hear the whole of it. I know you didn't understand a thing through my mess last night."

"No, Carly … if you don't want-"

"I want to, Sam. You're thinking it. And you have a right to. You saw the show. It's the same show that went on since I was twelve. I looked sixteen when I was twelve. My dad didn't look at me anymore like he used to. He was looking at me like all the old men around the neighborhood were. They were pigs. They were hosing cold water down their pants when I walked by. I ain't lying. Think I should have been real flattered, don't you?"

"No, Carly. That's really-"

"I could almost see him jerking himself off to me in the bathroom, Sam. I knew what jerking off was then too. I could almost see him closing his eyes and thinking of fucking his daughter."

"Yeah?" Sampson said and started to grow fidgety.

"You listening, Sam?"

"Yeah. Yeah, I am."

"Too much too soon?"

"Tell me, Carly. I mean … just do what you want, is what I'm saying."

"I've known all sorts of men, Sam. All sorts. I've known the great daddies and the bad ones. The real bad ones. I've known men that did to their daughters what my daddy done to me. And it always starts with medicine, Sam. *Medicine*. Doing it for your own good, and he's your daddy, so you figure you should trust him. I didn't, though, Sam. I told him not to do it *every* time, and when my mom came down and saw it was the same thing, she just went up again.

"He said he was checking down there to make sure I was all right. You know where. I knew he just wanted to touch it. And when mom didn't seem to stop him, he got bold enough to put it in me. He told me he had to. Then he told me it was our little secret." Carly's bottom lip began to quiver. "I *told* him I didn't like it!"

She turned from Sampson's face and looked up at the ceiling. Sampson tried to halt this confession. "Carly, if this is making you-"

"It was once a week at first and then whenever he wanted. He would just come in and tell me to take my clothes off." She gasped, but controlled the quiver in her lip. "I told my mom, Sam. I did. I told her. I told her every time it happened, and she just didn't care or didn't want to hear it."

"I know. You don't have to say anymore."

"I want to!" Carly said. The quiver stopped. "I ran away at sixteen. I hitch-hiked to Atlanta. I just walked around. I slept in parks or whatever. Some guys came along asking for a blowjob, and I figured what the hell. I started shooting up, doing blow, smoking whatever. I was gangbanged twice. I mean raped, Sam. I wasn't paid. Just taken off the street and fucked in the car by three sweaty old white guys. I had a pimp who fucked me when he wanted. Beat the shit out of me when he wanted to. I really grew to hate men, Sam. I still wanted to fuck them, but I wanted to hurt them more. Anyone who wanted me I wanted to hurt, no matter how good they were. I wanted punishment. They were all him to me. You were him to me, too, at first. I fucked for money or for revenge and that's all. And I thought that did the trick. I thought I had it beat. I thought he wouldn't touch me again because I was so fucking tough."

"It's over, Carly."

"Not in my head, Sam. I wish I could blow that part away."

*   *   *   *

Grayson's hands were not cooperating. They were like claws, scrunched up and inflexible. Somehow, he maneuvered them to empty the tiny bag of cocaine on his bedside table. He had just woken up and put his nose to the mound and sucked in a good sniff. Grayson heard something and looked up with a nose tipped with white powder to see his caretaker standing just before the threshold of his room.

"What are you doing?" the caretaker asked calmly.

"What does it look like?"

"You can lose your benefits if they find out you're doing illegal drugs."

"Yeah? You going to tell them?"

"It's not good for you."

"Not good for me? You're a part of hospice care. You know what that means, right? It means I'm *dying*. And I know *this* ain't the shit that's gonna kill me."

Grayson's caretaker shook her head and went into the bathroom to run his bath. Grayson was glad. He stunk. He wet himself last night. He had avoided defecating in the diaper, but he needed to release his bowels soon or he would.

In the place the caretaker had just stepped from, Billy now stood. He shook his head and tried to seem just as concerned as the woman.

"She's right," Billy said. "Might as well do what God intends to do to you anyway."

"Long as I have coke," Grayson said, smiling. The coke was bursting grandly in his head and he was feeling good. He would need another mound after his bath to maintain that feeling.

"You heard your dealer. Gonna be dry for a while. They just done a big sweep, like he said. You ain't gonna have any for awhile."

"Yeah, well we'll see. He isn't the only dealer around."

*   *   *   *

Sampson told Carly to wait in the car. Like Carly, before Sampson left the car he looked at his childhood home with reservation, though not nearly as much now that he realized his home was the paradise compared with others. He never really wanted to see his parents again. He wanted divorced from his past, because his past seemed full of so much ignorance, and he wasn't ignorant anymore. Looking at it when he didn't have to seemed akin to beating a dead horse that even the flies were done with.

But Sampson felt he had to now.

He went up those steps and sighed. While knocking hard, he tried to suck up some temporary strength so he wouldn't look the cracked-through man he had admitted being to Carly's father.

Sampson's father opened the door. It was his father, but Sampson thought for a moment it wasn't. Ed wasn't as fat as Sampson remembered him, and he seemed taller.

His eyes were different too. They were softer, almost kind. Maybe even understanding. *It must just be a vision,* Sampson thought, *of what I want to see.*

But the vision didn't retreat; it only became more confusing when his father started to cry, then reached out his arms and brought Sampson in and hugged him tight.

"I've missed you so much, Sam," he said.

"You have?"

"Yes, Sam. So much."

Ed released him, and Sampson, still bewildered, turned to motion Carly out of the car.

"Things have changed, Dad."

"I know it, Sam. I know what's happened to you."

"No. Mary and me … we're divorced."

"I know."

"How do you know?"

"Alice heard."

"Well … I have a new girl and … she's pregnant, Dad."

"Oh." His eyes became pensive. "That was quick, son."

"It wasn't planned. This is Carly," Sampson said, and Carly looked at the concrete underneath her feet while shaking Sampson's father's hand. It seemed she feared that if she looked into his father's eyes, he would read what had happened to her, in the past and just yesterday.

"Hello," Ed said.

"Hi," Carly's soft voice barely carried.

"Can we … can we stay here a while?" Sampson asked.

"Of course." Sampson wanted to ask his father what had happened to him. Something had. Something very real had happened to him. Something had turned him inside out and turned him into the father Sampson wished he had growing up.

Sampson's mother wasn't home. His father told him she had gotten a job as a secretary. Ed further told Sampson he had retired from the police force and was now working part-time at a hardware store. He had gotten rid of all his guns too.

"Why?" Sampson asked.

"When you disappeared, Sam," his father began, "they seemed mean to me. I seemed mean to me. I don't want to die mean, Sam."

*   *   *   *

Mary's daughter could hold her head up while she rested inside her crib. Cecilia smiled at Mary as if she knew how much of an accomplishment it was and Mary wished she could share her joy with someone, and then asked herself why. Wasn't her own joy enough for her?

Sheila continued to try to set Mary up with men she thought would suit her. None of them did. They all talked Jesus so much that Mary wanted to tell them to just shut up and have a goddamn beer. Sheila didn't understand. She seemed to think Mary had to sooth her loneliness with whoever presented himself. Her own advice to not force a romantic union seemed forgotten.

Mary was becoming so apathetic about relationships that Sheila's words of advice finally became a comfort. She didn't know when it happened, but it did. Maybe it was the third or fourth date with someone who carried a Bible every-where he went. She thought, *If this is the only kind of man that isn't expecting my flesh before I'm ready, my flesh can just relive the memories.*

And that's just what her flesh did. When Mary touched herself she thought of Sampson, no one else. She never had any fantasies about a mythical man with all the right muscles and tender touches. The best sex was with Sampson. Well, the only sex—besides the near rape—was with Sampson. She glorified Sampson, the man she married. The Sampson of late wasn't even a thought. If Mary wanted to come, he couldn't be.

She sometimes bought a few roses for herself and laid them on the bed. Lying naked on the bed, she closed her eyes and breathed in the roses as her hand went to her nipples and between her thighs. Mary wanted as much romance as she could have. The past was the only romance that seemed possible. After Mary opened her eyes, after the climax had rendered her motionless and then drifted off so she could open her eyes, she was Mommy, and the lone distinction didn't make her sad. She was Mommy. If ever she were someone else's embodiment of physical love again, it would be on her terms and her terms only.

*   *   *   *

Sampson's mother cooked them all a nice dinner. It was better than Carly's mother's cooking and better than the food Sampson remembered his mother making him when he was young.

His mother seemed happy. She smiled without strain. Sampson's father smiled back at her without menace or bitterness, without the aggressive grimace that Sampson saw his father offer her in the past.

Sampson thought, *Maybe I shouldn't have come. Maybe I was the reason they were so unhappy. Maybe they never should have had kids.*

Carly barely spoke. She was asked questions and answered them all, but only in one-word sentences. This brought no worry to Sampson's parents. They figured she was just shy.

Unlike Carly's and Aaron's rooms, Sampson's room still had his old furniture. It still had the posters on the walls of baseball and football stars. It still had clothes hanging in his closet in case Sampson ever needed them. His mother cleaned the room every week, but just of dust.

"I was raped too," Sampson confessed to Carly that first night inside his old room. The moon came through the blinds, shielded by some clouds. It was almost romantic. But not to them. Not today.

"You were?" said Carly and turned to him with another feature Sampson had never seen. She seemed concerned. She seemed actually interested in his feelings.

"An uncle. He died when I was fourteen. But when I was eleven, he … he brought me to the guest room and fucked me. He didn't try and mask it. He just threw me on the bed and told me to not make a noise. He was a big guy. It hurt really bad."

"Did you ever tell?"

"No. He said he would kill me. I believed him."

"Do you hate him?"

"Tell you the truth, I almost never think of him."

But Sampson did. Whenever he was with a man he did. He fucked them all like his uncle had fucked him: ruthless, every time

Sampson dreamed of Aaron that night. It was the first wet dream he'd had since he was fifteen. When he woke from the dream, Sampson went into the bathroom in the hall to clean himself so Carly wouldn't notice and ask why he was so horny at such a time like this.

He looked in the bathroom mirror and saw the feeling of comfort his parents had given, his old house had given ... that feeling was receding. Sampson was still just as desperate as before his father opened the door. He still needed everything he could get his hands on to distract himself from the schism in his brain.

"He's different isn't he?" Grouchy said standing behind Sampson and scaring him just a bit.

"Real different, Grouchy."

"Maybe he'll understand now."

"Or maybe he became that way so he didn't have to try to understand anymore. Not that he ever succeeded."

"It's something, Sam. Sometimes all you need is something."

CHAPTER 33

Billy was right. Grayson hobbled up to every dealer on the street he knew. None of them had his escape. His need erased his need for everything else.

Grayson didn't care if he never ate food again as long as could have cocaine. Piles of it to lie in all day. Grayson didn't care if his stomach corroded into bile and gagged his throat. If enough coke were in his head, he wouldn't feel it.

The dealers only had weed, and weed was like a decaffeinated coffee to an addict of a different sort. Grayson's escape was now a nightmare because it existed. It existed in plenty in the fields of Columbia, but the shipment was illegal because assholes who had never felt the pain Grayson was in enacted their moral compass to protect kids who would find it anyway.

So he bought bottles of liquor and emptied them quickly, waiting for the numbness he needed to distract himself from the sizzles of crying nerves that cried worst at night. But the liquor only made him throw up. It made Grayson's head heavier than his whole body. The liquor only made him want more, suffer more.

"I know somewhere," said Billy when Grayson's desperation had peaked; he was scratching his arms into raw, bloody appendages.

"You know where?" Grayson replied with great surprise while looking into eyes that he never truly believed in.

"Yeah, Grayson. I do."

"So … where?" Grayson imagined a baggy of white before his eyes.

"Well, you gotta drive."

"Fine. I'll drive! I'll drive!"

Hospice had found a truck for him and paid for it too. The doors were painted different from the rest of the body. It had no radio or air conditioning, and the windshield was cracked. Inside this truck, Grayson drove speedily with Billy by his side telling him where to go.

As Billy directed him, another ghost sometimes popped in the cab and whispered in Billy's ear. It was Georgie, the Vietnam vet who was thrust into quick duty once he died. Georgie's whispering was frantic. Once Georgie relayed his message to Billy, he left.

"Who's that?" Grayson asked distractedly. He didn't really care as long a dealer with the stuff was near.

"Just a friend. You'll get to know him soon," said Billy and couldn't help but smile a wicked smile.

"What does that mean?" Grayson said, finding more interest in a look that contradicted all of Billy's attempts to seem decent and sincerely concerned.

"Nothing. Turn here."

Grayson did. Georgie reappeared, whispered something, then disappeared again.

"Turn here!" said Billy, feeling an excitement Grayson didn't understand. "Here! Turn here!"

"It's red. The light is red, Billy."

"No it isn't! You're seeing things!"

"A car's coming!"

"No it isn't! Keep going! Turn! Turn or he'll go away!"

With Grayson's desperation overriding the truth he plainly could see through his watery eyes, he turned. The car that Billy tried to convince Grayson wasn't real was most certainly real. Grayson slammed into an SUV, just north of the driver's side. Without a seatbelt on, Grayson flew through his already half-cracked windshield and landed on the street, where his head was crushed and he instantly died.

Inside the other car two airbags had deployed. The two babies in the backseat weren't hurt. They were crying, but they weren't hurt. Sheila was sitting in the front passenger seat. Her shoulder strained heavy against the belt and was maybe dislocated. She looked at Tommy, who was shaking his head rapidly. Sheila saw blood from Tommy's nose but nowhere else. Tommy would only need to be looked over by a medic. But not Sheila. She would need to be observed for longer. And it had nothing to do with her shoulder.

Just before the accident, just before Sheila's life could have ended, she was close enough to death that she could see Grouchy's face in front of her. Grouchy screamed, "No!" just before the impact. Sheila saw Grouchy's desperation and then another face: the grey, awful face of Billy smiling cryptically, dripping saliva like a lion standing over crippled kill, as if she was for dinner. But Sheila didn't realize they were two faces. She had approached death and left it in such a short span of seconds that those two faces blended in her mind. The only face Sheila recognized was Grouchy's. She thought the evil she saw was Grouchy's; she was certain the accident was his design.

Billy's crew was called quickly to assembly on that street corner, where, just beyond, Grayson's grotesquely twisted body was taken from his pool of blood and wrapped in a heavy, black body bag.

Grouchy had grabbed Billy. Grouchy shook him fiercely, and when Billy cried for everyone to come help him and they all appeared, they were apprehensive when they saw Grouchy's state. His strength was greater than all of theirs combined at the moment. The other bullies watched him as if he were a strong, unstable psychopath they feared could injure them, though the feeling of injury would last a fraction of a fraction of a second. Once the impact was made, it would sting, then dissolve.

"I did it for you!" Billy screamed. "You wanted her! *You* wanted her!"

"You did it for *you*!" Grouchy screamed back.

"No! I did it for you! Only for you, damnit! Stop the bullshit! You know you wished she died! If he turned when I told him too, she would've!"

"Oh, you fucking asshole," Grouchy hissed. "You fucking, dumb, fucking asshole. You are rotten. You are rotten in every single way. Your soul is as rotten as your body two days after you died. You might be like this until the end of fucking time, but *not* me! I will *never* be a part of you! I will *never* be! And you didn't even succeed! You're not worth shit even *here*! You won't succeed, Billy. I will make sure of it."

"You can't be everywhere," Billy said. His smile had returned. "You can't be the angel you want to be to Sampson and the protector of your woman at the same time, every time."

"I will take Sampson out of danger and leave after that, and then you'll have no reason to bother her anymore. You won't even *think* about it. Because, you know when she dies, a long time for now when she dies, she won't want you either, and she won't even allow you an ear when she's near death."

"Don't underestimate me, David. I've been doing this a long time."

"And only succeeded in getting the weakest of the weak, and that *isn't* her!"

As Sheila was helped out of the car, her eyes were jittery and shifted. She didn't even think of her child and the other child in the car, who was essentially hers as well. The medics asked Sheila routine questions about the date, who the president was, and what her full name was. Sheila answered them all correctly, but was still so shaken by the view of a world that surrounded her for just seconds, that the medics told Tommy she should be seen by someone immediately.

"Sheila ... Sheila," Tommy said before he agreed. "We're OK. Elena, Tommy Junior, they're OK."

"David," Sheila eked out.

"What?"

"David. I saw him. He did this. He wanted me to die, Tommy."

"No. No, Sheila. You're just confused."

"I saw him, Tommy! Saw him plain as day. Right in front of me. Two inches from my face, Tommy! He did this!"

"Sheila," Tommy tried again, but the medics intervened and insisted she go with them *now*.

Inside the ambulance, Grouchy was by Sheila's side. But Sheila wasn't near death anymore. The truth of his love and concern and lack of desire to see Sheila leave the world—and most especially his daughter—in the way Billy had tried for couldn't be understood. Grouchy still said to Sheila what he felt he had to.

"It wasn't me, Sheila," he said into those twitching, red, greatly disturbed eyes. "It was someone else. I'll never let him get close enough again."

"David ... Why? Why?" Sheila said over and over again as the medics wheeled her into the hospital and placed her in a room until a doctor could see her.

*   *   *   *

Grayson was in line and was looking forward. He had no interest in hanging around. But Billy had an interest in keeping him around and assembled his crew to take him like they had taken Grouchy when Grouchy tried to leave.

When Grayson turned to Billy there was hate in his eyes. But it was directed only at Billy. It was enough of a hate to keep him strong, but not too much to disable Grayson's quest in seeking new life.

The crew's motions toward Grayson were useless. Their arms passed through the body that was his image on earth. Grayson had already imagined something like this. He imagined an endless death surrounded by the endlessly dead. So being familiar with Billy and his crew for some years allowed Grayson the sight of their desperation before they tried to make him one of them. He wasn't scared. Billy's sole purpose was something Grayson had never seen before on Billy's face, but one Grayson had already guessed as soon as he left his body.

"You were never my friend," Grayson told Billy as his virtual limbs tried to grab at him and grab again. "You used me. You thought you could use me forever, didn't you?"

"You belong with us," Billy said as the reality of his inability made him angry and scary, but only to one who wasn't expecting it, to one who could be susceptible to being overcome.

"I belong as far from you as I can get," Grayson said and stepped forward as the line progressed two steps ahead.

Billy's crew looked at him. Mutiny was in their eyes. But none of Billy's crew was strong enough to carry out what maybe some spine would allow them to. He had conditioned them for years and years. But two failures in a row had Billy worried his crew's conditioning could recede into a power-hungry revolt. A third failure would most certainly guarantee it.

*   *   *   *

"Mrs. Granville," said the psychiatrist on call to Sheila. He was dressed in a white lab coat, with circular spectacles around his eyes and a kind smile on his young, shaved face. "Tell me what you saw."

"I told you what I saw. I saw my ex—husband. He died. He didn't want me to marry again."

"Did he tell you that?"

"No. He told someone after he died."

"Told who?"

"A ... friend. A friend. His father told me everything was OK. But he lied. He lied to me. David tried to kill me. I ... thought it was OK."

"You're in shock, Mrs. Granville. Shock can make a person think they see all sorts of things."

"I saw it! I know what I saw! Ask anybody. I don't make things up. I don't have delusions."

"I didn't say you were making this up, Mrs. Granville. You've just gone through a traumatic experience. A mind is a complicated thing. It can force visions that aren't really there."

"I'm *not* crazy!"

"I didn't say you were. But ... your ex-husband is gone."

"No. He watches me. He was waiting until the right time. *He* did this. He'll do it again. I don't know when, but he will."

"Were you afraid of your ex-husband while he lived?"

"Never. He was the most beautiful man," Sheila said, and her eyes started to clear as she started to cry.

Grouchy reached his arms around Sheila and clasped his hands together to make himself feel like he was doing some good. He knew he wasn't, but unless Sheila had another near-death experience soon, she would believe what her mind had confused. Grouchy didn't know how Sheila would cope unless she could hear the truth from his own mouth. But hearing that truth would mean Billy would almost succeed again. Maybe this time Billy would actually render Sheila lifeless to face endless agony like him.

CHAPTER 34

Aaron's cell number was still in Sampson's wallet. Sampson opened it several times, only to close it when that ripped piece of paper peaked out at him. He shuddered when thinking of Aaron's small hands on his inner thigh.

Though the work required only one man, Sampson started working with his father at the hardware store and busied himself however he could. It helped with the confusion. It helped Sampson not to think of ways to divert the confusion. Aaron's number was like a flask, however. And just like a full flask, Sampson could hide it from himself for only so long.

Sampson's father didn't pry. It seemed he had no interest in prying. Sometimes Sampson thought he saw enough understanding in his father's eyes to spill his dilemma with alcohol and with Aaron. But, enough past rants by his father's against "faggots" made Sampson almost certain his father hadn't advanced that far.

Carly didn't drink for the first few days inside the Roy household. But Sampson handed some of the money he made at the hardware store over to her, and she left the house to numb herself solid. Just out of respect, she would sleep it off in her car and then come back into Sampson's boyhood room to sleep some more. Since she and Sampson were in Kennesaw again, Carly was tempted to visit the coke dealers who knew her by name. They gave her a nickname too: "Sweet Tits." It wasn't very original, but it stuck. Every dealer called her "Sweet Tits." She used to think of getting it tattooed. But Carly avoided them now. She avoided stopping at those corners, though she tempted herself by passing them every day.

Carly needed Sampson again. She asked him, politely this time, to please her again physically. She couldn't call Sampson those names anymore, though, and so the act was a confusing thing. Part of her wanted to scratch at Sampson's face, and the part that loved Sampson's protection wanted to kiss him tenderly. Those two forces battled and left her frozen. She needed him inside her, yet she did not know how to express the pleasure Sampson's tight arms and tingling sex sizzled into a brain that hadn't associated pleasure without pain for some time.

Sampson's interest was dipping so low he didn't know what to do. He tried running, but it made him tired. He tried watching those history shows with his dad, but he got bored. He didn't think getting drunk was an option because he would be ashamed if he did. His father was with him all day, and at night he couldn't sneak out without both his father and mother smelling the drink and noticing the sway of how much he had drunk when he returned.

One Sunday, when the hardware store was closed and Sampson's mother had taken Carly shopping, the phone number in his wallet was burning into his pocket, into his thigh, up into his mind, and into his rigid penis.

Aaron had been waiting for the call and was willing to leave his job with a claim of a stomach ache and drive the forty-five minutes to have that rough, unencumbered sex that left him numb and elated for hours.

They met on a street corner a few streets away from the Roy house. Sampson told his father he needed a long walk. Just as Sampson had figured, his father didn't ask questions. Sampson rented a room with Aaron's money, and Aaron sneaked into the room he saw Sampson unlocking from his car below the second floor balcony.

If they were trying to be discreet it didn't work. The loud banging on the wall behind the bed, the screams of Aaron with each insistent and desperate thrust, shattered any illusion that Sampson was just needing a room for his own rest.

The men lay next to each other, still in an afterglow they both needed more than the other knew. The smells of two sweaty men with sore penises permeated the air. Aaron lit a cigarette and handed Sampson a fresh one.

"I guess I'm Jack Twist and you're Ennis Del Mar," Aaron said, laughing.

Sampson blew out some smoke after lighting his cigarette from Aaron's red lighter that Aaron had tossed on to his sweaty, naked thigh. "Who?"

"You know, *Brokeback Mountain*."

"What?"

"Don't tell me you never heard of that movie."

"Don't ring a bell right now, but ... I might of."

"Jack Twist is the real queer. Ennis Del Mar is, too, but ... well, he's both, I guess you could say."

"I'm not both, Aaron," Sampson replied tightly, and the glow of his orgasm began to fade away.

"You're not both? You're fucking me like you like it, Sam."

"I do like it."

"OK. Fucking men usually means you're at least part queer."

"Yeah? Well, I'm not. I can't love a man."

"Loving's what you just did, sweetie."

"No, that was *fucking*!"

"Oh! Like in prison?" Aaron said with a grandly distasteful smile. The smile left him and he looked down into his hairless chest to whisper loud enough for Sampson to hear, "You think you're in prison, Sam? You think this just one big prison and that means you can fuck a man and not be a queer? That's the name for it, Sam. It's just a name, though. You'll get used to it."

"No! I mean ... I ain't ever gonna hold your hand, Aaron. I ain't ever gonna *kiss* you."

"You *have* kissed me, Sam," Aaron said angrily. Spit flew into Sampson's eyes as Aaron stretched his taut neck to look up into Sampson's guarded face.

"No, you kiss me."

"And you kiss back."

"No, you just kiss me."

"You let me."

"Not the same thing."

"So what do you feel for me, Sam? I mean *really* feel for me. If this is just sport fucking, I don't wanna do it no more."

"It *is* sport fucking, Aaron! Christ, what else could it *be*?"

"Why do you think it's so obvious to me, too, Sam?"

Sampson tried to cool down. He spoke while monitoring his tone, "Your sister and me are having a baby-"

"I don't give a shit, Sam! You think I give a shit about her?"

"Well, you *should*. She's ain't been treated right her whole life."

"Oh, you gonna give me that shit that my dad raped her? Don't try it with me. I've *known* her my whole life. You just haven't figured how much bullshit she's full of."

"He *did* rape her! I almost saw him do it with my own eyes!"

"She's just twisting your mind, Sam."

"No she isn't! Your dad's a piece of shit!"

"Don't you talk about my dad that way," Aaron said slowly while shaking his head just as deliberately.

"Oh? You that fond of your dad, huh? I bet you he didn't call you all sorts of names when you told him you was queer, did he?"

"Haven't told him, Sam. No reason to."

"Yeah, well make it official and let's see what he thinks."

"Good point, Sam. How 'bout while I'm at it I make what we have official to Carly and see what *she* thinks."

Sampson looked at Aaron. He examined Aaron for sincerity but couldn't spot a bluff, so he winced and said, "You ain't gonna do that."

"And why not? You care more about me than you do her."

"That ain't true."

"You telling me you like it with her as much as with me?"

"That ain't the point. It's got nothing to do with what I *think* about you."

"Yeah? So when you screw your hand do you get all hot and sweaty?"

"That makes no sense."

"It makes perfect sense. There's a reason you fuck me like that. You want me more. You want me way more than her. Maybe way more than anyone you've ever wanted. I don't think that should stay quiet. Not with me stuck as some side man, at least."

"Side man? Goddamn, Aaron! The first time we screwed was the second time I ever saw your face! This is nothing. This is just fun."

"Yeah, well, I don't like that I'm just fun, maybe."

"What the fuck did you think it would turn into?"

"Don't know, but it's turned into something for me," Aaron said rising and quickly snatching up his underwear and Kroger uniform trousers.

Still naked, Sampson got up and gripped Aaron's arm after scuttling to his side.

"Aaron ... don't do something stupid, OK? Your sister's in a state. A real state. This ain't the time to tell her all your goddamn feelings."

"That's your problem, Sam," Aaron said without looking at him as he tightened his belt.

"Aaron!" Sampson forced Aaron around to face him. "You listen to me," he said, holding up a finger in front of Aaron's face. "You don't do this. You don't want to be with me no more, then fine. We'll end it today. But don't go doing something to someone I gotta take care of."

"I already said it, Sam. That's your problem. You figure out what you wanna tell her, and I'll figure out what I want to. You can still be a father and a queer all at the same time."

"I ain't no queer!" Sampson struck Aaron hard across the mouth with a clenched fist.

Aaron fell to the floor. He looked up at Sampson with fear and confusion, until he noticed Sampson was sorry for what he'd done. After realizing no more violence was in store for him, Aaron started to laugh.

"Damn, you are way in, aren't you?" he said.

"Way in *what?*"

"The closet, moron! I know we're in Kennesaw. I know this is the Deep South, but it's 2007, damn it! People gotta deal with the truth these days."

"I'm not queer, Aaron, OK?" Sampson tried to say calmly. "I like it. I like to fuck men, sure. I mean … *sometimes.* It's been a while though. A long while. It could have never happened again. But it *did,* and you gotta turn my mistake into something it's not?"

"You don't want it to be something, but it is," Aaron said as he got back on his feet. He ignored his bloodied lip while putting on his light blue cotton uniform shirt.

"Just promise me, Aaron," Sampson said in a slow tone that almost veered into a demand. "Just promise me you ain't gonna say anything. Don't, Aaron, OK? You want to find love. That's your right. But it won't be with me."

"It's too late, Sam," Aaron said, edging past him. "I want a life too. I want a life with you, and I'm gonna get that life whether or not you realize you love me now."

Sampson was too ashamed to follow Aaron outside. He wanted to run after him and drag Aaron back inside and beat him black and blue until Aaron promised he'd never tell.

But maybe he won't, Sampson thought. *And me showing what this really is could spread throughout town if I go bring him back.*

Sampson wasn't calmed. He was just a coward, he knew. Aaron was serious. He wanted to tell, and maybe Sampson wanted him to tell. He didn't know. Sampson didn't love Aaron. And while he searched desperately for it, he couldn't find a love for Carly inside him either.

Maybe Aaron can set me free.

"He's gonna tell her," Grouchy said, looking out the window at Aaron speeding away.

"I know," Sampson replied.

"What will you do?"

"Lie, I guess."

"And what if that doesn't work?"

"It's gotta work, Grouchy. She's got no one but me."

CHAPTER 35

Sheila dreamed of Grouchy. After the accident, she remembered every single dream she had. And every single dream included him. Sometimes the dreams were sweet. Sometimes Grouchy was the David Sheila knew; sometimes he wasn't. Sometimes he was diabolical and threatening while shaking heavy chains or a fist.

Every morning when Sheila woke, she believed Grouchy's death was the true dream. But when she turned to see that it was Tommy she lay beside, she felt a pit digging itself further into her stomach and the certainty that this partnership doomed her life.

The accident left her so dazed that Sheila couldn't work. Tommy was afraid to leave her alone, but someone had to make sure their home remained their home and the food they ate was fresh. So Tommy left her alone to work, worried about her at work, called her every hour to hear the same depressing tone, came home right after work, and stayed with Sheila all day on his days off. She never engaged in any contact with him unless he asked.

When the children needed something out of their reach, Sheila got it. When they wanted love, Sheila mimicked it, but the children knew it wasn't love. They started looking at her differently. A stranger had donned the mask of their mother. The children almost cowered as this unsmiling woman picked them up every morning without saying anything.

Tommy didn't know how to ask her what was wrong. Tommy didn't know if he wanted to ask. Sheila had become someone else, even though she looked the same. Tommy called Sheila's friends. He called Mary, but she couldn't be bothered. She had shrouded herself inside a make-believe world where no effort was needed. Mary still worked and went through the motions of normal life, but the idea of engaging in her off time with anyone besides Cecilia and phantom images of Sampson left Mary breathless.

All of Sheila's other friends came over. They talked with her on the phone and tried desperately to get her head out of that moment, but that moment had seized every thought since.

"You gotta get her into therapy," one friend said to Tommy. All her friends said something similar. They all seemed to think the idea had never occurred to him.

"She won't go," Tommy replied.

"Then *make* her go."

"I can't strap her down."

"I've never seen her like this, Tommy," the friend said. "Even after David died she wasn't like this."

"David, give me a sign," Sheila often said out loud. Most of the time she was outside and talking upward to the heavens. Under a large poplar tree, she looked for a ray of sun or a whisper from God. But besides the swaying of grass in the wind or a rumble from a car, there were no signs. Everywhere she went she looked for signs that would clue her in to the next attempt on her life and convinced herself she saw them, only to realize later they were ordinary images she'd twisted into something important. Whatever needed to happen she was ready for. She just wanted it done.

The pictures of Grouchy returned. One day they were all over the house. Tommy went into every room and saw a new one. Each new picture was displayed in a new frame. Tommy stopped himself before confronting Sheila. He told himself, "Not yet," but that phrase had outlasted its welcome.

He closed the bedroom door behind him and looked at Sheila staring vacantly out at the empty street, as though maybe Grouchy would walk up at anytime and take her wherever he wanted. As though she wanted him to know she was ready to go with him.

"Sheila ... listen and listen for good now. He *didn't* do it," Tommy said.

"I know he did, Tommy."

"Sheila, it makes no sense."

"You're trying to make sense out of a ghost?" Sheila said as she turned away from the street. Bitter confusion was in her eyes, confusion of what it all meant, if it meant anything at all.

"He is *dead*, Sheila," Tommy said. "He's not haunting you. He doesn't want to hurt you. He's wherever they go when they go. Now, listen, we have a life together. You have a daughter and I have a son. They both rely on you. If you won't get help, you gotta shake it off. You tell me how I can help you and I will. But we gotta get this under control *now*."

"How do I shake off what has total power over me?" Sheila said. She turned back to the window and watched two cars pass before she turned away again.

"*You're* giving it power over you."

"He did it, Tommy. I've upset him. He wants me to know how much before he does it for good."

"Sheila … I know you loved him more than you'll ever love me. And I can accept that. But … you need love for your life today. If he doesn't like it then that's his problem."

"No, Tommy," Sheila said. "He's made sure to make it my problem too."

*   *   *   *

Carly was away, and Sampson was inside the bedroom. She had hidden a few bottles in some old shoebox inside Sampson's closet. He heard them clink when he stumbled trying to find a clean shirt. Carly's car came screeching up the driveway, and her footsteps were quick into the house.

She opened the bedroom door, smiling. It was the giddy, coke-ridden smile Sampson had seen so often before they came to this house. He didn't ask, though. He didn't feel he had any right to. He had taken one of those bottles from the shoebox and had drunk nearly all of it.

"I have to take you somewhere!" Carly exclaimed.

"Where?" Sampson said with no excitement. He just wanted to lie there and drift away.

"It's a surprise."

"Carly … I don't want to go anywhere."

"Come on! It's a surprise. Come on! You *have* to come."

Sampson got up from the bed gingerly. He put down the small bottle of vodka. He was nervous to leave a room where his parents could smell the wake of his disease.

Carly sped out of the driveway. She sped down streets where children were playing. They managed to get out of the way, but just barely.

"Carly, *slow* down! Jesus!" Sampson said. His previously contented body demonstrated its displeasure by giving him a sharp headache.

Carly didn't listen. She continued to speed. She turned up the radio to drown out Sampson's urgings and headed south on I-75. When they entered into the city limits of Marietta, Carly turned to him.

"Aaron tells me you're a faggot," Carly said. Her smile was gone. Her energy was still evident, but she was using it against him now. Inside a speeding mass of metal and plastic, Sampson was scared.

"What?"

"You've been fucking him, is that right?"

"N-No."

"Liar! He told me about that birthmark!"

"What birthmark?"

"You goddamn know it! No one could see that 'less they birthed you or are fucking you, Sam!"

"My birthmark?"

"*That* birthmark, damn it!" Carly said, and her speedometer hit ninety. Sampson quickly reached for the seatbelt and fastened it while watching the blur of cars Carly was passing, weaving in and out of. Brakes screeched, horns blared, and cops were on the pursuit. "You've been fucking him this whole time! You've been using me this *whole* time!"

"Carly! Slow down!"

"You don't love me!" she said and started to cry. "No one loves me! No one will *ever* love me!"

"Carly, come on. Carly. I … it was … I'm sorry. It won't happen again. I promise."

"No, it won't," she said, and on the overpass above the Chattahoochee River, just north of Mount Paran Road, Carly turned the wheel sharply into the concrete barrier. The barrier broke easily and the car started its dive toward the water.

Sampson's ribs cracked as the seatbelt stressed against his body. Carly had no seatbelt on, so she bounced against her seat, the wheel and the dashboard. She didn't scream, but Sampson did. He didn't want this. Carly did.

They crashed into the river. Water started filling up the car. Sampson was dazed and hurting badly. But he was conscious. Carly wasn't. Her head lay against the steering wheel. She was still. She looked dead.

Sampson could feel his lungs filling with water, but he still tried to grab her. Carly slipped away. Sampson could feel blackness come into his head. His fingers were numb. His arms were weakening. But Sampson still clutched and clutched toward Carly's body and the body growing within.

"Two lives can die here or three," Sampson heard in his ear, though he didn't recognize the voice.

"Get out, Sam. Get out, now."

Sampson's mind tried to override reality. He hoped this accident might result in broken bones, maybe the trauma unit, but not a death. *Not* a death.

Somehow, without knowing exactly how, he found himself on the bank. He watched the car go under. Sampson heard sirens. Blackness enveloped him, but he was alive.

*   *   *   *

Billy was smiling at Sheila. Her eyes were closed. When she opened them she screamed.

"It's OK. I'm a friend of David's," Billy said.

"What?" Sheila replied excitedly and looked around the bathroom for something to strike him. She was inside the tub, naked and too vulnerable to stop this intruder from doing whatever he wanted to her.

"A friend of David's," Billy said again and somehow managed to smile without looking corrupt. "See?" he said and reached out to touch her. Sheila flinched, but watched Billy's hand go through her body like a fog.

"Where … where is he?"

"Well, he's getting things ready," Billy said.

"Ready for what?"

"Ready for you."

"When … when will he try again?" Sheila looked at that face, trying to figure out where she'd seen it before.

"He won't. You have to."

"Have to what?"

"You have to decide to be with him. You have to do it yourself."

"I … I can't do it *myself.*"

"Then you'll feel more pain," Billy said and disappeared.

*   *   *   *

Once again Grouchy was being held in that dungeon reserved for the uncooperative and the feeble souls who hadn't left. He struggled against the arms of Billy's crew while Billy relayed a message that contained no truth.

"This was your doing," Billy said to him. "You could have done this without her, but you made me include her, didn't you?"

"She won't!" Grouchy shouted back.

"She will, David. She's cracked and no glue is gonna put her back together," Billy said and laughed. His crew laughed with him.

Billy had captured his crew's confidence again, and to keep it he needed Grouchy under control until the job was done. Grouchy would be their prisoner until Sheila passed into Billy's control. And with Sheila under his control, Grouchy would be under his control too.

"Life is just a blur to her now," Billy said. "She's figured how fucking meaningless it is without you."

CHAPTER 36

Sampson opened his eyes inside the hospital. Time had stopped for him on that bank, so it seemed just one second later when he saw himself inside a hospital room and a hospital bed. In reality, he'd been sleeping in this hospital bed for two days.

His neck was in a brace. His cracked ribs were secured by tight white plaster around his midsection. One loose bone had punctured a lung. His left shoulder, which was dislocated, almost broken, was secured with a metal rod that had Sampson's arm aimed straight towards a wall. His left leg, broken in three places, was elevated and cast up to his thigh. Sampson didn't realize the damage to his body while swimming away. He was in too much shock to realize anything except how much he wanted on solid ground.

The walls were blurry. Sampson's sheets were too. The nurses spoke in warped, swirly voices, and Sampson just nodded back. Weakly, he called Grouchy's name. He was told Carly died, and he understood. He was told that she was pregnant as well. In a soft voice, he told them he knew.

"Where are you, Grouchy? Grouchy, I need you," Sampson weakly repeated every time he woke.

*   *   *   *

Grouchy sometimes struggled against the crew's increasingly tired arms. He'd become a necessity, so when they needed energy to keep him restrained, they found it. The crew knew Grouchy wouldn't leave Sheila to their whims once she passed into their control. He would have to stay and find action besides mourn-ing a loss he didn't have to mourn anymore. The only action around here was cruelty or constant self-pity, and Grouchy wasn't meant for that. They were cer-tain that Grouchy could add to their numbers and make their power almost totally unbeatable to anyone who tried.

Grouchy soon stopped struggling. Slowly, without drama, he started to sound as though he would welcome Sheila's company soon and in whatever way.

"I love her, boys," Grouchy told the crew holding him tight.

"Then you know Billy is doing the right thing," said the bully holding his right leg.

"Well, maybe," he replied, just to sound as though he was slowly embracing an ideal he'd never believe in. Even if Grouchy had to hide from the bullies in the shadows, even if he were hunted day and night, he vowed never to allow himself to embrace their ways.

"Let him do his thing. You'll be with her soon if you do."

*   *   *   *

Sheila had started thinking of how to end her life. Tommy had a gun. She could stand in the backyard, in the very back corner. She could do it in just a small, dark space that no one would mind never going to again. But that didn't suit her. She wanted it to look like an accident. The guilt she imagined if it didn't was far beyond the sadness she could accept. Suicide would bring Tommy to a low that might prove the same result for him, and Sheila saw the revolving foster homes for her children if he took himself from the mix. She thought of going to a railroad crossing at night and inching her car into a train's path. But Sheila feared the terror in her ears before it slammed into her.

"You have medication," Billy reminded her, "those antidepressants the hospi-tal gave you. Swallow them all and down it with some whiskey."

"That wouldn't look like no accident!" Sheila said. "It's gotta look like an acci-dent!"

"Tommy's gonna tell your kids it was accident. He ain't gonna tell him you done it on purpose. Not till they're older at least."

"I'm worried about *Tommy* too! I don't want *no one* to know it was on pur-pose!"

"Who do you love, Sheila?" Billy asked.

"What do you mean?"

"Who? David or Tommy?"

"Tommy's a good man, damn it! He's a damn good man!"

"Not the question, Sheila. *Who* do you love?"

"You know who," Sheila answered bitterly.

"Tell me!" Billy demanded.

"David! David, OK?"

"Get it done, Sheila. Be with David forever. In bliss, with him, forever."

"Just …" Sheila sputtered, "just tell him to try again. I ain't gonna do this this way."

"He *won't* try again. You have to make the commitment soon or lose him forever."

"Forever?"

"Forever, Sheila. Remember the vows? Do you want to disappoint God?"

"I know damn well that it says in the Bible that you shouldn't kill yourself!"

"Who you gonna believe, Sheila?" Billy asked her with a smile. "Someone like me, who's dead, or twelve assholes who were alive when they wrote that mess?"

A day later Sheila got into the tub. Tommy was at work. He'd be home within two hours. The kids were asleep and would nap for at least two hours. Sheila took a full bottle of pills with her, a prescription she never once opened. She also took a half-filled bottle of bourbon. Billy watched with excitement. He couldn't hide it. The look on Billy's face was looking more familiar to Sheila as it veered from serious into a glad-frightening smile. But Sheila believed him. Billy had said it— David wanted her. Sheila loved David. She'd lose him if she didn't go now. If she could catch him, she should.

She lifted the bottle of pills to her lips.

The bullies were sure Grouchy had been convinced. They held him loosely now. Grouchy saw Sheila walk into the bathroom. He saw her disrobe and climb into a warm tub. He let his emotions rise while she opened the bottle and saw her looking at Billy's near orgasmic state as she lifted it to her lips.

"Yeah, guys, just wanted to tell you again, thanks," Grouchy said in a convincing tone. "Didn't know I was so wrong before."

"Yeah," some said and started to smile.

"Oh, yeah. What we get to do around here? We get to bugger some of these old guys?"

"Can't really," one bully said sadly. "We ain't really alive."

"But we get to rough them up?"

"Well, yeah. You see what happened to you?" another bully said, and they all started to laugh.

Grouchy broke from limbs that merely rested on top of him. He slammed through the wall, which vanished to let loose the trapped souls of the unsure and outright belligerent that wanted to go. The crew followed Grouchy, but he was too quick.

"No!" Grouchy screamed and swiped the air that held the bottle Sheila was raising to her lips. Somehow his most determined force broke Sheila's grip and sent those pills flying into the water.

Sheila looked up at Grouchy. She was afraid. *Does he want it more painful?* she thought and further worried he wanted their daughter dead as well. Confusion and fear lined Sheila's china white face with flushes of red. She saw Grouchy turn to Billy and the crew approaching him. She saw Grouchy push them all away and then pummel the goons and slam them against the bathroom walls. Sheila saw some too afraid to continue, so they disappeared.

Billy remained, however, and started to struggle with Grouchy. But Grouchy threw Billy off. He punched him about the head. He hoisted Billy up and slammed him against a wall. It sounded as though some of those decorative tiles were falling onto the floor, but Sheila looked and saw none. Again Grouchy picked up Billy whose depleting energy made it easy for Grouchy to throw him out of the closed bathroom window.

"It wasn't me, Sheila!" Grouchy said, turning back to her. "I didn't do anything! I don't want you to do this!"

"You ... what? David, I saw you that day. I *saw* you! You wanted it!"

"You saw us both!" Grouchy said, as Billy's desperation to hold on to his power brought him back through the bathroom window with a face that now looked as familiar as Grouchy's did on that traumatic day.

"Do you see?" Grouchy said. "It was him! He engineered it! Look at his *face!*" Grouchy gripped Billy's neck to show Sheila the demented mug that had blended with Grouchy's before her air bag cushioned the intended fatal blow. "He's like ... the devil! He's an evil, fucking *dead* man!"

"David, I don't ... I don't understand!"

"It isn't easy to explain, Sheila. And you don't need to know it. Just know I didn't do it. I didn't want this."

"So, you don't ... you don't want me?"

"Sheila, I've missed you. I used to watch you and Tommy and want nothing more than you with me. But not like this. *Not* like this, Sheila. You have a daughter. *Our* daughter. You have a man that loves you. You have a boy that needs a mother. *Not* like this! You're *alive*, Sheila. I had no say if I left or not. Don't you *dare* leave by your own hand. You're healthy. You're needed here. Don't! Don't ever listen to him again," Grouchy said pointing at Billy who'd been standing frozen with frustration. "I want nothing more than for you to live your life as best as you can. You don't have to forget me. But you can't join me. Not like this, Sheila. *Not* like this!"

Sheila started to cry. The shame of almost being fooled into a departure made her bury her eyes into water-wrinkled hands.

Billy was on his last reserve. He would have nothing if Sheila couldn't be convinced to come and Grouchy couldn't be convinced to stay. He would lose his crew, lose his status, and be ostracized. Nothing was worse than ostracism in Sheila's world or his.

"I will make sure of it!" Billy cried. "I will get it done!"

"You have no power now," Grouchy said, turning to him. "You're as useless to those fucking losers as you are to anyone on earth."

Sheila looked back up Grouchy. He blinked some and said with tenderness, "You will never see me again. Never believe anything bad that happens to you was a sign from me. It will never be. I love you. If I ever see you again, it will be after you lead a long, happy life."

Sheila nodded. And though Grouchy and Billy remained with her, Sheila's renewed commitment to life erased their images from her eyes.

CHAPTER 37

Sampson's father was by his side the third day after Sampson woke with itches only a coat hanger could scratch. Ed Roy was holding his son's hand and was crying. He held his lips together with his other hand so it wouldn't wake his son. But he woke him anyway.

"Dad?" Sampson said, and his father looked up. Ed dried his eyes and said, "Yes, Sam."

"She's dead, Dad."

"I know."

"It wasn't an accident, Dad."

"No. I know."

"I'm sorry, Dad."

"You weren't driving, Sam. I have to assume you didn't know it was going to happen."

"I didn't, Dad. I'm not sorry about that."

"Then what you sorry for, Sam?"

"I ... know I'm a disappointment, Dad. I know it. Carly was just someone ... I mean ... someone who I didn't even know. She just took me in, Dad. She wasn't someone I ever loved. And then when she got pregnant-"

"You ain't a disappointment to me, Sam," his father interrupted him.

"No, Dad, just listen. Please. Let me say what I need to say."

"OK. Say what you need to say to me, Sam. I'll shut up."

"Look, Mary divorced me. My child, I didn't know when I'd ever see her again. I just told myself it didn't matter. It didn't matter because I would be responsible to *this* woman. I didn't try and see it any other way, just do what I should. I thought I could handle anything. I handled everything before the war, Dad. Why can't I handle anything after?"

Ed looked at the sheets of Sampson's hospital bed, and then back up at his son with a pained expression. He looked almost as if he would start crying again. But he found a way to sturdy those emotions and replied, "You just a man, Sam. Just a man. You didn't have much of a man to raise you. Even if you did, Sam, no one could prepare you for war. I wished I went when you was young. I wished I had something about me people could look up to. Especially you. I know I said you'd be a real man. I know I drilled it into your head. But I didn't know *shit* about it. Still don't. But, I know war ain't something you can leave the same way you came into it. I don't care how tough you was going in. Maybe it's even worse. Maybe you feel a failure because when you macho going in and the death around you takes some of that away, you feel like you lost something."

"Sometimes when we was patrolling, sometimes when the bullets were flying around me, I wished something would hit me. I wished for you and Mom to go to my grave every Memorial Day and plant a flag and say a prayer. I wished you would look up to the sky and wear buttons with my face on it. I thought that was how it was supposed to be. When it didn't happen, when I came back and everyone told me how good I was supposed to feel, I wished something would kill me. But that ain't there anymore. I could have died in that car. I had a thought of letting it take me. Me dying with the woman holding my baby, I thought I finally could go and no one would blame me how it was done. But it just ain't true anymore. I want to see my daughter. I want to raise her. I want to do whatever Mary lets me do to raise her. I have to, Dad. I finally feel like I have to."

"OK, Sam, then you'll do it."

*   *   *   *

Sampson knocked on Sheila's door. He was still limping. His shoulder still hurt like hell. He took none of the pain medication he was given without nurses around pushing the paper cup forward. He figured he should feel everything life was, even the great pain he was in. Sampson was sure the accident hadn't taken away the need to float back on that fluffy cloud that silenced everything. The pills would just bring him right back to preferring sedation rather than a real life.

Tommy let Sampson into the house. Sheila was sitting on the porch with their kids. She was smiling, the sincere smile she had no trouble displaying before the accident and one that came back a day after Grouchy had told her the truth. The mask had come off. Elena and Tommy Junior were so glad Mommy was back and displayed it with joyful squeals and tugs on Mommy's arm. Sheila thanked the sun in the morning. She marveled at the strong storms in the late afternoon. Holding on to Tommy at night, she kissed his cheek and nuzzled him like she never had before.

Sheila asked about Sampson's physical state, his cane, his shoulder, and the cast on his leg. Sampson told her everything, including the details she'd guessed at. Sheila told him she was so sorry, and Sampson thanked her. But that wasn't why he was here.

"Where's Mary?" Sampson asked.

"She got her own place a while ago, Sam."

"Can you ... can you please tell me where?"

"Yeah ... I guess I could tell you. But ... Sam ... I have to know. I believe you. I know you saw David. I believe he talked to you. Was he ever really mad at me, Sam? Did he ever really tell you that? Please tell me the truth, whatever it is."

"No," Sampson said without thinking. "He never did, Sheila. He misses you. I know that. But he never wanted you unhappy. He never said he did. He never said he wanted you alone. Don't know if he ever felt it. But he never said it. Grouchy was never like that. Grouchy is probably the best person I've ever known. Probably the best person I ever will know. I didn't think about him at all until he came to me and told me how to carry on. He didn't have to do that, Sheila. We weren't really ever friends before. Others came to me too. And they wanted nothing more than to hurt who they left behind. He never did. He struggled with it, but he didn't give in."

"Listen, I ... was unhappy. I didn't want you to find happiness without him when I couldn't have Mary. I'm sorry. It was wrong. But I was hurting. I didn't want to be the only one."

"It's OK, Sam," Sheila said reaching over, putting her hand in Sampson's palm and squeezing it. He couldn't squeeze back because it would hurt that shoulder too much. "I had to go through it. If I didn't feel guilty then, I would feel guilty later. I appreciate everything now."

*   *   *   *

Sampson confided to his father his problem with the bottle. He also confided the reason Carly wanted them to die. He could see his father's surprise at having a son who had been with men, surprised by the side of a boy he thought was heterosexual through and through. But Ed had no unkind words about Sampson's confused sexuality. He had no words at all. He just said, "You will go with me tomorrow. I have a meeting I think you'll want to attend."

Coffee and doughnuts lay on a small coffee table in the basement of a church. Men and women, young and old alike, sat next to each other gripping the steaming coffee in their hands. The young looked shaken. The older members looked tough, but their watery eyes had yet to stop dreaming of life through chemicals. The veteran addicts still wanted to swallow enough every day to put them asleep or keep them awake with joys that vanished when every bottle, pill, powder, and smoke was gone.

Sampson's father rose and said, "I'm Ed. I'm an alcoholic. My son is here with us today. I'm ashamed to say he followed my path. I stopped drinking many years ago, but I didn't stop pressuring him to be someone that no one can be. I pressured him to go through life like a Mack truck. He did his best. But eventually, one realizes that in life pain is always around. He was ashamed of his pain and did what I used to do to bury it. I am ashamed I taught him to bury it."

Sampson rose after his father sat down. He used his cane as leverage to keep him up and said, "I'm Sam. I'm an alcoholic."

CHAPTER 38

Sampson feared Mary slamming the door in his face. If not that, he feared some legalize saying he was no longer Cecilia's rightful father. And, if not that, he feared being punched out by some man and waking up in another jail cell.

Leaving it all alone was a persistent thought as he stood before apartment number eight. Cecilia's life being better without him was another. He would just be a strain she could do without. When she grew old enough to understand, she would be pulled toward him and back to Mary with every surging feeling. Drinking would enter the picture, maybe drugs, maybe bad men. Or maybe just books, like Mary always found solace in, but *only* found solace in sometimes. Sampson feared the extremes of a wanton woman or a woman barricading all her thoughts and relations from the world. He wanted her normal and happy. He had never been either and neither had Mary, and he couldn't tolerate his child continuing that cycle.

Maybe a new man is inside, anyway, Sampson thought. *Maybe that same skinny dick in the glasses.*

Maybe that man had become Cecilia's father just like Tommy had become Elena's. Maybe that guy had taken on the duty even though Sampson was still alive to try. A lawsuit was an idea. Sampson imagined years inside some courtroom to establish that while he might be unfit to be a parent, he should still be allowed to see his flesh and blood. But maybe the law would take him away for invading the happiness Mary had finally found without him, and the court records would show his resistance when they did and brand him completely unfit for any part in Cecilia's life.

Despite these thoughts, Sampson knocked anyway. Despite these thoughts, he put a heavy hand to the door and stomached all his fears while hoping for the best, but expecting the worst.

Mary looked into the peephole and believed she was seeing a vision, the vision she thought of nightly while kissing her pillow, imaging it was the love of her life, the vision that she could swear kissed her back. It had kept her contented because it was a vision with words and feelings Mary had invented herself. But even if this was the same vision, she didn't care. If her mind were becoming so unglued that her visions had manifested themselves into a physical delusion outside of her bed, she'd still welcome it.

This vision was broken though. Sampson was bandaged up and looked older. Mary opened the door and looked into those beautiful, though nervous, shocking blue eyes. This man was real, because he was unpredictable. And though Mary knew the mythical Sampson would never disappoint her, the real Sam in front of her felt so good.

Emotions came into Mary's throat, but they stopped there. In a forced, cool tone, Mary asked Sampson in, and he came in cautiously, half expecting this to be a trap and he'd be immediately pummeled by Mary's bespectacled lover once the door was closed to hide them from all cooperating witnesses.

"What … what happened to you, Sam?" Mary said, looking at Sampson's heavily cast leg that he didn't let anyone sign.

"An accident," Sampson replied. "Just an accident, Mary."

"So, where have you been?"

"Oh … everywhere."

"We were really worried about you."

This struck Sampson as funny, because it was *she* who had left him in jail. She didn't bail him out. She just left him to rot and figure out his choices with a mind that couldn't figure out much. But the past was just the past, and he was ready to stop living through it. So he said, "I thought of you all the time, Mary. I thought of her too."

The crib started to rattle within the silence just after Sampson's statement. Cecilia's tiny hands had grabbed the bars and shook as much as she could. It seemed to Mary that she understood her father's subtle asking, so she invited Sampson's limping frame into the bedroom to see Cecilia. Sampson noticed how much more animated she was compared with the last time he held his daughter.

Sampson limped to the crib and looked closely into Cecilia's smiling face. She was smiling at him, just him. And those eyes, they were his. *She* was his. This was his—something he could believe in. Unlike Mary, Sampson's emotions rushed past his throat and into his mouth and eyes and Cecilia's smile became restrained, a little worried perhaps. But as Sampson took Cecilia in his arms, her happy smile returned in full.

Sampson kissed Cecilia and held her to his chest. He said, "Oh, Cecilia," over and over again in a whisper made husky by his tender throat.

Seeing this, Mary broke from her emotion inhibition. Her relief and joy at the sight matched Sampson's while she embraced her ex-husband from behind.

"You're different, Sam," Mary said, though Sampson's broken soul had yet to heal so he could become the confident man she had first fallen in love with. It probably never would. But this real man, with a softness that the past Sampson would never completely show, was like a real ray of sun inside a head that had manufactured every glow besides the one her daughter provided her every day.

Sampson put Cecilia back down into her crib and turned to Mary. She kissed him immediately and after being stunned by such intensity, Sampson kissed back. They held on to each other, kissing, hugging tighter. Mary started to kiss Sampson's neck, which elicited a sigh. Sampson was experiencing a real feeling of love for the first time in many months. They walked with each other to the side of the bed, their desire slowed by Sampson's limp. The couple lowered themselves to the mattress while undressing and made love in a manner that caused Sampson no pain. Mary's unbridled tenderness filled Sampson with euphoria he had never known.

*   *   *   *

Billy was battered daily. His past crew, with no respect for him anymore, with not a trace of the fear that had kept them within his powers, unleashed what power they had on to his apparition. It was so brutal and so continuous that Billy showed the physical results of the damage upon his image as though he were truly flesh and blood. He was the limping dead. Even members of the world he inhabited who had never before joined him, who had been his and his crew's playthings, reveled in their ability to strike him down. He would never find friends again.

Grouchy was in line. The line had no real connection to time on earth. A step forward could mean three seconds on earth or three weeks. There was no rhyme or reason, and it mattered none to those in line because they couldn't feel the time. Each step forward happened in a short enough span to them. There weren't any long pauses, just a gradual procession that those participating had the patience for.

Occasionally Billy came to Grouchy's side. Billy's gums bled. His arms were out of their sockets. His feet were so twisted that he shuffled when he walked. He was so desperate he would threaten Grouchy, though Grouchy laughed at him as dismissively as a muscle man would laugh at a skinny geek trying to flex muscles that didn't exist. With a cracked, raw voice, Billy called for his past crew, but none came. They only laughed at him, too, and waited for him to embarrass himself before he limped back to be brutalized some more. Billy was the raving ex-pugilist with so much brain damage that he thought he was still champ. This was all he had—just the memories of power and the insane notion that he still wielded a big stick.

*   *   *   *

A family that acted as if they missed a gathering that never once occurred came together at Sampson's boyhood home. Sampson, Mary, Cecilia, Sampson's father and mother, his sister, Alice, and her two children and husband all gathered together at the homestead and beamed like they were expected to. Mary had only met Sampson's parents only twice; Alice, just once. She'd never once seen Alice's kids or her husband in person.

The smiles seemed sincere, but also strangely unrelenting in Sampson's eyes. They overwhelmed him with an earnestness that he wasn't ready for, that he couldn't truly believe. Even Alice, who Sampson knew was miserable from age fourteen on, smiled truly, though he detected just enough makeup on her face to cover what her husband did to her last night.

Alice wondered aloud where the wine was. She drank it by the bottle every night. Even Mary wondered, though Sampson had told her he wouldn't ever drink again. Mary didn't seem to understand. She understood *he* couldn't drink, but why couldn't she?

Mary drank in front of him. She enjoyed a glass nightly. Sampson wanted to stress that he couldn't be around alcohol, but he also didn't want to create any waves in an ocean he was enjoying. He became so jittery while watching Mary consume what he couldn't anymore that he started taking long showers while she enjoyed her drink. While the water beat down on him, Sampson's need for release had him touching himself, and his thoughts veered back to Aaron.

This is all Sampson would ever have of Aaron again. He hated Aaron for killing his sister, yet he couldn't help wanting him.

Sampson told the AA meetings of his ex-wife's lack of consideration. He expressed his anger at her only at these meetings. Privately, his father told Sampson he had to lay down the law or the recovering alcoholic would become the renewed one in no time time. The group said this too. They all seemed to gang up on him with the same level of anger Sampson held inside. Every single member knew too well what it was like to avoid telling someone with no clue that they were enabling a certain fall.

Alone, Sampson sometimes went to the cupboard and took that wine bottle out. He stared at it while it invited him to just have a taste.

"Come on, Sam," it always said. The voice in his head mimicked Billy, though it was Sampson's own. "Come on. A drink? One fucking drink, Sam? Shit, you survived! Celebrate!"

But Sampson never did. He had to tear himself away, but he never drank a red drop. Before leaving the kitchen, he would slam the wine bottle inside the cupboard with so much force the glass almost broke against the cheap wood.

Sampson and Mary didn't talk much. They never did before, so Sampson figured he shouldn't be worried that they didn't now. Mary buried her head in books or gave her attention to Cecilia. Sampson was still a vision she engaged to meet her needs. And when this vision had some comment about the wine that was tempting his downfall, she dismissed the vision until she desired it again.

Sampson was starting to open his eyes and realize it couldn't work like this. He would become a drunk again. He would become useless again. He would blow this shot and believed Mary would never understand her part in any of this when he did. So he finally found the courage. He finally told himself that if he had a shot, if they had a shot, he couldn't stand idly by while his resistance weakened each time he saw someone with no sickness imbibe something that might take him back to the woods—or to the hope for death.

He told Mary she could have a drink with some friends, but not near him, and he preferred that she wash her mouth out with mouthwash so he couldn't smell it. He told Mary that he really wanted a second chance with her, with their child, but that second chance would be his last chance if she ignored what he needed for his recovery.

She didn't really protest, really. She seemed annoyed as she sighed and took the wine out of the cupboard and put it in her car. Mary had no friends to drink with. She didn't tell Sampson this. Mary wanted no friends to drink with. She didn't tell him this either. If he was ready for life with her he could deal with it. Mary didn't say this. But Sampson could feel her lack of understanding. Mary's pleas for him to try to recover before seemed so hollow to Sampson now and made their sleeping together an act, which reminded him of Carly, the Carly

Sampson first met, the Carly who wanted what she wanted and could care less if it pleased him or not.

Sampson wanted Grouchy back. But he wanted to live, so Grouchy wouldn't come back. Even if Sampson had visions of suicide or self-destruction, Grouchy was in line and wouldn't be turning around. He was strong now. He'd had the opportunity to explain to Sheila what he couldn't before. He needed to leave all things on Earth behind now.

A vision appeared to Grouchy. These visions ran in a loop around the dead so quickly they were mostly a blur. However, when the dead recognized a vision it seemed to slow down. It enlarged, and they could see every detail. Every tear. Every call. Every stitch of clothing. Every movement of breath.

Grouchy wanted to ignore it. He tried to ignore it. But the image wouldn't go away, so he hadn't convinced himself he didn't care. His past vow to help the near-damned became whole again and cried inside of him. Grouchy felt selfish for only thinking of his path. He was strong, he told himself this. He couldn't be touched. He knew this. Grouchy's eagerness to end the chapter of pain in this murky afterlife told him to just move forward. But he couldn't, because he wasn't ignorant and he couldn't leave this plane pretending to be.

He turned around and got out of line.

CHAPTER 39

The grocery list was missing an item. Though Sampson did all the shopping, Mary compiled the list. She had forgotten to write down *diapers*. So Cecilia woke very late with her last diaper full and she wanted another, a desire she expressed loudly in the only way she knew how.

Mary was sleeping in her nightgown when Cecilia began to cry. Sampson was watching TV in clothes permissible to the outside world, so Mary asked if he could fetch some diapers from the convenience store still open on the corner.

Sampson readily agreed. Being out on his own had become such a luxury; he was in the apartment all day. Mary had cancelled daycare, so Sampson spent all day with Cecilia, changing her, holding her, watching her sleep. Sometimes Sampson would stroll Cecilia around the greens. But mostly he sat stir-crazy in the apartment because he had no car.

She handed the keys to her car, a car that thankfully didn't require his left leg to press on a clutch, and he grabbed them as if they were clanging one hundred dollar bills. The sky was cloudy, but the moon shone so brightly it could be seen through a haze that doubled its efforts with every passing hour.

Sampson hobbled inside the store, his cane clacking the floor. He swiveled his unbending left leg so stridently it almost knocked over a display. The diapers were in a back corner, between motor oil and a stack of teenybopper magazines that Sampson perused only to discard each one disgustedly when seeing what young girls were wearing these days. When Sampson got in line, he wasn't the lone customer in the store anymore. A woman was at the front of the line buying cat food. Behind her, a nervous man stood with no goods in his hands, and he was fidgeting while staring aimlessly at the brown tiled floor.

When the nervous man faced the clerk, he asked for a few things behind the counter and then another few other things when the clerk returned. Sampson became impatient when he asked for yet another package of cigarettes as the clerk returned for a third time placing the package the customer had just asked for on the counter. The clerk was showing his impatience, too, with grunts and a tiring expression.

The nervous man's gun came out when the clerk returned with the second package of cigarettes. The gun was black, the bullets held in a chipped black cylinder. It was old and looked almost fake. But Sampson and the clerk believed it was real. The man shook the rusted barrel in the clerk's face and demanded all the money. The clerk held up his hands and said OK. But the gunman cocked the gun and thrust it like he was about to fire.

"He said he's getting the money!" Sampson said, and the gunman turned around and stuck the gun up into Sampson's face. "Calm down!" Sampson said. "He said he's getting you the money."

The gunman said nothing. The sweat on his face dripped past his neck and into his ragged white t-shirt. His eyes were bloodshot. They communicated nothing but drug addiction and fear. When Grouchy appeared in the space next to him, Sampson looked at the gunman with muted sadness on his face and said, "You going to kill me, aren't you?"

The gunman said nothing. He lowered the gun and blasted a charge into Sampson's chest. Sampson fell, and the lights on the ceiling blared violently into his eyes. The lights began to dance. Pixilated dark started surrounding his vision, coming ever closer to consuming it with every black dot. Soon, the lights were like weak, white, blinking Christmas lights on a faraway house that was speeding farther away.

The clerk retrieved the gun he kept behind the counter and fired into the back of the gunman's head. The gunman fell, dead. He lie dead next to a dying Sampson, who had no flash of his past life, nor any thoughts or words to tell his ex-wife, his daughter, his parents, or anyone. When those blinking lights left him completely, Sampson felt sucked into a hallway that echoed with voices fading away.

Grouchy took his hand. He rushed Sampson into the line that faced the beckoning cloud of shifting shades. The line was long but moving steadily. Grouchy told him to stay strong, to look forward, to not, *not* turn around.

"Sam," Billy said, shuffling next to him. Sampson saw him because he was still unsure, though didn't know it yet. Billy spoke happily, as though Sampson were a long—lost friend who had finally moved cross-country just to live near him.

"Don't look at him, Sam. Don't even listen to him," Grouchy warned.

"Your wife ... your kid ...," Billy said. "Don't you miss your wife and your kid?"

Sampson hadn't yet missed anything because he hadn't any time to. But the question instilled him with the reality. What *would* become of Mary? She felt the worst was behind her, and now she would have a corpse to bury while thinking of what might have been.

So Sampson ignored Grouchy's continual insistence that he pay no attention to Billy. He turned to Billy with the part of himself Grouchy didn't yet control.

"What are you saying?" Sampson said.

Billy saw the concern. He felt the power. Sampson hadn't been present for his dramatic fall, so he couldn't dismiss him as quickly as everyone else did, everyone who took shots at Billy as if he were a pliable punching bag. Billy would exploit this light of hope even if he tempted more failure that would diminish him to a complete cripple. He had no choice; he'd be one anyway without this victory.

"Don't you want to help them?" Billy asked.

"Don't listen to him, Sam!" Grouchy said and gripped Sampson tighter.

"Of course I want to help them ... if I can," said Sampson, his voice wavering, uncertain of the trust he was giving to someone he never trusted.

"You can! You gotta stay, though. You go into the cloud, you never come back. You never see them again. Not ever! You can help them only if you stay!"

"He's trying to catch you, Sam," Grouchy said. "Take it from me, Billy has no good intentions, Sam. And you *know* this. He *said* it to you! You *know* what he's doing!"

Sampson did know this. But though he knew it, Billy had stirred up the feelings everyone has when they leave behind a young wife and child. Sampson didn't truly realize what Grouchy knew. Being newly dead, he didn't quite realize that all his watching would accomplish nothing, that the complete insignificance he would eventually feel would turn to bitterness or sadness that could keep him trapped forever if he never found the strength back to this line. He *certainly* didn't realize the strength he had now was stronger than anything he'd ever have later.

But Grouchy couldn't allow any real hesitation. He didn't care what Sampson thought he wanted. What he wanted *right* now at *this* moment would be cursed and shame Sampson into becoming an unwilling bully. Sampson would be diving into the shallowest of murky water. The mud would trap his feet; he would be surrounded and would never leave.

Grouchy swiped at Billy. Billy somehow darted away and started to laugh. Grouchy swiped at him again. Billy's past crew was watching. If Sampson could come into their fold they would have one more—one more eager soul, and that would buck up the whole crew. Morale would swell. What they could accomplish seemed limitless. Billy would never regain the power he once had. But if Billy could make progress, even with his broken, desperate self, they could easily finish the job and instill Billy as the most subservient part of the flock. He'd gladly take the position.

"Go away!" Grouchy said, but Billy continued to laugh even though Grouchy was striking him hard and he was feeling it. Billy was struck every day and with far more force than Grouchy could ever manage, so these strikes were quite tame to him.

Grouchy observed the crew approaching. The fold of twenty came closer. They looked at Sampson as if he were a piece of meat for a pack of dogs left starving for weeks.

"Stay away!" Grouchy said, but they didn't. They tried to take Sampson from his hand, but Grouchy held on tight. "Stay away!" Grouchy struck one, then another. They bristled but remained determined. His force brushed them back, but they reared back stronger. When he brushed them back again, the crew reared back just as strong but now with rage filling their eyes. Grouchy's fear of being taken along with Sampson made him almost let Sampson go to save himself.

"I … think … I want to stay, Grouchy," Sampson said to him. "Just for a while."

"No!" Grouchy said. "No! No! A while is forever, Sam! It's forever to them. You aren't strong enough. You'll *never* be! You'll just be a fucking ghost if you stay. Just a *fucking* ghost, Sam!"

Sampson tried to take his hand from Grouchy's, but Grouchy gripped it so tight he would have broken that hand if Sampson were still made of flesh and bone. Grouchy turned him from the crew. He held on to Sampson's neck with his other hand and kept it forward. He needed to keep Sampson's eyes averted from ones that dripped with awful desire.

Though it started to buckle from such stress, Grouchy was able to hold on to his own strength as well. He trembled. But he knew once they entered the cloud it was over. Everything would dissipate—this stress, his memories. And while he once wanted to hang on to the latter, he'd accepted that he couldn't, and he wouldn't allow himself to allow Sampson the choice.

Sampson wriggled fiercely. The crew tugged and tugged at him, but Billy's laughter kept Grouchy strong. This would be the last nail in Billy's virtual coffin, and Grouchy would have his final revenge when he won this fight. The glory would last only a split second, but that brief feeling was just enough motivation to prod himself and Sampson toward the swirling void.

The fog crept on to their feet. It was a mist that reminded Sampson of some concerts he went to. That mist crept off the stage and into his nostrils with the smell of clean chemicals.

But there was no smell. Sampson had no smell. The closer they came, the less sight he had. He was feeling light. He was feeling free. He said a silent word to Mary and Cecilia. To his father and his mother. To his sister. To the friends he had known. To the warriors still in the sand. Sampson said his words, and then he and Grouchy started into the cloud and were taken from all they had known into a world that would try them as relentlessly as the last.

978-0-595-47205-5
0-595-47205-2

Printed in the United States
201258BV00002B/133-261/A

9 780595 472055